The Darkness Reveals . . .

"The strange woman sat in the semi-darkness. In the light of the shaded lamp I could see the gleam of white teeth through her veil, but could not imagine why she swathed herself in that manner. In spite of this enwrapping she could not disguise the fact that she possessed remarkably large and beautiful eyes . . .

"As she rose to depart the hand of fate intervened. I had only one lamp burning in the room, and at this moment the filament expired, plunging the room into darkness! Looking across the darkened room to the chair upon which she was seated, I saw a pair of blazing eyes regarding me fixedly!"

When Jack Addison first encounters THE GREEN EYES OF BAST, he is horrified. But the worst is yet to come. For the strange and astounding secret that lurks behind those blazing feline lights will not rest until it has found revenge in murder—again, and again, and again . . .

THE
GREEN EYES
OF BÂST

SAX ROHMER

PYRAMID BOOKS • NEW YORK

THE GREEN EYES OF BAST

A PYRAMID BOOK

Published by arrangement with Paul R. Reynolds, Inc.

Pyramid edition published February 1971

PYRAMID BOOKS are published by Pyramid Publications
A Division of The Walter Reade Organization, Inc.
444 Madison Avenue, New York, New York 10022, U.S.A.

CONTENTS

CHAPTER I

I SEE THE EYES

"Good evening, sir. A bit gusty?"

"Very much so, Sergeant," I replied. "I think I will step into your hut for a moment and light my pipe, if I may."

"Certainly, sir. Matches are too scarce nowadays to take risks with 'em. But it looks as if the storm had blown over."

"I'm not sorry," said I, entering the little hut like a sentry-box which stands at the entrance to this old village high street for accommodation of the officer on point duty at that spot. "I have a longish walk before me."

"Yes. Your place is right off the beat, isn't it?" mused my acquaintance, as, sheltered from the keen wind, I began to load my briar. "Very inconvenient I've always thought it for a gentleman who gets about as much as you do."

"That's why I like it," I explained. "If I lived anywhere accessible I should never get a moment's peace, you see. At the same time, I have to be within an hour's journey of Fleet Street."

I often stopped for a chat at this point, and I was acquainted with most of the men of P Division, on whom the duty devolved from time to time. It was a lonely spot at night when the residents in the neighbourhood had retired, so that the darkened houses seemed to withdraw yet farther into the gardens separating them from the high road. A relic of the days when trains and motor-buses were not, dusk restored something of an old-world atmosphere to the village street, disguising the red brick and stucco which in many cases had displaced the half-timbered houses of the past. Yet it was possible in still weather to hear the muted bombilation of the sleepless city, and when the wind was in the north to count the hammer strokes of the great bell of St. Paul's.

Standing in the shelter of the little hut, I listened to the rain dripping from overreaching branches, and to the gurgling of a turgid little stream which flowed along the gutter near my feet, whilst now and again swift gusts of the expiring tempest would set tossing the branches of the trees which lined the way.

"It's much cooler to-night," said the sergeant.

I nodded, being in the act of lighting my pipe. The storm had interrupted a spell of that tropical weather which sometimes in July and August brings the breath of Africa to London, and this coolness resulting from the storm was very welcome. Then:

"Well, good night," I said, and was about to pursue my way, when the telephone bell in the police hut rang sharply.

"Hullo!" called the sergeant.

I paused, idly curious concerning the message, and:

"The Red House," continued the sergeant, "in College Road? Yes, I know it. It's on Bolton's beat, and he is due here now. Very good; I'll tell him."

He hung up the receiver, and turning to me, smiled and nodded his head resignedly.

"The police get some funny jobs, sir," he confided. "Only last night a gentleman rang up the station and asked them to tell me to stop a short, stout lady with yellow hair and a big blue hat (that was the only description) as she passed this point, and to inform her that her husband had had to go out, but that he had left the door-key just inside the dog-kennel!"

He laughed good-humouredly.

"Now to-night," he resumed, "here's somebody just rung up to say that she thinks—only *thinks*, mind you—that she has forgotten to lock the garage, and will the constable on that beat see if the keys have been left behind. If so, will he lock the door from the inside, go out through the back, lock that door, and leave the keys at the station on coming off duty!"

"Yes," I said. "There are some absent-minded people in the world. But do you mean the Red House in College Road?"

"That's it," replied the sergeant, stepping out of the hut and looking intently to the left. "Ah, here comes Bolton."

He referred to a stolid, red-faced constable who at that moment came plodding across the muddy road, and:

"A job for you, Bolton," he cried. "Listen. You know the Red House in College Road?"

Bolton removed his helmet and scratched his closely-cropped head.

"Let me see," he mused; "it's on the right——"

"No, no," I interrupted. "It is a house about half-way down on the left, very secluded, with a high brick wall in front."

"Oh! You mean the *empty* house?" inquired the constable.

"Just what I was about to remark, Sergeant," said I, turning to my acquaintance. "To the best of my knowledge, the Red House has been vacant for twelve months or more."

"Has it?" exclaimed the sergeant. "That's funny. Still, it's none of my business. Besides, it may have been let within the last few days. Anyway, listen, Bolton. You are to see if the garage is unlocked. If it is, and the keys are there, go in and lock the door behind you. There's another door at the other end; go out and lock that too. Leave the keys at the station when you go off. Got that fixed?"

"Yes," replied Bolton, and he stood, helmet in hand, half inaudibly muttering the sergeant's instructions, evidently with the idea of impressing them upon his memory.

"I have to pass the Red House, constable," I interrupted, "and as you seem doubtful respecting its whereabouts, I will point the place out to you."

"Thank you, sir," said Bolton, replacing his helmet and ceasing to mutter.

"Once more—good night, Sergeant!" I cried, and met by a keen gust of wind which came sweeping down the village street, showering cascades of water from the leaves above, I set out in step with my stolid companion.

It is supposed poetically that unusual events cast their shadows before them, and I am prepared to maintain the correctness of such a belief. But unless the silence of the constable who walked beside me was due to the unseen presence of such a shadow, and not to an habitual taciturnity, there was nothing in that march through the deserted streets calculated to arouse me to the fact that I was entering upon the first phase of an experience more strange and infinitely more horrible than any of which I had ever known or even read.

The shadow had not yet reached me.

We talked little enough on the way, for the breeze when it came was keen and troublesome, so that I was often engaged in clutching my hat. Except for a dejected-looking object, obviously a member of the tramp fraternity, who passed us near the gate of the old chapel, we met never a soul from the time that we left the police-box until the moment when the high brick wall guarding the Red House came into view beyond a line of glistening wet hedgerow.

"This is the house, constable," I said. "The garage is beyond the main entrance."

We proceeded as far as the closed gates, whereupon:

"There you are, sir," said Bolton triumphantly. "I told you it was empty."

An estate agent's bill faced us, setting forth the desirable features of the residence, the number of bedrooms and reception rooms, modern conveniences, garage, &c., together with the extent of the garden, lawn and orchard.

A faint creaking sound drew my glance upward, and stepping back a pace I stared at a hatchet-board projecting above the wall which bore two duplicates of the bill posted upon the gate.

"That seems to confirm it," I declared, peering through the trees in the direction of the house. "The place has all the appearance of being deserted."

"There's some mistake," muttered Bolton.

"Then the mistake is not ours," I replied. "See, the bills are headed 'To be let or sold. The Red House, &c.' "

"H'm!" growled Bolton. "It's a funny go, this is. Suppose we have a look at the garage."

We walked along together to where, set back in a recess, I had often observed the doors of a garage evidently added to the building by some recent occupier. Dangling from a key placed in the lock was a ring to which another key was attached!

"Well, I'm blowed," said Bolton, "this *is* a funny go, this is!"

He unlocked the door and swept the interior of the place with a ray of light cast by his lantern. There were one or two petrol cans and some odd lumber, suggesting that the garage had been recently used, but no car, and indeed nothing of sufficient value to have interested even such a derelict as the man whom we had passed some ten minutes before. That is, if I except a large and stoutly-made packing-case, which rested only a foot or so from the entrance so as partly to block it, and which from its appearance might possibly have contained spare parts. I noticed, with vague curiosity, a device crudely representing a seated cat which was painted in green upon the case.

"If there ever was anything here," said Bolton, "it's been pinched, and we're locking the stable-door after the horse has gone. You'll bear me out, sir, if there's any complaint?"

"Certainly," I replied. "Technically I shall be trespassing if I come in with you, so I shall say good night."

"Good night, sir!" cried the constable, and entering the empty garage he closed the door behind him.

I set off briskly alone towards the cottage which I had made my home. I have since thought that the motives which had induced me to choose this secluded residence were of a peculiarly selfish order. Whilst I liked sometimes to be among my fellowmen, and whilst I rarely missed an important first night in London, my inherent weakness for obscure studies and another motive to which I may refer later had caused me to abandon my chambers in the Temple and to retire with my library to this odd little backwater where my only link with Fleet Street, with the land of theatres and clubs and noise and glitter, was the telephone. I scarcely need add that I had sufficient private means to enable me to indulge these whims, otherwise as a working journalist I must have been content to remain nearer to the heart of things. As it was, I followed the careless existence of the independent free-lance, and since my work was accounted above the average I was enabled to pick and choose the subjects with which I should deal. Mine was not an ambitious nature—or it may have been that stimulus was lacking—and all I wrote I wrote for the mere joy of writing, whilst my studies, of which I shall have occasion to speak presently, were not of a nature calculated to swell my coffers in this commercial-minded age.

Little did I know how abruptly this chosen calm of my life was to be broken nor how these same studies were to be turned in a new and strange direction. But if on this night which was to witness the overture of a horrible drama, I had not hitherto experienced any premonition of the coming of those dark forces which were to change the whole tenor of my existence, suddenly, now, in sight of the elm tree which stood before my cottage the *shadow* reached me.

Only thus can I describe a feeling otherwise unaccountable which prompted me to check my steps and to listen. A gust of wind had just died away, leaving the night silent save for the dripping of rain from the leaves and the vague and remote roar of the town. Once, faintly, I thought I detected the howling of a dog. I had heard nothing in the nature of following footsteps, yet, turning swiftly, I did not doubt that I should detect the presence of a follower of some kind. This conviction seized me suddenly and, as I have said, unaccountably. Nor was I wrong in my surmise.

Fifty yards behind me a vaguely defined figure showed for an instant outlined against the light of a distant lamp—ere melting into the dense shadow cast by a clump of trees near the roadside.

Standing quite still I stared in the direction of the patch of shadow for several moments. It may be said that there was nothing to occasion alarm or even curiosity in the appearance of a stray pedestrian at that hour; for it was little after midnight. Indeed thus I argued with myself, whereby I admit that at sight of that figure I had experienced a sensation which was compounded not only of alarm and curiosity but also of some other emotion which even now I find it hard to define. Instantly I knew that the lithe shape, glimpsed but instantaneously, was that of no chance pedestrian—was indeed that of no ordinary being. At the same moment I heard again, unmistakably, the howling of a dog.

Having said so much why should I not admit that, turning again very quickly, I hurried on to the gate of my cottage and heaved a great sigh of relief when I heard the reassuring bang of the door as I closed it behind me? Coates, my batman, had turned in, having placed a cold repast upon the table in the little dining-room; but although I required nothing to eat I partook of a stiff whisky and soda, idly glancing at two or three letters which lay upon the table.

They proved to contain nothing of very great importance, and having smoked a final cigarette, I turned out the

light in the dining-room and walked into the bedroom—
for the cottage was of bungalow pattern—and crossing the
darkened room stood looking out of the window.

It commanded a view of a little kitchen garden and
beyond of a high hedge, with glimpses of sentinel trees lining the main road. The wind had dropped entirely, but
clouds were racing across the sky at a tremendous speed so
that the nearly full moon alternately appeared and disappeared, producing an ever-changing effect of light and
shadow. At one moment a moon-bathed prospect stretched
before me as far as the eye could reach, in the next I
might have been looking into a cavern as some angry
cloud swept across the face of the moon to plunge the
scene into utter darkness.

And it was during such a dark spell and at the very moment that I turned aside to light the lamp that I saw *the
eyes*.

From a spot ten yards removed, low down under the
hedges bordering the garden, they looked up at me—those
great, glittering cat's eyes, so that I stifled an exclamation,
drawing back instinctively from the window. A tiger, I
thought, or some kindred wild beast, must have escaped
from captivity. And so rapidly does the mind work at such
times that instinctively I had reviewed the several sporting
pieces in my possession and had selected a rifle which had
proved serviceable in India ere I had taken one step towards the door.

Before that step could be taken the light of the moon
again flooded the garden; and although there was no opening in the hedge by which even a small animal could have
retired, no living thing was in sight. But, near and remote,
dogs were howling mournfully.

CHAPTER II

THE SIGN OF THE CAT

When Coates brought in my tea, newspapers and letters in the morning, I awakened with a start, and:

"Has there been any rain during the night, Coates?" I asked.

Coates, whose unruffled calm at all times provided an excellent sedative, replied:

"Not since a little before midnight, sir."

"Ah!" said I, "and have you been in the garden this morning, Coates?"

"Yes, sir," he replied, "for raspberries for breakfast, sir."

"But not on this side of the cottage?"

"Not on this side."

"Then will you step out, Coates, keeping carefully to the paths, and proceed as far as the tool-shed? Particularly note if the beds have been disturbed between the hedge and the path, but don't make any marks yourself. You are looking for *spoor*, you understand."

"Spoor? Very good, sir. Of big game?"

"Of big game, yes, Coates."

Unmoved by the strangeness of his instructions, Coates, an object-lesson for those who decry the excellence of British Army disciplinary methods, departed.

It was with not a little curiosity and interest that I awaited his report. As I sat sipping my tea I could hear his regular tread as he passed along the garden path outside the window. Then it ceased and was followed by a vague muttering. He had found something. All traces of the storm had disappeared and there was every indication of a renewal of the heatwave; but I knew that the wet soil would have preserved a perfect impression of any imprint made upon it on the previous night. Nevertheless, with the early morning sun streaming into my window out of a sky

14

as near to turquoise as I had ever seen it in England, I found it impossible to recapture that uncanny thrill which had come to me in the dark hours when out of the shadows under the hedge the great cat's eyes had looked up at me.

And now, becoming more fully awake, I remembered something else which hitherto I had not associated with the latter phenomenon. I remembered that lithe and evasive pursuing shape which I had detected behind me on the road. Even now, however, it was difficult to associate one with the other; for whereas the dimly seen figure had resembled that of a man (or, more closely, that of a woman) the eyes had looked out upon me from a point low down near the ground, like those of some crouching feline.

Coates's footsteps sounded again upon the path and I heard him walking round the cottage and through the kitchen. Finally he re-entered the bedroom and stood just within the doorway in that attitude of attention which was part and parcel of the man. His appearance would doubtless have violated the proprieties of the Albany, for in my rural retreat he was called upon to perform other and more important services than those of a valet. His neatly shaved chin, stolid red countenance and perfectly brushed hair, were unexceptionable of course, but because his duties would presently take him into the garden he wore, not the regulation black, but an ancient shooting-jacket, khaki breeches and brown gaiters, looking every inch of him the old soldier that he was.

"Well, Coates?" said I.

He cleared his throat.

"There are footprints in the radish-beds, sir," he reported.

"Footprints?"

"Yes, sir. Very deep. As though someone had jumped over the hedge and landed there."

"Jumped over the hedge!" I exclaimed. "That would be a considerable jump, Coates, from the road."

"It would, sir. Maybe she scrambled up."

"She?"

Coates cleared his throat again.

"There are three sets of prints in all. First a very deep one where the party had landed, then another broken up like, where she had turned round, and the third set with

the heel-marks very deep where she had sprung back over
the hedge."

"*She?*" I shouted.

"The prints, sir," resumed Coates, unmoved, "are those
of a lady's high-heeled shoes."

I sat bolt upright in bed, staring at the man and scarcely
able to credit my senses. Words failed me. Whereupon:

"Will you have tea or coffee for breakfast?" inquired
Coates.

"Tea or coffee be damned, Coates!" I cried. "I'm going
out to look at those footprints! If you had seen what I saw
last night, even your old mahogany countenance would
relax for once, I assure you."

"Indeed, sir," said Coates; "did you see the lady, then?"

"Lady!" I exclaimed, tumbling out of bed. "If the eyes
that looked at me last night belonged to a 'lady' either I
am mad or the 'lady' is of another world."

I pulled on a bath-robe and hurried out into the garden,
Coates showing me the spot where he had found the mysterious footprints. A very brief examination sufficed to
convince me that his account had been correct. Someone
wearing high-heeled shoes clearly enough had stood there
at some time whilst the soil was quite wet; and as no track
led to or from the marks, Coates's conclusion that the person who had made them must have come over the hedge
was the only feasible one. I turned to him in amazement,
but recognizing in time the wildly fantastic nature of the
sight which I had seen in the night, I refrained from
speaking of the blazing eyes and made my way to the
bathroom wondering if some chance reflection might not
have deceived me and the presence of a woman's foot-
marks at the same spot be no more than a singular coincidence. Even so the mystery of their presence there remained unexplained.

My thoughts were diverted from a trend of profitless
conjecture when shortly after breakfast time my 'phone
bell rang. It was the editor of the *Planet*, to whom I had
been indebted for a number of special commis-
sions—including my fascinating quest of the Giant Gnu,
which, generally supposed to be extinct, was reported by
certain natives and others to survive in a remote corner of
the Dark Continent.

Readers of the *Planet* will remember that although I

failed to discover the Gnu, I came upon a number of notable things on my journey through the almost unexplored country about the head-waters of the Niger.

"A most extraordinary case has cropped up," he said, "quite in your line, I think, Addison. Evidently a murder, and the circumstances seem to be most dramatic and unusual. I should be glad if you would take it up."

I inquired without much enthusiasm for details. Criminology was one of my hobbies, and in several instances I had traced cases of alleged haunting and other supposedly supernatural happenings to a criminal source; but the ordinary sordid murder did not interest me.

"The body of Sir Marcus Coverly has been found in a crate!" explained my friend. "The crate was being lowered into the hold of the ss. *Oritoga* at the West India Docks. It had been delivered by a conveyance specially hired for the purpose apparently, as the *Oritoga* is due to sail in an hour. There are all sorts of curious details, but these you can learn for yourself. Don't trouble to call at the office; proceed straight to the dock."

"Right!" I said shortly. "I'll start immediately."

And this sudden decision had been brought about by the mention of the victim's name. Indeed, as I replaced the receiver on the hook I observed that my hand was shaking and I have little doubt that I had grown pale.

In the first place, then, let me confess that my retirement to the odd little retreat which at this time was my home, and my absorption in the obscure studies to which I have referred were not so much due to any natural liking for the life of a recluse as to the shattering of certain matrimonial designs. I had learned of the wreck of my hopes upon reading a Press paragraph which announced the engagement of Isobel Merlin to Eric Coverly. And it was as much to conceal my disappointment from the world as for any better reason that I had slunk into retirement; for if I am slow to come to a decision in such a matter, once come to it is of no light moment.

Yet although I had breathed no word of my lost dreams to Isobel but had congratulated her with the rest, often and bitterly I had cursed myself for a sluggard. Too late I had learned that she had but awaited a word from me; and I had gone off to Mesopotamia, leaving that word unspoken. During my absence Coverly had won the prize which

I had thrown away. He was heir to the title, for his cousin, Sir Marcus, was unmarried. Now here, a bolt from the blue, came the news of his cousin's death!

It can well be imagined with what intense excitement I hurried to the docks. All other plans abandoned, Coates, arrayed in his neat blue uniform, ran the Rover round from the garage, and ere long we were jolting along the hideously uneven Commercial Road East, dodging traction engines drawing strings of lorries, and continually meeting delay in the form of those breakdowns which are of hourly occurrence in this congested but rugged highway.

In the West India Dock Road the way became slightly more open, but when at last I alighted and entered the dock gates, I recognized that every newspaper and news agency in the kingdom was apparently represented. Jones, of the *Gleaner*, was coming out as I went in, and:

"Hallo, Addison!" he cried, "this is quite in your line! It's as mad as 'Alice in Wonderland.'"

I did not delay, however, but hurried on in the direction of a dock building, at the door of which was gathered a heterogeneous group comprising newspaper men, dock officials, police and others who were unclassifiable. Half a dozen acquaintances greeted me as I came up, and I saw that the door was closed and that a constable stood on duty before it.

"I call it damned impudence, Addison!" exclaimed one pressman; "the dock people are refusing everybody information until Inspector Somebody-or-other arrives from New Scotland Yard. I should think he has stopped on the way to get his lunch."

The speaker glanced impatiently at his watch and I went to speak to the man on duty.

"You have orders to admit no one, constable?" I asked.

"That's so, sir," he replied. "We're waiting for Detective-Inspector Gatton, who has been put in charge of the case."

"Ah! Gatton," I muttered, and stepping aside from the expectant group I filled and lighted my pipe, convinced that anything to be learned I should learn from Inspector Gatton, for he and I were old friends, having been mutually concerned in several interesting cases.

A few minutes later the inspector arrived—a thick-set, clean-shaven, very bronzed man, his dark hair streaked with grey, and with all the appearance of a retired naval officer, in his well-cut blue serge suit and soft felt hat; a very reserved man whose innocent-looking blue eyes gave him that frank and open expression which is more often associated with a seaman than with a detective. He nodded to several acquaintances in the group, and then, observing me where I stood, came over and shook hands.

"Open the door, constable," he ordered quietly.

The constable produced a key and unlocked the door of the small stone building. Immediately there was a forward movement of the whole waiting group, but:

"If you please, gentlemen," said Gatton, raising his hand. "I must make my examination first; and Mr. Addison," he added, seeing the resentment written upon the faces of my disappointed *confrères*, "has special information which I am going to ask him to place at my disposal."

The constable stood aside and I followed Inspector Gatton into the stone shed.

"Lock the door again, constable," he ordered, "no one is to be admitted."

Thereupon I looked about me, and the scene which I beheld was so strange and gruesome that its every detail remains imprinted upon my memory.

The building then was lighted by four barred windows set so high in the walls that no one could look in from the outside. Blazing sunlight poured in at the two southerly windows and drew a sharp black pattern of the bars across the paved floor. Kneeling beside a stretcher, fully in this path of light, so that he presented a curious striped appearance, was a man who presently proved to be the divisional surgeon, and two paces beyond stood a police inspector who was engaged at the moment of our entrance in making entries in his note-book.

On the stretcher, so covered up that only his face was visible, lay one whom at first I failed to recognize, for the horribly contorted features presented a kind of mottled green appearance utterly indescribable.

Stifling an exclamation of horror I stared at that ghastly face, then:

"My God!" I muttered. "Yes! it *is* Sir Marcus!"

The surgeon stood up and the inspector advanced to meet Gatton, but my horrified gaze had strayed from the stretcher to a badly damaged and splintered packing-case, which was the only other object in the otherwise empty shed. At this I stared as much aghast as I had stared at the dead man.

The iron bands were broken and twisted and the whole of one side lay in fragments on the floor; but upon a board which had formed part of the top I perceived the figure of a cat roughly traced in green paint.

Beyond any shadow of doubt this crate was the same which on the night before had lain in the garage of the Red House!

CHAPTER III

THE GREEN IMAGE

"Yes," said Gatton, "I was speaking no more than the truth when I told them that you had special information which I hoped you would place at my disposal. Some of the particulars were given to me over the 'phone, you see, and I was glad to find you here when I arrived. I should have consulted you in any event, and principally about—that."

He pointed to an object which I held in my hand. It was a little green enamel image; the crouching figure of a woman having a cat's head, a piece of Egyptian workmanship probably of the fourth century B.C. Considered in conjunction with the figure painted upon the crate, the presence of this little image was so amazing a circumstance that from the moment when it had been placed in my hand I had stood staring at it almost dazedly.

The divisional surgeon had gone, and only the local officer remained with Gatton and myself in the building. Sir Marcus Coverly presented all the frightful appearance of one who has died by asphyxia, and although of course there would be an autopsy, little doubt existed respecting the mode of his death. The marks of violence found upon the body could be accounted for by the fact that the crate had fallen a distance of thirty feet into the hold, and the surgeon was convinced that the injuries to the body had all been received after death, death having taken place, in his opinion, fully twelve hours before.

"You see," said Gatton, "when the crate broke several things which presumably were in Sir Marcus's pockets were found lying loose amongst the wreckage. That cat-woman was one of them."

"Yet it may not have been in any of his pockets at all," said I.

"It *may* not," agreed Gatton. "But that it was some-where in the crate is beyond dispute, I think. Besides, this is more than a coincidence."

And he pointed to the painted cat upon the lid of the packing-case. I had already told him of the episode at the Red House on the previous night, and now:

"The fates are on our side," I said, "for at least we know where the crate was dispatched from."

"Quite so," agreed Gatton. "We should have got that from the carter later, of course, but every minute saved in an affair such as this is worth considering. As a pressman you will probably disagree with me, but I propose to sup-press these two pieces of evidence. Premature publication of clues too often handicaps us. Now, what *is* that figure exactly?"

"It is a votive offering of a kind used in Ancient Egypt by pilgrims to Bubastis. It is a genuine antique, and if you think the history of such relics is likely to assist the investi-gation I can give you some further particulars this evening if you have time to call at my place."

"I think," said Gatton, taking the figure from me and looking at it with a singular expression on his face, "that the history of the thing is very important. The fact that a rough representation of a somewhat similar figure is paint-ed upon the case cannot possibly be a coincidence."

I stared at him silently for a moment, then:

"You mean that the crate was specially designed to con-tain the body?" I asked.

"I am certainly of that opinion," declared Inspector Heath, the local officer. "It is of just the right size and shape for the purpose."

Once more I began to examine the fragments stacked upon the floor, and then I looked again at the several ob-jects which lay beside the crate. They were the personal

belongings of the dead baronet, and the police had carefully noted in which of his pockets each object had been
found. He was in evening dress and a light top-coat had
been packed into the crate beside him. In this had been
found a cigar-case and a pair of gloves; a wallet containing
£20 in Treasury notes and a number of cards and personal papers had fallen out of the crate together with the cat
statuette. The face of his watch was broken. It had been in
his waistcoat pocket, but it still ticked steadily on where it
lay there beside its dead owner. A gold-mounted malacca
cane also figured amongst the relics of the gruesome
crime; so that whatever had been the object of the murder,
that of robbery was out of the question.

"The next thing to do," said Gatton, "is to trace Sir
Marcus's movements from the time that he left home last
night to the time that he met his death. I am going out
now to 'phone to the Yard. We ought to have succeeded in
tracing the carter who brought the crate here before the
evening. I personally shall proceed to Sir Marcus's rooms
and then to this Red House around which it seems to me
that the mystery centres."

He put the enamel figure into his pocket, and taking up
the broken board which bore the painted cat:

"You are carrying a top-coat," he said. "Hide this under
it!"

He turned to Inspector Heath, nodding shortly.

"All right," he said, with a grim smile, "go out now and
talk to the crowd!"

Having issued certain telephonic instructions touching
the carter who had delivered the crate to the docks, and
then imparting to the representatives of the Press a guarded statement for publication, Inspector Gatton succeeded
in wedging himself into my little two-seater, and ere long
we were lurching and bumping along the ill-paved East
End streets.

The late Sir Marcus's London address, which had been
unknown to me, we had learned from his cards, and it was
with the keenest anticipation of a notable discovery that I
presently found myself with Gatton mounting the stairs to
the chambers of the murdered baronet.

At the very moment of our arrival the door was opened
and a man, quite obviously a constable in plain clothes,
came out. Behind him I observed one whom I took to be

the late Sir Marcus's servant, a pathetic and somewhat di-shevelled figure.

"Hallo, Blythe!" said Gatton, "who instructed you to come here?"

"Sir Marcus's man—Morris—telephoned the Yard," was the reply, "as he couldn't understand what had become of his master, and I was sent along to see him."

"Oh," said Gatton, "very good. Report to me in due course."

Blythe departed, and Gatton and I entered the hall. The man, Morris, closed the door, and led us into a small library. Beside the telephone stood a tray bearing decanter and glasses, and there was evidence that Morris had partaken of a hurried breakfast consisting only of biscuits and whisky and soda.

"I haven't been to bed all night, gentlemen," he began the moment that we entered the room. "Sir Marcus was a good master, and if he was sleeping away from home he never failed to advise me, so that I knew even before the dreadful news reached me that something was amiss."

He was quite unstrung and his voice was unsteady. The reputation of the late baronet had been one which I personally did not envy him, but whatever his faults, and I knew they had been many, he had evidently possessed the redeeming virtue of being a good employer.

"A couple of hours' sleep would make a new man of you," said Gatton kindly. "I understand your feelings, but no amount of sorrow can mend matters, unfortunately. Now, I don't want to worry you, but there are one or two points which I must ask you to clear up. In the first place, did you ever see this before?"

From his pocket he took out the little figure of Bâst, the cat-goddess, and held it up before Morris.

The man stared at it with lack-lustre eyes, scratching his unshaven chin; then he shook his head slowly.

"Never," he declared. "No, I am positive I never saw a figure like that before."

"Then, secondly," continued Gatton, "was your master ever in Egypt?"

"Not that I am aware of; certainly not since I have been with him—six years on the thirty-first of this month."

"Ah," said Gatton. "Now, when did you last see Sir Marcus?"

"At half-past six last night, sir. He was dining at his club and then going to the New Avenue Theatre. I booked a seat for him myself."

"He was going alone, then?"

"Yes."

Gatton glanced at me significantly and I experienced an uncomfortable thrill. In the inspector's glance I had read that he suspected the presence of a woman in the case, and at the mention of the New Avenue Theatre it had instantly occurred to me that Isobel Merlin was appearing there! Gatton turned again to Morris.

"Sir Marcus had not led you to suppose that there was any likelihood of his *not* returning last night?"

"No, sir; that was why, knowing his regular custom, I became so alarmed when he failed to come back or to 'phone."

Gatton stared hard at the speaker, and:

"It will be no breach of confidence on your part," he said, speaking slowly and deliberately, "for you to answer my next question. The best service you can do your late master now will be to help us to apprehend his murderer."

He paused a moment, then:

"Was Sir Marcus interested in someone engaged at the New Avenue Theatre?" he asked.

Morris glanced from face to face in a pathetic, troubled fashion. He rubbed the stubble on his chin again and hesitated. Finally:

"I believe," he replied, "that there was a lady there who——"

He paused, swallowing, and:

"Yes," Gatton prompted, "who?"

"Who—interested Sir Marcus; but I don't know her name nor anything about her," he declared. "I knew about —some of the others, but Sir Marcus was—very reserved about this lady, which made me think——"

"Yes?"

"That he perhaps hadn't been so successful."

Morris ceased speaking and sat staring at a bookcase vacantly.

"Ah," murmured Gatton. Then, abruptly: "Did Sir Marcus ever visit anyone who lived in College Road?" he demanded.

Morris looked up wearily.

"College Road?" he repeated. "Where is that, sir?"

"It doesn't matter," said Gatton shortly, "if the name is unfamiliar to you. Had Sir Marcus a car?"

"Not latterly, sir."

"Any other servants?"

"No. As a bachelor he had no use for a large establishment, and Friar's Park remains in the possession of the late Sir Burnham's widow."

"Sir Burnham? Sir Marcus's uncle?"

"Yes."

"What living relatives had Sir Marcus?"

"His aunt—Lady Burnham Coverly—with whom I believe he was on bad terms. Her own son, who ought to have inherited the title, was dead, you see. I think she felt bitterly towards my master. The only other relative I ever heard of was Mr. Eric—Sir Marcus's second cousin—now *Sir* Eric, of course."

I turned aside, glancing at some books which lay scattered on the table. The wound was a new one, and I suppose I was not man enough to hide the pain which mention of Eric Coverly still occasioned me.

"Were the cousins good friends?" continued the even, remorseless voice of the inquisitor.

Morris looked up quickly.

"They were not, sir," he answered. "They never had been. But some few months back a fresh quarrel arose, and one night in this very room it almost came to blows."

"Indeed? What was the quarrel about?"

The old hesitancy claimed Morris again, but at last:

"Of course," he said, with visible embarrassment, "it was—a woman."

I felt my heart leaping wildly, but I managed to preserve an outward show of composure.

"What woman?" demanded Gatton.

"I don't know, sir."

"Do you mean it?"

A fierce note of challenge had come into the quiet voice, but Morris looked up and met Gatton's searching stare unflinchingly.

"I swear it," he said. "I never was an eavesdropper."

"I suggest it was the same woman that Sir Marcus went to see last night?" Gatton continued.

The examination of Morris had reached a point at

which I found myself hard put to it to retain even a seeming of composure. All Gatton's questions had been leading up to this suggestion, as I now perceived clearly enough; and from the cousins' quarrel to Isobel, Eric's *fiancée*, who was engaged at the New Avenue Theatre, was an inevitable step. But:

"Possibly, sir," was Morris's only answer.

Inspector Gatton stared hard at the man for a moment or so, then:

"Very well," he said. "Take my advice and turn in. There will be much for you to do presently, I am afraid. Who was Sir Marcus's solicitor?"

Morris gave the desired information in a tired, toneless voice, and we departed. Little did Gatton realize that his words were barbed, when, as we descended to the street, he said:

"I have a call to make at Scotland Yard next, after which my first visit will be to the stage doorkeeper of the New Avenue Theatre."

"Can I be of further assistance to you at the moment?" I asked, endeavouring to speak casually.

"Thanks, no. But I should welcome your company this afternoon at my examination of the Red House. I understand that it is in your neighbourhood, so perhaps as you are also professionally interested in the case, you might arrange to meet me there. Are you returning home now or going to the *Planet* office?"

"I think to the office," I replied. "In any event, 'phone there making an appointment and I will meet you at the Red House."

CHAPTER IV

ISOBEL

Ten minutes later I was standing in a charming little boudoir which too often figured in my day-dreams. My own photograph was upon the mantelpiece, and in Isobel's dark eyes when she greeted me there was a light which I lacked the courage to try to understand. I had not at that time learned what I learned later, and have already indicated, that my own foolish silence had wounded Isobel as deeply as her subsequent engagement to Eric Coverly had wounded me.

The psychology of a woman is intriguing in its very *naïveté*, and now as she stood before me, slim and graceful in her well-cut walking costume, a quick flicker of red flaming in her cheeks and her eyes alight with that sweet tantalizing look in which expectation and a hot pride were mingled, I wondered and felt sick at heart. Desirable she was beyond any other woman I had known, and I called myself witling, coward, to have avoided putting my fortune to the test on that fatal day of my departure for Mesopotamia. For just as she looked at me now she had looked at me then. But to-day she was evidently on the point of setting out—I did not doubt with the purpose of meeting Eric Coverly; on that day of the irrevocable past she had been free and I had been silent.

"You nearly missed me, Jack," she said gaily. "I was just going out."

By the very good-fellowship of her greeting she restored me to myself and enabled me to stamp down—at least temporarily—the monster through whose greedy eyes I had found myself considering the happiness of Eric Coverly.

"I am afraid, Isobel," I replied, "that what I have to tell you is not by any means pleasant—although——"

"Yes?" she prompted, noting how I hesitated.

"Although it means that you are now the future Lady Coverly."

The bright colour left her cheeks. That some black tragedy underlay my words she had intuitively perceived, but I could see that she failed to grasp the whole meaning of my bald statement. She sank down slowly into a cushioned chair, so that a beam of golden light pouring in through the opened window set aglowing the russet tints in her dark brown hair.

"Did you know Sir Marcus?" I asked, speaking as gently as I could.

With what intense, if hidden, emotion I awaited her answer it were impossible to describe.

"Do you mean——"

She met my glance, and I nodded gravely.

"Oh, Jack! When did it happen?"

"Last night. But you have not told me if you knew him?" I persisted.

Isobel shook her head.

"Not in any way—intimately," she replied. "Eric"—she hesitated, glancing up quickly and as quickly down again —"and he were not on good terms."

"But you had met him?" I persisted; for I had detected in her manner a reluctance to discuss Sir Marcus which I failed to understand.

"I used to meet him, Jack, when—when you were away. He came once or twice with Eric. They were not good friends, even then. But I never liked him. I quite lost sight of him from the time that he came into the title—about four years ago, was it not?—until quite recently. He had been in Russia, I think. Then he——" Again she hesitated. It was odd how often people hesitated, as if seeking for words, when speaking of the late baronet. "He called at the theatre. Considering that he knew of my engagement to Eric his manner was not quite nice. But I was anxious to prevent trouble, and did not mention the visit to Eric. Sir Marcus was very persistent, however. One night Eric saw him leaving the stagedoor, and I believe there was a dreadful scene at Sir Marcus's rooms."

"And that is all you know of him, Isobel?"

"Practically all, except what I have heard, of course. I might add that I instructed Marie to tell Sir Marcus I was engaged whenever he might call in future."

"And did he call again?"

"Marie said that he sent his card up on several occasions, but she knew how the affair worried me and did not tell me at the time. I saw him in the stalls occasionally, and—oh!"

The last word was a mere murmur. Isobel's expression grew more than ever troubled.

"He was there last night," she whispered, and raising her eyes to me: "Tell me how it happened, and where——"

But ere I had time to begin there was an interruption. Dimly, a telephone bell rang. I could hear the voice of Marie, Isobel's maid, answering the call, then:

"Mr. Coverly to speak to you, madam," said Marie, entering the room.

"He must have only just heard the news!" cried Isobel, rising swiftly and going out.

Consumed by impatience I walked up and down the dainty apartment listening to Isobel's muffled voice speaking in the lobby. Twice I went to the window and peered down into the street, expecting to see the thick-set figure of Inspector Gatton approaching. My frame of mind was peculiar and troubled. Gatton's inquiries pointed unmistakably to a suspicion that Sir Marcus's last hours had been spent if not actually with, at any rate near to Isobel. And since the man who would most directly profit by the baronet's death happened also to be Isobel's *fiancé*, I foresaw a dreadful ordeal for both if Eric Coverly was not in a position to establish an alibi.

I had been about to ask her if Coverly had been in her company on the previous night when the interruption had occurred. Now, if Gatton should arrive and find me in Isobel's flat, what construction would he put upon my presence?

Yet again I went to the window and peered anxiously up and down the street. Every cab that approached I expected to contain the inspector, and I heaved a sigh of relief as one after another passed the door. Pedestrians who turned the distant corner I scrutinized closely and was so employed when Isobel came running back to the room.

All her colour had fled and her eyes were wide and fear-stricken.

"Oh, Jack, Jack!" she cried, "it is horrible, horrible! Eric is at his solicitors' and they tell him that suspicion is bound to fall on *him!* It's preposterous—unthinkable. It must have been some fiend who committed such a crime, not a human being——"

"Then," I interrupted excitedly, "Coverly was not with you last night?"

"No! That is the crowning tragedy of it all. He 'phoned me early in the evening saying that he had an unavoidable business appointment to keep. From the tone of his voice——"

She ceased speaking abruptly, and stared at me rather wildly.

"Isobel," I said, "you should surely know that you can trust your life to me—and the life of anyone dear to you."

She quickly laid her hand on my arm and her face flushed sweetly. I fear I had infused my words with an ardour which exhibited at an earlier and more opportune moment might have changed the course of both our lives.

"Of course I know, Jack," she said. "But I am so frightened that I distrust my very self. Well, then, I thought that I noticed a change in Eric's manner last night—in the tone of his voice. In fact, I asked him if I had done anything of which he had disapproved." She gave me a quick little embarrassed glance. "He is somewhat exacting, you know. He laughed at the idea, but in rather a forced way it seemed. Then he arranged to meet me for lunch at the Carlton today."

"But surely he can satisfactorily account for his movements? He must have been seen by those who know him."

Isobel frowned in a troubled manner that awakened strange, wild longings.

"I cannot make it out," she replied. "He appears to be keeping something back."

"He is very ill-advised. He will certainly have to make up his mind to speak out when Inspector Gatton examines him. I cannot disguise from you, Isobel, that the police know that Sir Marcus was at the New Avenue last night, and since his death occurred some hours later the nature of their suspicion is obvious enough. Are you joining him at the solicitors', Isobel?"

"Yes, he asked me to do so."

"Then come along at once. I expect a Scotland Yard man to arrive at any moment, and it would be advisable to see Coverly and to take a legal opinion before you give your testimony."

"But, Jack!" Isobel confronted me. "You don't think that I or Eric have anything to hide?"

"Certainly not. You must know that I do not think so. But, on the other hand, the legal mind being used to considering problems of evidence, a solicitor will be able to advise you of the best course to adopt, and that most likely to result in your being spared all association with the inquiry. Meanwhile—let us hurry. I prefer to give Inspector Gatton my own account of this visit rather than to be discovered here by him. He will learn from Marie that I have called, of course, but that doesn't matter."

We had now quitted the flat and were descending the stairs. On reaching the street I glanced sharply to right and left. But Gatton was not in sight.

I secured a taxi at the corner and Isobel set out for the office of Coverly's solicitor. I stood looking after the cab until it was out of sight, and then I set out to walk to the *Planet* office. By the time that I had reached Fleet Street I had my ideas in some sort of order, and I sat down to write the first of my articles on the "*Oritoga* mystery"— for under that title the murder of Sir Marcus Coverly was destined to figure as the *cause célèbre* of the moment. I had more than one reason for reticence, and indeed I experienced no little difficulty in preparing the requisite amount of copy without involving Isobel and Eric Coverly. Half-way through my task I paused, laid down my pen, and was on the point of tearing up the pages already written and declining the commission at the eleventh hour.

A few minutes' reflection, however, enabled me to see that the best service I could offer to the suspected man (always assuming that he had no alibi to offer) was that of representing the facts as I saw them to the vast public reached by this influential journal. In my own mind I had never entertained a shadow of suspicion that Coverly was the culprit. Underlying the horrible case I thought I could perceive even darker things—a mystery within a mystery; a horror over-topping horror.

I had just resumed work, then, when a boy came in to inform me that Gatton had rung up and wished to speak to me.

Half fearful of what I should hear, I went to the adjoining room and took up the receiver. Presently:

"Hallo! Is that Mr. Addison?" came Gatton's voice.

"Yes, speaking. What developments, Gatton?"

"Several. I've got the report of the estate agent, and I've seen the stage-doorkeeper of the New Avenue! You mustn't write anything until I see you, but in order to regularize things a bit I've spoken to the Chief and formally asked his permission to consult you on the case—about the Egyptian figures, you know. He remembered you at once, so it's all square. But I've got a bone to pick with you."

"What is that?"

"Never mind now. Can you meet me at the Red House at five o'clock?"

"Yes. I will be there."

"Good. I don't hope for much. It's the strangest case I ever touched. We are dealing with unusual people; not ordinary criminals."

"I agree."

"If there is any man in London who can see daylight through the mystery I believe you are the man. Do you know on what I think the whole thing turns?"

"On some undiscovered incident in Sir Marcus's past, beyond a doubt. Probably an amorous adventure."

"You re wrong," said Gatton grimly. "It turns on the figure of the green cat. Good-bye. Five o'clock."

CHAPTER V

THE INTERRUPTED SUPPER

I arrived at the Red House before Inspector Gatton. A constable was on duty at the gate, and as I came up and paused he regarded me rather doubtfully until I told him that I had an appointment with Gatton. I stared up the drive towards the house. It was not, apparently, a very old building, presenting some of the worst features of the mid-Victorian period, and whence it derived its name I could not conjecture unless from the fact that the greater part of the façade was overgrown with some kind of red creeper.

The half-moon formed by the crescent-shaped carriage-way and the wall bordering the road was filled with rather unkempt shrubbery, laurels and rhododendrons for the most part, from amid which arose several big trees. In the blaze of the afternoon sun the place looked commonplace enough with estate agents' bills pasted in the dirty windows, and it was difficult to conceive that it had been the scene of the mysterious crime of which at that hour all London was talking and which later was to form a subject of debate throughout the civilized world.

Gatton joined me within a few minutes of my arrival. He was accompanied by Constable Bolton with whom I had first visited the Red House. Bolton was now in plain clothes, and he had that fish-out-of-water appearance which characterizes the constable in mufti. Indeed he looked rather dazed, and on arriving before the house he removed his bowler and mopped his red face with a large handkerchief, nodding to me as he did so.

"Good afternoon, sir; it was lucky you came along with me last night. I thought it was a funny go, and I was right, it seems."

"Quite right," said Gatton shortly, "and now here are the keys which you returned to the depot this morning."

From his pocket the inspector produced a steel ring bearing a large and a small key, which I recognized as that which had hung from the lock of the garage door on the previous night.

We walked along to the garage, and Inspector Gatton placed the key in the lock; then turning to Bolton:

"Now," he directed, "show us exactly what you did."

Bolton replaced his bowler, which hitherto he had carried in his hand, hesitated for a moment, and then unlocked the door.

"Of course I had my lantern with me last night," he explained, "and this gentleman and myself stood looking in for a moment."

"Mr. Addison has already described to me exactly what he saw," said Gatton. "Show us what you did after Mr. Addison left you."

Bolton, with a far-away look in his eyes betokening an effort of retrospection, withdrew the key from the lock and entered the garage, Gatton and I following. There was a sky window to light the place, so that when Bolton reclosed the door we could see well enough. His movements were as follows: Relocking the door from the inside he walked slowly along to a smaller door at the opposite end, and with the other key attached to the ring unfastened it.

"Wait a moment," said Gatton. "Did you look about you at all before opening this door?"

"Only long enough to find where it was, sir. Just about as long as I showed you."

"All right. Go on, then."

We followed Bolton out into a very narrow hedge-bordered path, evidently a tradesman's entrance, and he turned and locked the door behind him. Slipping the keys into his pocket he tramped stolidly out to the main road whereon we emerged immediately beside the garage.

"Ah," murmured Gatton. "Now give me the keys," and as the man did so: "Throughout all this time did you see or hear anything of an unusual nature?"

Bolton removed his bowler once more. I had gathered by this time that he regarded fresh air as an aid to reflection.

"Well, sir," he replied in a puzzled way, "that first door——"

"Well," said Gatton, as the man hesitated.

"It seemed to open more easily just now than it did last night. There seemed to be a sort of hitch before when it was about half-way open."

"Perhaps the crate was in the way?" suggested Gatton. "Except for the absence of the crate do you notice anything different, anything missing, or anything there now that was not there before?"

Bolton shook his head.

"No," he answered, "it looks just the same to me—except, as I say, that the door seemed to open more easily."

"H'm," muttered Gatton; "and you carried the keys in your pocket until you went off duty?"

"Yes, sir."

"All right. You can go now."

Bolton touched his bowler hat and departed, and Gatton turned to me with a grim smile.

"We'll just step inside again," he said, "so as not to attract any undue attention."

He again unlocked the garage door and closed it as we entered.

"Now," said he, "before we go any farther, what was your idea in keeping back the fact that one of the missing links in the chain of evidence was already in your possession?"

"No doubt," I said rather guiltily, "you refer to the fact of my acquaintance with Miss Isobel Merlin?"

"I do!" said Gatton, "and to the fact that you nipped in ahead of me and interviewed this important witness before

I had even heard of her existence." He continued to smile, but the thoroughness and unflinching pursuit of duty, which were the outstanding features of the man, underlay his tone of badinage. "I want to say," he continued, "that for your co-operation, which has been very useful to me on many occasions, I am always grateful, but if in return I give you facilities which no other pressman has, I don't expect you to abuse them."

"Really, Inspector," I replied, "you go almost too far. I have done nothing to prejudice your case nor could I possibly have known until my interview this morning with Miss Merlin that it was she in whom the late Sir Marcus was interested."

"H'm," said Gatton, but still rather dubiously, his frank, wide-open eyes regarding me in that naïve manner which was so deceptive.

"All that I learned," I continued, "is unequivocally at your disposal. Finally I may tell you—and I would confess it to few men—that Miss Merlin is a very old friend and might have been something more if I had not been a fool."

"Oh!" said Gatton, and his expression underwent a subtle change. "Oh! That's rather awkward; in fact"—he frowned perplexedly—"it's damned awkward!"

"What do you mean?" I demanded.

"Well," said he, "I don t know what account Miss Merlin gave to you of her relations with Sir Marcus——"

"Relations!" I said hotly; "the man was a mere acquaintance; she hadn't even seen him, except from the stage, for some months past."

"Oh," replied Gatton, "is that so?" He looked at me very queerly. "It doesn't seem to dovetail with the evidence of the stage-doorkeeper."

I felt myself changing colour, and:

"What, then, does the stage-doorkeeper assert?" I asked.

Gatton continued to look at me in that perplexed way, and believing that I detected the trend of his reflections:

"Look here, Inspector," I said, "let us understand one another. Whatever may be the evidence of stage-doorkeepers and others, upon one point you can be assured. Miss Merlin had nothing whatever to do with this horrible crime. The idea is unthinkable. So confident am I of this, that you can be perfectly open with me, and I give you my word of honour that I shall be equally frank with you. The truth of the matter cannot possibly injure her in the end, and I am as anxious to discover it as you are."

Gatton suddenly extended his hand, and:

"Good!" he said. "We understand one another, but how is Miss Merlin going to explain this?"

He drew a notebook from his pocket, turned over several leaves, and then:

"On no fewer than six occasions," he said, "I have approximate dates here, Sir Marcus sent his card to Miss Merlin's dressing-room."

"I know," I interrupted him; "he persecuted her, but she never saw him."

"Wait a minute. Last night"—Gatton glanced at me sharply—"Marie, the maid, came down after Sir Marcus's card had been sent to the dressing-room and talked for several minutes to the late baronet, just by the door-keeper's box, but out of earshot. That was at ten o'clock. At eleven, that is after the performance, Sir Marcus returned, and again Marie came down to see him. They went out into the street together and Sir Marcus entered a cab which was waiting and drove off. Miss Merlin left a quarter of an hour later."

Our glances met and a silence of some moments' duration fell between us, then:

"You suggest," I said, "that Miss Merlin had arranged a rendezvous with him, and to save appearances had joined him there later?"

"Well"—Gatton raised his eyebrows—"what do *you* suggest?"

I found myself temporarily at a loss for words, but:

"Knowing nothing of this," I explained, "naturally I was not in a position to tax Miss Merlin with it. Possibly you have done so. What is her explanation?"

"I have not seen her," confessed Gatton; "I arrived at her flat ten minutes after she had gone out—with you."

"You saw Marie?"

"Unfortunately Marie was also out, but I saw an old charwoman who attends daily, I understand, and it was from her that I learned of your visit."

"Marie," I said, "may be able to throw some light on the matter."

"I don't doubt it!" replied Gatton grimly. "Meanwhile

we have sufficient evidence to show that Sir Marcus drove from the New Avenue Theatre to this house."

"He may not have driven here at all," I interrupted; "he may have driven somewhere else and performed the latter part of his journey here——"

"In the crate!" cried Gatton. "Yes, you are right; his body may actually have been inside the crate at the time that you and Bolton arrived here last night; for that would be fully an hour after Sir Marcus left the stage-door."

"But who can have rung up the police station last night?" I cried, "and what can have been the object of this unknown person?"

"That we have to find out," said Gatton quietly; "undoubtedly it formed part of a scheme planned with extraordinary cunning; it was not an accident or an oversight, I mean. The men who are assisting me haven't been idle, for we have already learned some most amazing facts about the case. I haven't yet visited the house myself, but I have here the report of one of my assistants who has done so; also I have the keys. The garage I will inspect more carefully later on."

He glanced quickly about the place before we left it, then, leaving the door locked behind us, we walked along to the gate before which the constable stood on duty, and from thence proceeded up the drive to the front entrance. There was a deep porch supported by pillars and densely overgrown with creeper. I noted, too, a heavy and unhealthy odour as of decaying leaves, and observed that a perfect carpet of these lay on the path. In the shade of the big trees it was comparatively cool, but the heavy malarious smell did not please me and I imagined that it must have repelled more than one would-be lessee.

As we approached the porch I saw that the windows of the rooms immediately left and right of it had been stripped of the agents' bills, for I could see where fragments of paper still adhered to the glass. There were no bills in the porch either; but when Gatton opened the front door I uttered an exclamation of surprise.

We stood in a small lounge-hall. There was a staircase on the left, and three doors opened on to the hall. But although the Red House was palpably unoccupied, the hall was furnished! There were some rugs upon the polished floor, a heavy bronze club-fender in front of the grate, several chairs against the walls and a large palm in a Chinese pot.

"Why," I exclaimed, "the place is furnished and the stairs are carpeted too!"

"Yes," said Gatton, looking keenly about him, "but according to report if you will step upstairs you will get a surprise."

"What do you mean?"

"Well, suppose we go and see."

Gatton led the way and I followed up the stairs as far as the first landing. Here I paused in amazement. For at this point all attempts at furnishing ceased. The landing was quite bare and so were the stairs above it. Seeing my expression of incredulous surprise:

"Yes," said Gatton smiling, "it's a strange arrangement, isn't it?"

We descended again to the furnished hall.

"Look here," continued my companion.

He unlocked a door on the left, having tried several keys from the bunch he carried without success, but finally discovering the right one.

A long rectangular room was revealed, evidently intended for a dining-room. It was empty and unfurnished, odds and ends of newspaper and other rubbish lying here and there upon the floor. My astonishment was momentarily increasing. A second door, that in the centre, Gatton opened, revealing another empty room, but:

"I have reserved this one for the last," he said; "you will find that it is unlocked."

He pointed to the third door, that on the right, and as he evidently intended me to open it, I stepped forward, turned the handle and entered a small square room, exquisitely furnished.

A heavy Persian carpet was spread upon the floor and the windows were draped with some kind of brightly coloured Madras. Tastefully-framed water-colours hung upon the wall. There was a quaint cabinet in the room, too; a low cushioned settee and two armchairs. In the centre was a table upon which stood a lamp with a large mosaic shade. Two high-backed chairs were set to the table—and the table was laid for supper! A bottle of wine stood in an ice-pail, in which the ice had long since melted, and a tempting cold repast was spread. The table was decorated with a bowl of perfect white roses. The silver was good; the napery was snowy.

Like a fool I stood gaping at the spectacle, until, noting the direction of Gatton's glance, I turned my attention to the mantelpiece, upon which a clock was ticking with a dull and solemn note.

Standing beside the clock, in a curious carved frame, was a large photograph of Isobel!

CHAPTER VI

THE VOICE

"This is where the mystery centres," said Gatton.

I made no reply, for I had not yet recovered from the shock of that discovery in the deserted supper-room. It was so wholly unexpected and yet it so cruelly confirmed the inspector's undisguised suspicions that it seemed to me to have created a sort of impalpable barrier between us. Of this Gatton was evidently conscious. He endeavoured to arouse my interest in the inquiries which he was conducting in the garage, but for long enough I saw nothing of the place in which we stood; I could only see that photograph smiling at me inquiringly through a haze of doubt, and my companion's words reached me in a muffled fashion. Finally, however, I succeeded in rousing myself from this dazed condition, and confident as ever that Isobel was innocent of all complicity in the matter:

"The presence of the photograph," I said, "takes us a step farther. Don't you see, Inspector, that this is a deeply and cunningly laid trap? What I had taken for a series of unfortunate coincidences I perceive now to be the workings of an elaborate scheme involving perfectly innocent people in the crime."

"H'm," said Gatton doubtfully; "it may be as you suggest; at any rate it is a new point of view and one which I confess had not occurred to me. There is one witness who can clear up any doubt on the subject."

"You mean Marie?"

"Exactly. She will lie, beyond doubt, but we shall find means to reach the truth."

"Would it not be advisable, Inspector," I asked excitedly, "to make sure of her at once?"

Gatton smiled grimly, and:

"Marie would have to make herself invisible to evade Scotland Yard now," he replied. "She is being watched closely. But," he continued, "what do you make of these marks on the door?"

We had reclosed the garage door and now were standing immediately inside. The marks to which my companion had drawn my attention were situated high up near the roof.

"This may account for the statement of Bolton that the door seemed more difficult to open last night than to-day," he said. "Unless I am greatly mistaken, some sort of attachment existed here until quite recently."

"Possibly a contrivance for reclosing the door?" I suggested.

The marks in fact roughly corresponded to those which would be made by the presence of such a contrivance, and there seemed to have been some attempt where it had been removed to disguise the holes left by the screws.

"But the purpose of it?" muttered Gatton helplessly.

"God knows," I said; "the purpose of the whole thing is a mystery beyond me entirely."

"Assuming that such a piece of mechanism as you suggest had been attached to the door," mused Gatton, "you would have noticed its operation last night, unless one of you held the door open."

"Neither of us held the door!" I interrupted excitedly. "I remember that we stood just outside looking in. I was behind the constable and he was directing the rays of his lantern into the place."

"H'm," muttered Gatton. "Then it wasn't a contrivance for closing the door; it was something else. Suppose we investigate the other door?"

We proceeded to the other door and I became aware of an intense curiosity respecting what we should find, and of a conviction too that there would be evidence here of another attachment. In this I was quite correct. Some piece of mechanism had evidently been fastened to this door also. Together we stood staring up at these tell-tale screw-holes and then rather blankly we stared at one another.

"We only lack one thing," said Gatton; "the scheme upon which all these contrivances, and apparently isolated episodes, were hung together. Nothing, as we have already assumed, was accident, and nothing coincidence. It was with some deliberate purpose that the constable was instructed to walk through this garage, opening and shutting the doors behind him."

"From whom did these instructions come?"

"That is one of the minor points which I have already cleared up," he replied. "On my way here I called at the house agent's, as you know, since I have the keys; I also called at the station. The sergeant who was on duty last night I could not see, unfortunately, but I learned—that it was a woman who rang up."

My heart sank lower and lower. It seemed to me as we stood in that empty garage that an invisible hand was drawing a net closer and closer about Isobel and my ideas became increasingly chaotic, for the purpose of it all eluded me, try how I would to conceive of a scheme by which anyone could profit which necessitated the imprisonment, or worse, of Isobel.

"And the agent?" I asked in a rather toneless voice.

Gatton shook his head.

"I have no reason to doubt the word of this man of business," he replied; "because at the time when I saw him he could not possibly have learned of the crime, but nevertheless his account is almost unbelievable. It appears, then, he, too, received his instructions throughout by telephone."

"What?" I exclaimed.

"By telephone," repeated Gatton. "He was rung up about ten days ago by someone who made a verbal offer to lease the Red House for a period of twelve months. A foreigner, who in lieu of the usual references was prepared to pay the annual rent in advance. As the Red House, to use an Irishism, was regarded as something of a white elephant, the agent was interested, apparently; and when on the following day the sum agreed upon arrived by post, he did not demur about delivering the keys to the prospective lessee, who desired to take certain measurements in regard to carpets and so forth."

"Wait a moment," I interrupted, "to whom did he deliver these keys?"

"To a district messenger who called for them, as the agent had been advised that one would do."

"Very well. What then?"

"That is all that the agent had to say."

"What, that is all?"

"Substantially there is nothing more. It is quite evident that the sole intention of this unknown lessee was to secure possession of the house for the purpose of the crime only."

"Do you mean that from first to last no one but the district messenger appeared in the matter?"

"No one," Gatton assured me, "and the rent, payment of which quite disarmed the agent of course, was sent in the form of Treasury notes and not by cheque."

"But surely some name, some address, must have been given?"

"A name was given," replied Gatton, "and an hotel address, but confirmation of its accuracy was never sought, after the receipt of the money."

"And the voice on the telephone?"

Again I saw that odd expression creep over Gatton's face, and:

"It was a woman's voice," he answered.

"Great heavens!" I muttered—"what does it all mean?"

That the evidence of the cabman when he was discovered and of the carter who had taken the box from the garage to the docks, and (for it was possibly the same man) who had first delivered it at the Red House, would but tighten the net about Isobel, whom I knew to be innocent, I felt assured.

"Gatton," I said, "this case appears to me to resolve itself into a deliberate conspiracy of which the end was not the assassination of Sir Marcus, but the conviction of Miss Merlin!"

Gatton looked at me with evident complexity written all over him.

"I begin to think the same," he confessed. "This business was never planned and carried out by a woman, I'll swear to that. There is a woman concerned in it, for at every point we come upon evidence of her voice issuing the mysterious instructions; but she is not alone in the matter. Already the intricacy of the thing points to a criminal of genius. When we know the whole truth, if we ever do, the fact that the crime was planned by a man of amazing, if perverted, intellect, will be put beyond dispute, I think."

"What is puzzling me, Gatton," I said, "is the connexion existing between the incidents which took place in this garage and those, unknown at present, which took place in the furnished room in the Red House."

"Obviously," replied Gatton, "a supper for two had been prepared, and that one of those two was the late Sir Marcus is perfectly obvious. That he expected the other to be Miss Merlin is at least suggested by the presence of her photograph in the room; for you will have noticed that it is the *only* photograph there."

"Nevertheless," I said firmly, "I am positive that no one would be more surprised than herself to learn of its presence."

"And as I have already said," replied Gatton, "I am rapidly coming round to your way of thinking. But even if I were quite sure of it, the evidence at the moment is all the other way, you will admit. As to the connexion between this garage and the interrupted supper party (for obviously it was interrupted) this it must be my business to find out."

"Don't you think," I said, "that we are attaching perhaps undue importance to the fact that some kind of fittings have been removed from the doors? They may have been removed by the late occupier, and the call to the police station may have been made with the idea of securing a witness, and a credible one, to the presence of the crate here on the night of the murder."

"At the moment," replied Gatton musingly, "I cannot see that this would have served any useful purpose; but nevertheless you may be right. I am going to assume, however, that you are wrong, and that the object of sending Bolton here last night was to open and shut these doors. I propose now to return again to the scene of the interrupted supper."

Leaving the garage not very much wiser than when we had entered it, we paced once more up the drive in the shade of the big trees and were greeted again by the malarious smell of rotting leaves. Entering the Red House, Gatton and I proceeded first to that incredible oasis in the

desert of empty rooms and my companion made a detailed
examination of everything in the place, even sounding the
walls, examining the fittings of the door, and finally proceeding through the hall in the direction of the south wing
of the house—that nearest to the garage.

What he expected to find I had no idea, but his attention
seemed to be more particularly directed towards the wain-
scot and the picture-rails of the empty and uncarpeted
rooms which we entered. Whatever he had sought he
failed to find, and at last we stood in a desolate apartment
looking out into the tangled shrubbery before the windows.
The back of the garage was visible from there and I
viewed it dully, wondering what evil secret it held, and
marvelling at the trick of fate which had made me witness
of an act in this gruesome drama.

"Of course, Gatton," I said, "we are all along assuming
that Sir Marcus actually met his death in this house. We
must remember that he may merely have been brought
here after the crime."

"Such a short period elapsed," replied the inspector,
"between his leaving the New Avenue Theatre and the approximate time of his death that it seems unlikely that he
visited any intermediate spot."

"But he may not have been in the crate when Bolton
and I saw it."

"I don't believe he was," replied Gatton, "but I think he
was at the Red House nevertheless."

I stared at him with curiosity.

"You mean that he was in the house at the time that the
constable and I opened the garage?"

"I do. I think he was in that room where supper was
laid for two."

"Good God!" I exclaimed; for there was something horrible in the idea of the man who now lay murdered having
been in the house presumably alive, whilst Bolton and I
had stood within forty yards of him; in the idea that it had
lain in our power, except for those human limitations
which rendered us ignorant of his presence, to have averted his fate, perhaps to have checked the remorseless movement of this elaborate murder machine which seemingly
had been set up in the Red House.

"Someone was here last night," declared Gatton suddenly as we turned to leave the deserted room, "after you and

Bolton had gone. Everything incriminating the assassin has been removed. Looking at the matter judicially it becomes quite evident that anyone clever enough to have planned this crime could not possibly have been guilty of an act of such glaring stupidity as that of accidentally leaving a photograph planted upon the mantelpiece."

That this fact had presented itself to the inspector with such a force of conviction raised a great load from my mind. It had all along been evident to me, but I had feared that to the official outlook of my companion, and the official outlook is always peculiar, it might have seemed otherwise.

"The clever and cunning villain who planned this thing," I said, "has overstepped himself, as you say, Gatton. If the murder was planned artistically, in his attempt to throw the onus of the crime upon innocent shoulders he has been guilty of a piece of very mediocre work. It would not deceive a child."

"No, I agree with you there. The discovery of that photograph has done more to convince me of the innocence of Miss Merlin than any amount of testimonials to her good character could ever have done. You see," he added, smiling whimsically, "all sorts of people hitherto unsuspected by their closest friends of criminal tendency develop that taint, so that I am never surprised to find a convicted thief or assassin possessed of credentials which would do justice to an archbishop. But when I see an obviously artificial clue I recognize it a mile off. Real clues never stare you in the face like that."

Coming out of the front door, we walked down the leaf-strewn drive to find that the constable on duty at the gate had been joined by a plain-clothes man who was evidently waiting to speak to the inspector.

"Yes?" said Gatton eagerly at sight of the newcomer.

"We have her, sir," he reported tersely.

"Does he refer to Marie?" I asked.

Gatton nodded.

"I think, Mr. Addison," he said, "I will proceed immediately to Bow Street, where she has been taken to be interrogated. Will you come with me or are you otherwise engaged?"

I hesitated ere I replied:

"I do not particularly want to confront this woman, but

I should be much indebted if you could let me know the result of your examination."

"I shall do that without fail," said Gatton, "and some time to-day I should be obliged if you could provide me with the facts concerning the little cat-images which you said you had in your possession."

"Certainly," I agreed. "You are still of the opinion that the mark upon the crate and the image of the cat-woman have an important bearing upon the crime?"

"I don't doubt it," was the reply. "If the photograph clue is a false one, the cat clue is a true one and one to be followed up. Perhaps," he added, "it would be as well if you returned now and looked out the points which you think would be of interest, as when I come I may not have long to stay."

"I will do so," I said, "although I think I can lay my hands upon the material almost immediately."

Accordingly Gatton set off with the detective who had brought the news of Marie's arrest, and I, turning in the opposite direction, proceeded towards my cottage in such a state of mental tumult respecting what the end of all this would be and what it might mean for Isobel that I found myself unable to think connectedly; and needless to say I failed to conjure up by any stretch of the imagination a theory which could cover this amazing and terrible sequence of events.

CHAPTER VII

THE CAT OF BUBASTIS

"She belongs to the innumerable family of cats which suddenly came forth from the ruins of Tell Bastah in 1878," I wrote, Sir Gaston Maspero's "Egyptian Art" lying before me on the table, "and were in a few years scattered over the whole world.

"She is Bâst, a goddess of good family, the worship of whom flourished especially in the east of the delta, and she is very often drawn or named on the monuments, although they do not tell us enough of her myths or her origin. She was allied or related to the Sun, and was now said to be his sister or wife, now his daughter. She sometimes filled a gracious and beneficent role, protecting men against contagious diseases or evil spirits, keeping them off by the music of her sistrum: she had also her hours of treacherous perversity, during which she played with her victim as with a mouse, before finishing him off with a blow of her claws. She dwelt by preference in the city that bore her name, Poubastit, the Bubastis of classical writers. Her temple, at which Cheops and Chephren had worked while building their pyramids, was rebuilt by the Pharaohs of the 22nd Dynasty, enlarged by those of the 26th; when Herodotus visited it in the middle of the fifth century B.C., he considered it one of the most remarkable he had seen in the parts of Egypt through which he had travelled.

"The fêtes of Bâst attracted pilgrims from all parts of Egypt, as at the present day those of Sidi Ahmed el-Bedawee draw people to the modern fair of Tantah. The people of each village crowded into large boats to get there, men and women pell-mell, with the fixed intention of enjoying themselves on the journey, a thing they never failed to do. They accompanied the slow progress of navigation with endless songs, love songs rather than sacred hymns, and there were also to be found among them flute-players and castanet-players to support or keep time to the voices. Whenever they passed by a town they approached the bank as near as they could without landing, and then, while the orchestra redoubled its noise, the passengers threw volleys of insults and coarse remarks at the women standing on the banks; they retorted, and when they had exhausted words——"

I finished my notes at this point; the improper behaviour of the Ancient Egyptians mentioned by the great Egyptologist having no possible bearing upon the matter in hand, I thought. I then proceeded to add some facts directly relating to the votive offerings laid at the feet of the goddess.

"The greater number of pilgrims, before returning home, left a souvenir of their visit at the feet of Bâst. It was a votive stele with a fine inscription, and a picture showing the donor worshipping his goddess; or a statuette in blue or green pottery, or, if they were wealthy, in bronze, silver, or sometimes gold: the goddess would be standing, seated, crouching, with a woman's body and a cat's head, a sistrum or an ægis in her hand. During the Greek period the figures were in bronze or in painted or gilded wood surmounted by a cat's head in bronze, many were life-size and modelled with elaborate art; they had eyes of enamel and amulets on the forehead."

The learned authority went on to explain that these accumulated offerings were after a time stored by the priests in cellars or in pits dug expressly for them, "veritable *favissæ* similar to those of classical times." They accumulated in thousands, large and small, some intact and fresh as when just made, others already out of shape and of no value. The places of concealment were soon forgotten, and the stores hidden therein reposed beyond the reach of men until the day when the chances of excavation brought them to light.

My notes completed, I turned my attention to the little image of green enamel ware which Gatton had left with me for examination. It was not possible to determine the period at which it was buried, but judging from the contours and general form, together with the aspect of the enamel, I thought I recognized the style of the second Saïte Period, and attributed the piece to the early Ptolemies, or the fourth century B.C. It was the time when the worship of Bâst and her subordinate forms, Pakh, Mait, was most popular, the period when the most extensive cemetery of cats was established in Egypt. The execution of the little figure was pure Egyptian, and in no way betrayed Greek influence.

So far had my studies proceeded when I heard the door-bell ring, and Coates entered the room.

"Detective-Inspector Gatton to see you, sir."

Gatton came in looking if anything more puzzled than when I had left him at the Red House; also I thought he looked tired, and:

"Mix yourself a drink, Inspector," I said, pointing to a side-table upon which refreshments were placed.

"Thanks," replied Gatton. "I have not had time to stop for a drink or even a smoke since I left you; but evidence is coming in quickly enough now."

He helped himself to a whisky and soda, being an old visitor and one used to the Bohemian ways of my household; then, setting his glass upon a corner of my writing-table, he dropped into the armchair and began in leisurely fashion to fill his pipe.

Although the hour was growing late, sunset was still a long way off, and the prospect visible through the open window was bathed in golden light. From where I sat I could catch a glimpse of the tree-lined road, and for the first time since that strange experience had befallen me I found myself wondering if the vaguely perceived follower whom I had detected on the previous night, and those blazing feline eyes which had looked out at me from beneath the shadow of the hedge, could have had any possible connexion with the tragedy which at about the same hour was being enacted in the Red House. I determined presently to confide the strange particulars to my friend, but first I was all anxiety to learn what evidence Marie had given, and that this evidence to which he had referred had done little more than to increase Gatton's perplexity was clear enough from his expression. Therefore:

"Tell me about Marie," I said.

Gatton smiled grimly, took a drink from his glass, and then:

"She began, of course, as I had anticipated, by denying all knowledge of the matter, but recognizing that she was in a tight corner, she presently changed her tactics, and although every available plan was tried to induce her to change her ground, she afterwards stuck to the extraordinary story which we first extracted from her. Briefly it was this:

"The late Sir Marcus had been paying unwelcome attention to Miss Merlin for a long time, and Marie had instructions that he was to be discouraged as much as possible. In fact, I am pleased to say that your theory of Miss Merlin's ignorance respecting the murder plot is borne out by the testimony of her maid. On several occasions, it appears, when he sent his card to the dressing-room, Marie returned equivocal messages and did not even inform her mistress of Sir Marcus's visit. This had been going on for some time, when one night, whilst Miss Merlin was on the stage, a telephone call came for Marie and a certain proposal was made to her.

"It was this: if on the following night Sir Marcus should present himself, she was to tell him that Miss Merlin would take supper in his company after the performance, but that he was to observe every possible precaution. Marie, according to her account, at first declined to entertain the proposal, but being informed that it was merely intended to play a practical joke upon the baronet, she ultimately consented. I may add that the promise of a ten-pound note undoubtedly hastened her decision, and it was on her receipt of the amount by post on the following morning that she determined to carry out her part of the bargain.

"Her instructions had been explicit. She was to tell Sir Marcus that Miss Merlin would see him after the performance, then when he presented himself to inform him that her mistress had decided it would be more prudent for him to proceed to the rendezvous alone, where she would join him in a quarter of an hour. She was to give him the door-key (which had arrived with the money) and to direct him to enter and wait in the room on the right of the hall. A cabman who knew the address would be waiting at the stage-door."

Gatton paused, puffing slowly at his pipe, then:

"Unknown to Miss Merlin," he continued, "this scheme was carried out. Sir Marcus presented himself at ten o'clock and received Marie's message; he returned about eleven, and she told him, as she had been instructed, that her mistress would join him in a quarter of an hour. Curiosity respecting the joke which she believed was being played upon the baronet prompted her to go outside the stage-door to see if there was actually a cab waiting. There was, and she heard Sir Marcus ask the man if he knew the address to which he was to drive.

"The cabman replied that he did, and Marie claims to know no more about the matter, except that Sir Marcus drove off in the cab, and that her mistress returned to her flat alone about a quarter of an hour later. Next point. Inquiries for the cabman have been made at all the ranks since early this morning, and he turned up at the Yard about a couple of hours ago. His story is simple enough; someone called up the rank where he chanced to be standing that evening, instructing him to call for Sir Marcus at the stage-door of the New Avenue Theatre and to drive him to——"

He paused.

"Yes?"

"To the Red House!"

"At last we have it!" I cried excitedly.

"There is no doubt of it," answered Gatton; "the cab-man drove him there, and it was certainly at the Red House that he met his death. Indeed, the cabby appears to be the last witness who spoke to the murdered man. He inquired his way to the Red House from a chance pedestrian, a tramp, whom he met at the corner of College Road. He has even described this person to us, but I don't think his evidence of sufficient importance to justify our searching for him. On reaching the Red House the cabman and his fare found it to be vacant. Sir Marcus, however, who had a very brusque manner with his inferiors, having paid the cabman, curtly dismissed him, and the man, who admits having bargained for a double fare for the journey because it was such an out-of-the-way spot, drove away vaguely curious, but not so curious as another might have been, since London cabmen are used to strange jobs."

"We are getting near the heart of the mystery."

"H'm," said Gatton, "I'm not so sure. The deeper we go the darker it gets. A man has been scouring the neighbourhood all day in quest of the carter who delivered the crate to the docks, but so far without result. I consider it a very important point that we should learn not only how and when the crate was collected, but when and by whom it was delivered at the garage."

"Another question," I said, "although I believe I know the answer. Was it a man or a woman who ordered the cab?"

"Both in the case of Marie and in the case of the cab-rank," replied Gatton, "it was a woman's voice that spoke."

"Thank God, one doubt is resolved!" I said. "It cannot possibly have been Isobel in either of these cases!"

"Right!" agreed Gatton, promptly. "I am as glad as you are. There is clearly a second woman in the case; yet I can't bring myself to believe that this elaborate scheme was the work of a woman."

"Not of a *jealous* woman?" I suggested.

"Not of any woman," he replied. "Besides—who put the body into the crate? What kind of a woman would it be who could do a deed like that?"

"In other words," said I, "you are still without a ghost

of a clue to the identity of the person who committed the murder and to the means employed?"

Resting his pipe upon an ash-tray, the inspector took up from my writing-table the little image of Bâst and held it up between finger and thumb.

"We always come back to the green cat," he said slowly. "I will trouble you now, Mr. Addison, for the history of such a little image as this."

"Yes," I replied abstractedly. "But there is a matter about which I have not spoken to you hitherto because, quite frankly, I had doubted if it had any existence outside my imagination; but every new development of the case is so utterly fantastic that I no longer regard my experience as being in the least degree outside the province of possibility. Before we go further, therefore, into the purely archæological side of the inquiry (and I have still serious doubt respecting the usefulness of such a quest), let me relate a peculiar experience which I had last night after I had left Bolton."

Gatton listened in silence whilst I gave him an account of that evasive shadow which I had perceived behind me, and then of the great cat's eyes which had looked in through the window.

His expression of naïve wonderment was almost funny, and when I had concluded:

"Well, Mr. Addison," said he, "if you had told me this story before I had taken up 'the *Oritoga* mystery,' for so I observe"—drawing an evening paper from his pocket—"the Press has agreed to entitle the case, I should have suggested that your peculiar studies had begun to tell upon your nerves; but this voice on the 'phone and this empty house in which only one room was furnished, finally the green cat painted on the packing-case and the green cat which stands there upon the table have prepared me for even stranger things than your adventure of last night."

"Yet," I urged, "there is no visible connexion between the episodes of the case and this strange apparition which I saw in the garden last night."

"There was no visible connexion between Sir Marcus's body in a packing-case in the hold of the *Oritoga* and the garage of the house in College Road until we found one," retorted Gatton. "Anyway, I am glad you mentioned the matter to me; I will take a note of it, for it may prove to provide a link in the chain. And now"—taking out a note-book and pencil—"for the history of these cat things."

I sighed rather wearily as I crossed the room to my bookcase and took down the volume of Gaston Maspero, the same which I had been reading but had returned to its shelf as Gatton had been admitted.

"We have it here in a nutshell," I said.

Gatton methodically noted the passages which I read to him. The task concluded:

"H'm," he muttered, scanning his notes, "very strange, very strange indeed. 'She had also her hours of treacherous perversity, during which she played with her victim as with a mouse, before finishing him off with a blow of her claws.'"

He raised his eyes and stared at me strangely.

"She played with her victim as with a mouse," he murmured, "before finishing him off with a blow——"

CHAPTER VIII

MY VISITOR

For long enough after Gatton's departure I sat thinking over our conversation. Despite the lateness of the hour at which he had departed, he had had no thought of rest, and was setting out in quest of further evidence to point to the author of Sir Marcus's death. The room was laden with to-bacco smoke, for our conference had lasted more than two hours, but dusk was very fully established, and when presently as I sat there in the dark contemplating the horrible labyrinth into which my steps had drifted, Coates entered.

"Ah, Coates," I said, "light up."

He switched on the electric light, and I saw layers of smoke-clouds drifting from the open window toward sthe newly opened door.

"Shall you be going out again to-night, sir?" asked Coates, standing rigidly to attention, as was his custom when addressing me.

"I think not, Coates," I replied. "I have done enough for one day, but I should be glad if you would ring up the New Avenue Theatre and inquire if Miss Merlin will speak to me. It will be about time now for the performance to have finished."

"Very good, sir," said Coates, and proceeded to make the call, whilst I sat listessly smoking and listening to his voice. Presently:

"Miss Merlin did not appear to-night, sir," he announced; "she is indisposed."

"I thought as much," I muttered. "I could hardly have expected after such a day of horror and excitement that she would have been capable of appearing tonight. Ring up her flat, Coates," I added. "I should like to speak to her, for I know she is in great trouble."

"Indeed, sir," Coates permitted himself to remark. "Is it something to do with the discovery at the docks this morning, sir?"

"It is, Coates," I replied. "It is an utterly damnable business."

"Indeed, sir," said Coates again, and went to the telephone.

Three minutes later I was talking to Isobel.

"I find it utterly impossible to tell you what has happened," she declared, "since I saw you last. I feel incapable of thinking, and, of course, it was quite out of the question for me to go to the theatre to-night. But it is not so bad as it might have been." She hesitated, then: "I was only able to give them very short notice, unfortunately, but from a selfish point of view, as you know—I was leaving the stage—very shortly——"

"Yes," I answered dully, "I know; but have you seen the police?"

"I have seen Inspector Gatton," she replied; "but as he told me that he was coming along to you, no doubt you know what took place."

"No," I replied, "he did not mention the visit, but you quite recognize the fact, Isobel, that he does not regard you as being in any way concerned in this ghastly affair."

"He was awfully kind," she admitted; "in fact, I quite changed my opinion regarding the methods of the police authorities after my interview with Inspector Gatton; but although he was so extremely tactful with me, I really cannot forgive him his suspicions, which he was at scarcely any pains to disguise, regarding Eric."

"Regarding Eric!" I exclaimed.

"Oh," continued Isobel, "he may have concealed his views from you, as he knows that you are—a friend of Eric's; but he was less careful about concealing them from me. To all intents and purposes Eric is under police surveillance!"

"But this is utterly incredible!" said I. "You don't mean to tell me, Isobel, that Coverly has persisted in his silence respecting his movements last night? If he has done so, in the circumstances he has only himself to thank. Social position and everything else counts for nothing when an inquiry concerning a murder is concerned. He knows that perfectly well."

I think I spoke hotly, and certainly I spoke with a certain indignation, for I very strongly resented Coverly's attitude in the case, which could only add to the difficulties and sorrows of Isobel's position.

Yet a moment afterwards I regretted that I had done so, for:

"Are *you* going to quarrel with me too?" she asked pathetically.

"What do you mean? Who has been quarrelling with you?"

"Eric quarrelled with me fiercely at the solicitors' today, and when I begged of him to be frank respecting his movements last night, his attitude became"—she hesitated—"almost unbearable. He did not seem to realize that I was only thinking of him, nor did he seem to realize the construction which I might have placed upon his silence. I mean, Jack, what can he possibly have to conceal?"

Temporarily I felt myself to have become tongue-tied. What *could* it be that Coverly was concealing? The idea of complicity in the crime I scouted; nothing could have induced me to believe it. Only one explanation presented itself to my mind, as evidently it had presented itself to Isobel's—another woman. However:

"You may depend," I said, endeavouring to speak soothingly, "that he has some good and sufficient reason for this silence, one which is not in any way discreditable. Nevertheless, he will have to reconsider his attitude in the near future. Of course there are times when almost every one of us would be hard put to it to establish an alibi if we were called upon to do so—as regards witnesses of our movements, I mean; but at least we can state roughly where we were during any hour of the day, even if we have to trust to luck to find witnesses to prove the truth of our words. His attitude of silence, Isobel, is ridiculous."

"Have you seen the evening papers?" she asked pathetically.

"Some of them," I replied.

"They have got my name in already!" she continued, "and my photograph appears in one. It is outrageous how they leap at an opportunity for scandal."

"It will all be cleared up," I said, speaking with as much confidence as I had at my command. "You know and I know that Coverly is innocent, and I don't believe that Gatton thinks him guilty."

A while longer we talked, and then I returned rather wearily to my chair in the room where the air was still laden with tobacco fumes.

Without believing it to contain any very special significance, as I had supposed, but merely attracted by the strangeness of the passage, I remembered how Gatton had harped upon Maspero's description of the attributes of Bâst. "Sometimes she plays with her victim as with a mouse," etc. The big book with its fine plates, several of them representing cats similar to that which Gatton had left behind for my more particular examination, still lay open upon the table, and I re-read those passages appertaining to the character of the cat-goddess which I had marked for Gatton's information. Scarce noting what I read—for all the time I was turning over in my mind the manifold problems of the case—I sat there for an hour perhaps, in fact until I was interrupted by the entrance of Coates.

"Shall you require me again to-night, sir?" he inquired.

"No," I replied; "you had better turn in now, as in all probability we shall be early afoot to-morrow, Coates. Inspector Gatton will probably be calling for me."

"Very good. Good night, sir," said Coates, and performing a smart about-turn, he walked out of the room.

I went on reading, not in quest of any particular information, but in that idle mood when one reads anything interesting or otherwise. For a time I heard my conscientious batman fastening doors and windows, as was his nightly custom; then the door of his own room closed and I heard him no more.

When I first became aware of the howling of distant dogs I know not, but it was with a great start that I was aroused from my semi-reverie by the ringing of the door-bell. I realized that I had sat much longer than I had supposed. It was a quarter to one.

Gatton was my first thought; there must be an unexpected development in the case calling in some way for my services. Coates was a sound sleeper and evidently had not been awakened by the ringing of the bell; therefore, arrayed as I was in pyjamas, slippers and bath-robe (for this, during the hot weather, was my indoor costume), I walked out along the little corridor, unbolted the front door and opened it.

A woman stood there.

For a moment I thought foolishly that it was Isobel, and my heart gave a great leap. But the delusion was instantly dispelled when my visitor spoke.

Her voice had a totally different tone from that of Isobel—it was a low, almost caressing voice, with a vaguely husky note in it, fascinating in a way, yet although I found myself unable to account for the fact, vaguely uncanny, queer.

"Please excuse me," she said. "You will naturally wonder what has brought a visitor to your door at this hour of the night, and indeed my explanation is a strange one."

She glanced apprehensively over her shoulder as she spoke, out into the darkness of the roadway. I observed that she was apparently in evening-dress and wore a very handsome cloak, having a thick silk scarf so draped about her head and shoulders that her face was quite concealed. Very clearly now I could hear the howling of dogs.

Instinct is a curious thing, and that which it prompted me to do at the moment when I found myself confronting this strange woman was instantly to awaken Coates! Honestly I was afraid of her, and wished for nothing better than to have the closed door between us. This was all the more unaccountable as she had the appearance and manners of a cultured woman, presenting, indeed, a figure of great elegance as she stood there with her tall slender form outlined by the moonlight which slanted down through the trees to form a scimitar of light upon the path behind her.

Of course I could never have acted upon this singular instinct, but the decision was taken out of my hands, for suddenly my visitor uttered a low cry of fear, swayed dizzily, and seemed about to fall.

Perforce I stepped forward to support her, and before I knew what had happened she had tottered into the passage, resting heavily upon my shoulder.

"Close the door!" she said in that low, husky voice. "Quick! Quick! I have seen them again!"

An unpleasant chill communicated itself to me.

"The eyes!" she whispered. "Two great eyes have followed me! That was why I knocked at your door. I was afraid."

It was enough, the mention of two great eyes. Leaving my visitor temporarily to take care of herself, I sprang to the door and closed it hurriedly. As I turned, in the light from the partly open study door, I saw the woman walking slowly ahead of me. I overtook her, holding the door fully open for her to pass in.

"Please sit down awhile," I said. "You have evidently been seriously alarmed."

Still there was no sign from Coates, whose voice would have been welcome music to my ears, for I could not reconcile myself to this woman's presence, strive how I might, nor could I understand how she had come to be wandering alone in such a place at that hour. One bond of sympathy there was between us. I could forgive anyone fearing those awful eyes, for I had feared them myself, and since I could no longer doubt that some strange apparition was haunting the vicinity:

"Believe me, I quite understand," I said, turning to my visitor. "It is most extraordinary, but I believe there is some unusually large cat frequenting the neighbourhood at present."

I stood by the side-table, and was on the point of pouring out a glass of water, when the woman raised her white-gloved hand in a gesture of refusal.

"Thank you," she said, "thank you, but I am quite recovered, and, indeed, if the cause of my alarm is no more than a cat, as you say, I will proceed."

She laughed, and her laughter was low-pitched but very

musical. In the light of the shaded table-lamp I could see the gleam of white teeth through her veil, but I could not imagine why she swathed herself in that manner. Yet in spite of this enwrapping she could not disguise the fact that she possessed remarkably large and beautiful eyes. She seemed now to have recovered her composure, but I noted that she made no attempt to remove her veil.

"Are you quite sure that you will not be nervous on your way?" I asked.

"Oh, no. I am staying with some friends quite near," she explained, detecting my curiosity, "and I was indiscreet enough to wander out at this hour to post a letter."

Possibly this explanation might have satisfied me; it is even possible that I should have thought little more about the incident at that time, when I lived in a constant turmoil of episodes even stranger, but by one of those accidents which sometimes seem to be directed by the hand of an impish fate, I was to learn who or what my visitor was. When I say I was to learn what she was, perhaps I err; more correctly I was to learn what she was not, namely, an ordinary human being.

It was as she rose to depart that the hand of fate intervened. I had only one lamp burning in the room, a table-lamp; and at this moment, preceded by a sudden accession of light due to some flaw of the generating plant, the filament expired, plunging the room into darkness! I stood up with a startled cry. I do not deny that I felt ill at ease in the gloom with my strange visitor; but worse was to come. Looking across the darkened room to the chair upon which she was seated, I saw a pair of blazing eyes regarding me fixedly!

Something in their horrid, luminous watchfulness told me that my slightest movement was perceptible to my uncanny visitor, of whom I could see nothing but those two fiery eyes.

What I did or what occurred within the next few seconds I am not prepared to state in detail. I know I uttered a hoarse cry and threw myself back from those dreadful eyes which seemed to be advancing upon me. The cry awakened Coates. I heard the pad of his bare feet upon the floor as he leapt out of bed, and an instant later his door was opened and he came blundering out into the darkened passage.

"Hallo, sir!" he cried in a half-dazed voice.

"Here, Coates!" I replied, and my tones were far from normal.

Falling over a chair on his way, Coates came running into the study. An impression I had of a flying shape, and the dimly seen square of the open window (for that side of the cottage lay in shadow) seemed momentarily to become blackened.

"Bring a light, Coates!" I cried. "The lamp has gone out."

"Matches on the table, sir," said Coates.

Instantly I remembered that this was the case, that they lay, in fact, near to my hand. I struck one, and in its flickering light looked about the room. My visitor had gone— palpably through the window, for certainly the front door had not been opened.

"She has gone, Coates!" I exclaimed.

And on this occasion it was Coates who repeated in an amazed voice:

"She?"

But even as he spoke, my attention had become diverted.

I was staring at that portion of the table upon which Maspero's book lay. Beside it had stood the little Bubastite statuette . . . but the statuette was there no longer!

CHAPTER IX

THE VELVET CURTAIN

"This gets me well out of my depth, Mr. Addison," said Inspector Gatton.

We were standing in the garden at a point near to my open study window. A small flower-bed intervened between the path and the high privet hedge. It lay much in shade, and Coates had set tobacco plants there. But the soil was softer here than elsewhere.

Clearly marked upon it were the imprints of little high-heeled shoes.

"It seems to take us back to the days of 'Spring-heeled Jack,'" my friend continued, "which was before my time! I don't think *that* mystery was ever cleared up?"

"No," I replied, meeting his questioning glance; "it never was—satisfactorily. Therefore the analogy is an unfortunate one. But as you say, it certainly looks as though my visitor had sprung across a six-foot hedge!"

"It's absolutely mad," said Gatton gloomily. "Far from helping us, it only plunges us deeper in the mire."

We returned to the study, and:

"You will have seen the daily papers?" asked the inspector.

I nodded.

"Practically all of them. They give a hateful prominence to the name of Miss Merlin."

"And to that of the new baronet—Sir Eric," said Gatton significantly.

I stared at him straightly.

"Do you seriously believe," said I, "that Eric Coverly had anything whatever to do with the death of his cousin?"

Gatton stirred uneasily in his chair.

"Well," he answered, "ignoring everything else for the moment, who else benefits by Sir Marcus Coverly's death?"

It was a poser—a question which I had dreaded because I had known it to be unanswerable.

"He inherits the title," continued Gatton, "and on the death of Lady Burnham Coverly he inherits Friar's Park. There is some clause or entail or legal hotch-potch whereby the estate and revenue remain hers during her lifetime."

"But I understand that the estate is mortgaged?"

"That I have to confirm, Mr. Addison," replied Gatton. "Sir Eric's solicitor has no information on the point, and that of Sir Marcus's man of business is inexact. But even supposing that only the title is concerned, many a man has lost his life for less. Then you have to consider Miss Merlin."

"In what way?" I demanded.

"In relation to the attitude of Sir Marcus. Jealousy makes men (and women) do strange and desperate things.

The character of Eric Coverly, the new baronet, is a very odd one."

"He is headstrong and in some respects weak," I admitted. "But otherwise he is an ordinary English gentleman, with the traditions of an old name and a public school to back him up. I tell you, Gatton, it's nonsense. His army career alone shows him to be a sound man."

"Yes," murmured Gatton; "he was awarded a decoration for distinguished service in Egypt."

That seemingly simple remark struck me with all the force of a physical blow. Gatton began quietly to load his pipe, without even glancing in my direction; but the covert significance of his words was all too apparent.

"Gatton," I said, "what the devil are you driving at?"

He slightly shrugged his shoulders.

"What you may term the hocus-pocus side of the case," he replied, "turns on matters Egyptian, doesn't it? Very well. Who else, that we know about, is associated, or ever has been associated with Egypt?"

"But—the woman?"

"Ah!" said Gatton, "now you are getting down to the depths. But assuming that the extraordinary characteristics of this visitor of yours can be explained in some way, by deliberate trickery, for example, might she not be a woman whom Eric Coverly met in Egypt?"

I stared silently awhile, and then:

"In short, a rival of Miss Merlin's?" I suggested.

"Precisely. The trick with the photograph was just of the kind one would expect from a madly jealous woman. Everything planned with supreme cunning, but the scene at which the hated rival enters the scheme badly overdone."

"And you believe Coverly's silence to be due to the fact that he is shielding someone?"

"Well, that or shielding himself. What else can it mean? A man suspected of murder doesn't hesitate to establish an alibi unless he is in a desperately tight corner. The exact position of your strange-eyed acquaintance in the case is not apparent to me at the moment, I'll admit, but I seem to have heard that there have been rare instances of human beings with luminous eyes."

"Quite right, Inspector," I agreed. "I hope very shortly to have some further particulars for you bearing upon this point. I am endeavouring to obtain a work by Saint-Hilaire dealing with teratology."

"As to her extraordinary activity and agility," Gatton continued, "we must remember that a privet hedge is not like a stone wall. I mean she may not have actually cleared the whole six feet, and after all, this is the age of the athletic girl. There are women athletes who can perform some extraordinary feats of high jumping. Of course, there are still a number of witnesses to be discovered and examined, but I know by now exactly what to expect. It's an ingenious idea, although not entirely new to me.

"The whole thing has been managed by means of the telephone—a powerful ally of the modern criminal. Briefly what happened was this: The Red House—selected because of its lonely position, but also because it was fairly accessible—was leased by our missing assassin without any personal interview taking place. We have to look, then, in the first instance for someone possessing considerable financial resources. It was by the effective substitution of a year's rent—in cash—for the more usual references, that our man—or woman—whom I will call 'A,' secured possession of the keys and right of entry to the premises. A limited amount of furniture was obtained in the same manner. We haven't found the firm who supplied it, but I don't doubt that the business was done over the telephone, cash being paid as before. Duplicate keys must have been made for some of the doors, I think—a simple matter. We shall find that the furnishing people as well as the caterer who later on supplied the supper were admitted to the Red House by a district messenger, or else had the keys posted to them for the purpose.

"The whole business was built up around a central idea, simple in itself, that of inveigling Sir Marcus into the prepared supper-room. His attendance at the New Avenue Theatre last night was doubtless assured—although we may never prove it, by another of these mysterious telephone messages, probably purporting to come from Miss Merlin. The cold-blooded thoroughness with which 'A' arranged for a crate to be delivered at the garage and for the body of the murdered man to be taken to the docks and shipped to the West Indies illuminates the character of the person we have to seek.

"Discovery sooner or later was inevitable, of course. It

came sooner because of the accident at the docks. Had it come later, I don't doubt that 'A' would have dismantled the Red House again so that the investigation would have been severely handicapped. As it is, the only dismantling done was the most important of all."

"You mean——" I said with keen interest.

"The death-machine," answered Gatton. "The cunning device around which all these trappings were erected. We don't have to wait for the coroner's inquest nor the pathologist's report to know that Sir Marcus was asphyxiated."

"In that room where supper was laid for two?" I muttered.

"Can you doubt it?"

"No," I said, "and I don't."

"I have allowed nothing to be touched," continued Gatton, "and I am going around there now to make a final attempt to unravel the mystery of how Sir Marcus met his death."

"There is one detail," said I, "which it seems impossible to fit into its proper place in the scheme. The figure of Bâst painted upon the crate—you have that at Scotland Yard—and the little image of the goddess which was stolen from my table last night."

Gatton stood up, uttering a sigh.

"I have always found, Mr. Addison," he replied, "that it is these outstanding features of a case, these pieces which don't seem to fit, that are the most valuable clues. It's the apparently simple cases in which there is no outstanding point that are the most baffling."

I laughed shortly.

"One could not very well complain of the lack of such features in 'the *Oritoga* mystery,'" I said. "As a confrère of mine remarked when the body of Sir Marcus was discovered in the crate, the whole thing is as mad as 'Alice in Wonderland'!"

Gatton presently departed for the Red House and I accompanied him, for I was intensely curious to learn by what means the murder of Sir Marcus had been accomplished. As I proposed later in the morning to call on Isobel, Coates drove Gatton and myself as far as the Red House, and I instructed the man to wait for me.

Although the morning was still young, the prominence given by the Press to this sensational crime had resulted in the presence of quite a considerable group of pilgrims who even thus early had arrived to look upon the scene of the mysterious tragedy. London is a city of onlookers. The most trivial street accident never lacks its interested audience, and a house in which a murder is reputed to have taken place becomes a centre upon which the idly curious focus from the four points of the compass.

Our arrival created a subdued excitement amongst the nondescript group gathered upon the pavement. Despite the efforts of a constable on duty, men, women and children persistently gathered before the gates of the drive peering up at the empty house as if they anticipated seeing the face of the murderer or an apparition of the victim appear behind one of the windows. A considerable group, too, was gathered before the garage, but as Gatton and I descended and began to walk up the drive there was a general movement in our direction.

"I wonder," said I, "if 'A,' the wanted man, is among the crowd? One reads that murderers are irresistibly drawn back to the scene of their crimes."

"He may be," replied Gatton; "anyway, there are two C.I.D. men there for certain, so that 'A' will do well to be upon his guard."

A few moments later I found myself again in the lounge-hall of the Red House; and the place now seemed to me to have taken on an air of oppressive mystery. In the very deserted silence of the house I detected something sinister. Of course, no doubt, this was merely an effect created upon my mind by the ghastly associations of the place; but I know that whereas on the previous day surprise and curiosity had been the most characteristic emotions aroused by our discoveries there, this morning something darker seemed to have taken their place, and I found myself listening for a sound that never came and wondering vaguely and vainly what secret was hidden in this desolate mansion.

By Gatton's orders the room in which that gruesome supper was laid had been left undisturbed and once more we stood surveying the spotless napery and sparkling silver. I listened to the ticking of the clock upon the mantelpiece and stared dully at the wine resting in the ice-pail which now contained nothing but dirty water. A big dish of fruit stood upon the table, peaches and apricots and

nectarines; and several large wasps had entered through
one of the windows which someone had opened, and were
buzzing sleepily around the dish. Lastly—there beside the
clock stood Isobel's photograph.

For any evidence of a struggle I looked in vain, but the
nature of my companion's investigation was more obscure.
Again the whole of his attention seemed to be directed
upon the wall, the window-ledges and the door-frame.
Suddenly:

"Ah!" I said, "I know what you are looking for! Some
connexion between this room and the garage?"

Gatton, who was kneeling examining a lower panel of
the door, looked up with a grim smile.

"Perhaps I am," he replied.

By the tone of his voice I knew that whatever he had
sought he had failed once more to find. Presently, desisting
from this quest of his, he stood and stared curiously for
some time at a recess immediately behind one of the high-
backed chairs drawn up to the supper-table. We had already explored this recess and found it to be vacant. Gatton advanced towards it and drew aside the curtain which
was draped in the opening.

It was a recess about four feet wide by three feet deep
and it contained nothing in the nature of furniture or or-
nament.

"Does anything strike you as curious about this arrangement?" said my companion.

I looked for a long time, but failed to detect anything of
a notable nature.

"Nothing," I said, "except that it seems a peculiar idea
to drape a curtain before a recess in that way."

"And such a curtain!" said Gatton, fingering the texture.

I in turn touched the material with my fingers and
found it to be an extremely heavy velvet. Looking upward
I noticed that it was attached to a rod set so high in the
wall on either side that the top of the drapery actually
touched the ceiling.

"Well," said Gatton, looking at me oddly, "in addition
to the texture of the curtain, do you notice anything else?"

"No," I confessed.

"Well," he continued, "you may remember that yesterday when I examined this place I had to drape the curtain

over a chair, which I moved here for the purpose, in order to see the recess."

"So you did," I said; "I remember."

"Well, doesn't it strike you as odd? If you'll notice the way it is fastened above, you will see that it is not upon rings. In other words, it is not intended to be opened. You see that it is one piece, so that anybody having occasion to enter the recess would have to lift it aside and let it fall to behind him."

I studied the arrangement of the drapings more closely and saw that his statement was correct. Also I saw something else, and:

"This room has been lighted by gas at some time!" I cried. "Here, up under the picture-rail, is a plug."

"Most houses are provided both with gas and electric light about here," replied Gatton abstractedly.

But even before he had finished speaking I saw his expression change, and in a moment he had dragged a chair into the recess.

"Hold the curtain back," he directed sharply.

Standing on the chair, he began to examine the little brass plug to which I had drawn his attention. For some time I watched him in silence, and then:

"What do you think you have found?" I inquired.

He glanced down over his shoulder.

"I think I have found a *clue!*" he replied.

CHAPTER X

"HANGING EVIDENCE"

Isobel came into the room and approached the chair from which I had arisen. In her plain morning-frock, with the sun bringing out those wonderful russet tints in her hair, but having that frightened look still in her eyes, she had never seemed more beautiful. Yet I saw as I rose to greet her that she was labouring under the influence of dangerous nervous excitement.

"You are worried about Eric?" I said, when we had exchanged those rather formal greetings in which I think we took mutual shelter. Certainly I did, and later I was to know that Isobel did so too.

"Every day seems to make the case grow blacker against him," she replied, sinking down upon the settee beside me.

And indeed the shadow which had fallen upon all of us seemed at that moment almost palpable, a thing to be felt like the darkness of Egypt and not to be dispelled even by the brightness of the morning.

"When did you last see Coverly?"

Isobel raised her head wearily.

"Last night, and he seemed to think that someone was following him—a detective."

I noticed that Isobel spoke of Eric Coverly with a certain manner of restraint for which I could not account. Yet perhaps it was only natural that she should do so, but at the time I was foolishly blind to the opposing emotions which fought and conflicted within her.

"He still refused to explain his movements on the night of the murder?" I asked.

"Yes, he persisted in his extraordinary silence," said Isobel.

The look of trouble in her eyes grew more acute.

"What I cannot understand is a sort of attitude of resentment which he has lately adopted."

"Of resentment? Towards whom?"

"Towards *me*."

"But——"

"Oh, it's quite incomprehensible, Jack, and it is making me horribly unhappy. He complained so bitterly, too, about this police surveillance to which he is subjected. He realizes that the coroner is almost certain to put a wrong construction on his silence, but instead of being frank about it he adopts, even when alone with me, this incomprehensible attitude of resentment. In fact his behaviour almost suggests that *I* am responsible for his present misfortunes."

"He must be mad," I said, and I expect I spoke bitterly, for Isobel lowered her eyes and her face flushed with embarrassment.

"Don't think that I condemn him," I added hastily, "but really in justice to you, if not in order to clear his own good name, he should speak out at once. Are you expecting to see him to-day?"

Isobel nodded.

"I am expecting him at almost any moment," she replied; then, glancing aside at a number of daily papers which lay littered upon the floor beside the settee: "Of course you have seen what the Press has to say about it?" she added.

I nodded.

"What can you expect?" said I. "It is one of those cases in which practically all the evidence, although it is of a purely circumstantial nature, points to an innocent man as the culprit. I feel very keenly annoyed with Coverly, for not only is he involving both of you in a most unsavoury case but he is also hindering the work of justice. In fact by his inexplicable silence he is, although no doubt unconsciously, affording the murderer time to elude the law."

Even as I spoke the words I heard a cab draw up in the street below, and, glancing out of the window, I saw Coverly alight from the cab, pay the man and enter the doorway. His bearing was oddly furtive, that, as I thought with a sudden pang, of a fugitive. A few moments later he came into the room, and his expression when he found me there was one of marked hostility.

Eric Coverly bore no resemblance whatever to the deceased baronet from whom he inherited the title, belonging as he did to quite another branch of the family. Whereas Sir Marcus had been of a dark and sallow type, Eric Coverly was one of those fair, fresh-coloured, open-air English types, handsome in an undistinguished way, and as a rule of a light and careless disposition. There had never been any very close sympathy between us, for the studies to which I devoted so much time were by him regarded as frankly laughable absurdities. Although well-enough informed, he was typical of his class, and no one could justly have catalogued him as an intellectual.

"Good morning, Addison," he said, having greeted Isobel in a perfunctory fashion which I assumed to be accounted for by my unwelcome presence. "The men of your Fleet Street tribe have conspired to hang me, I see."

"Don't talk nonsense, Coverly," I said brusquely; "this misapprehension is bound to arise if you decline to give any account of your movements."

"But it is an outrage!" cried Coverly hotly. "What the devil do *I* know about Marcus's death?"

"I am perfectly convinced that you know nothing whatever; but then I have known you for many years. The 'Fleet Street tribe' to whom you refer merely regard you as a unit of our rather large population. In a case of this kind, Coverly, all men are equal."

Whilst I had been delivering myself of this somewhat priggish speech—designed, I may add, in self-defence, to spur Coverly to a rejoinder which might throw some light upon the mystery—he had regarded me with an expression of ever-increasing dislike. I noted that there were shadows under his eyes, and that he was in a highly nervous and excited condition. He had slept but little, I judged, during the last forty-eight hours, and had possibly had recourse to stimulants to enable him to face the new trials which arose with every day.

"I don't feel called upon," he said angrily, "to give an account of my movements to every policeman who cares to inquire. I know nothing whatever about the matter. I have said so, and I am not accustomed to have my word doubted."

"My dear Coverly," said I, "you must be perfectly well aware that sooner or later you will have to relinquish this heroic pose. Will you allow no one to advise you? You will have to answer the coroner, and if you persist in this extraordinary refusal to give a simple answer to a simple question, surely you realize that the matter will be transferred to a higher tribunal?"

"Oh, I told you that they had hanged me in Fleet Street already, Isobel!" cried Coverly, with a burst of unmirthful laughter.

But (and no man could have construed the thing favourably to Coverly) to my anger and amazement, he added:

"Let them do it! I'll speak if I choose, but not otherwise!"

That I was annoyed with the young fool already, my remarks to him, which had transgressed every code of good taste, must sufficiently have shown. But I had hoped to provoke him to a declaration which would clear his name from the shadow which was settling darkly upon it, and which would raise that shadow from the girl who stood beside him, watching me with a sort of reproachful look in her dark eyes.

Now I recognized that I could remain no longer and keep the peace, therefore:

"Perhaps it is time that I went about my own business," I said, conjuring up a smile, although it must have been a dreary one, "and ceased to interfere with the affairs of other people. Good-bye, Isobel. Anything I can do, you know you may command. Good-bye, Coverly. I am deeply sorry about this business."

He barely touched my extended hand, but instantly turned and walked to the bay window. Descending to the street, I had immediate confirmation of Coverly's statement that his movements were watched.

In the porch below a man stood talking to the hall-porter. As I appeared he immediately averted his face and began to light a cigarette. Nevertheless, I had had time to recognize him as the man who had brought Gatton news of Marie's detention.

It was in a truly perturbed frame of mind that I proceeded on my way to the *Planet* offices. I would have sacrificed much to have been afforded means to comfort Isobel; a furious anger towards the man who thus deliberately had brought doubt and unhappiness upon her had taken up permanent quarters in my mind. I counted Coverly's declination to clear himself little better than the attitude of a cad.

I read religiously through a pile of cuttings bearing upon the case, and found the unmistakable trend of opinion to be directed towards Coverly as the culprit. The use made of Isobel's name enraged me to boiling point, and I presently took up the entire bundle of cuttings and crammed them into a wastepaper basket. I was engaged in stamping them down with my foot when I was called to the telephone.

Inspector Gatton was speaking from New Scotland Yard; and his voice was very grave.

"Can you possibly come along at once?" he asked. "There is a new development; a most unpleasant one."

He would say no more over the telephone. Therefore I hurried out to where Coates was waiting, and in ten minutes found myself in one of those bare, comfortless apartments which characterize the headquarters of the Metropolitan Police Force.

With his hat off Gatton looked more like a seaman than ever, for he had short, crisply curly hair, and that kind of bull-dog line of cranium which one associates with members of the senior service. Upon a chair set in a recess formed by one of the lofty windows a leather grip rested. It was wet and stained, and had palpably been recovered but recently from the water. Seeing my glance straying towards this object at the moment of my entrance, the inspector nodded.

"Yes," said he, "it has just come in."

"What is it?"

"Well," replied Gatton, sitting upon a corner of the table and folding his arms, "it is a piece of evidence sufficient to hang the most innocent man breathing."

He eyed me in a significant manner, and I felt my heart beginning to beat more rapidly.

"May I know the particulars?"

"Certainly. I asked you to come along for the purpose of telling you. Sir Eric Coverly's refusal to answer the questions put to him had necessitated his being watched, as you know. I mean to say, it's sheerly automatic; the Commissioner himself couldn't make an exception. Well, last night he left his chambers and started for Miss Merlin's flat. He came out of a back door and went along a narrow passage, instead of going out at the front. He evidently thought he had got away unobserved. He was carrying—that."

"Good heavens!" I said. "The young fool seems determined to put a rope around his own neck."

"As a matter of fact," continued Gatton, "he was *not* unobserved. He was followed right across St. James's Park. By the lake he lingered for some time, and the man tracking him kept carefully out of sight, of course. There was nobody else about at the moment, and presently thinking himself safe, Coverly dropped his bag in the water! Immediately he set off walking rapidly again, and he was followed right to Miss Merlin's door. But the spot where he had dropped the bag had been marked, of course, and when I came in here to-day it had been fished up—and placed there for my inspection."

With ever-growing misgivings:

"What does it contain?" I asked.

Inspector Gatton walked across to the chair and threw the bag open. First he took out several lumps of wet coal.

"To weight it, of course," he said.

Then, one by one, he withdrew from the clammy interior a series of ragged garments, the garments of a tramp. A pair of heavy boots there were, a pair of patched trousers, and an old shabby coat, a greasy cap, and finally a threadbare red muffler!

Gatton looked hard at me.

"He will have to break his obstinate silence now," he said. "Failing our discovery of new clues pointing in another direction, this is hanging evidence!"

"It is maddening!" I cried. "Can nothing be done, Gatton? Is there no possible line of inquiry hitherto neglected which might lead to the discovery of the truth? For whatever your own ideas may be, personally I am certain that Coverly is innocent."

Gatton replaced the sodden garments one by one in the bag, frowning as he did so, and:

"It occurred to me this morning," he replied, "that there *is* one inquiry which in justice to the suspected man, and in order to round off the investigation, should be instituted. I'm afraid Coverly will have a bad time in the coroner's court, but it is even possible that something might be done before the inquest. Now——"

He looked at me quizzically, and:

"Knowing your keen personal interest in the case, I am going to make a suggestion. It is probably going outside the intentions of the Chief in regard to your share of the inquiry, but I'll risk that. I stipulate, however, that anything you learn is to be communicated direct to me, not to the *Planet*. Is this arrangement consistent with your journalistic conscience?"

"Quite," I said eagerly. "My contributions to the *Planet* are always subject, of course, to your censorship. What is it that you propose I should do?"

"This," said Gatton tersely. "I should like to know under what circumstances Mr. Roger Coverly died."

"Roger Coverly?" I echoed.

"The son of Sir Burnham Coverly," continued Gatton, "and therefore the direct heir to the title. He died somewhere abroad about five or six years ago, and as a result the late Sir Marcus inherited the baronetcy on the death of his uncle, Sir Burnham. You will remember that the man, Morris, spoke of the ill-feeling existing between Lady Burnham Coverly and Sir Marcus, because of the premature death of her own son, of course."

"I follow you," I said eagerly. "You suggest that I should go down to Friar's Park and interview Lady Burnham Coverly?"

"Exactly," replied Gatton. "It's very irregular, of course, but I know you well enough to take my chance of a carpeting. I may send a C.I.D. man down as well. I've too much to do in town to think of going myself, but I will advise you of any such step."

The motive underlying Inspector Gatton's suggestion was perfectly evident to me, and I experienced a feeling of gratitude for the humanity which directed it. I held out my hand, and:

"Thanks, Gatton," I said; "you can leave the matter in my care with every confidence. I will start for Friar's Park to-day."

"Good," replied Gatton. "Let me give you a hint. Take a good pistol with you!"

CHAPTER XI

THE SCARRED MAN

It was towards the hour of seven in the evening that I reached the Abbey Inn at Upper Crossleys, itself among the most hoary buildings of the ancient village. It belonged to the days when white-clad brethren from the once great monastery of Croix-de-Lis had laboured in the abbey meadows and fished in the little stream which ran slowly through a neighbouring valley. Time had scarred it deeply, and the balcony overhanging the coachyard sagged in a rather alarming fashion as though about to drop down from sheer old age.

The surrounding country had impressed me at first

sight. There were long billowing hills and vales, much of their surface densely wooded, but with wide spaces under cultivation and even greater tracts of a sort of heath land very wild in aspect and conjuring up pictures of outlaws' camps and the clash of battling feudal days. Hard by had resided of old a warden of the marches and the ruins of his stronghold might still be seen on the crest of a near-by hill.

From the room allotted to me I could look out over a varied prospect of farmland and heath, terminated by the woody slopes which everywhere hemmed in the valley. Peeping above the outer fringe of trees showed a tower of some old house whereof the rest was hidden by verdure.

Having partaken of a typical country dinner, the small number of courses being amply compensated for by their quantity, I lighted my pipe and went down to the bar-parlour, being minded to learn something of the neighbourhood at first hand from any chance visitor who might serve my purpose.

The landlord, a somewhat taciturn member of his class, sat behind the bar, pipe in mouth, as I entered, and only one other man was in the room. This was a gipsy-looking fellow, with a very wild eye, attired in the manner of a gamekeeper, and wearing leggings and a fur cap. A sporting rifle stood in the corner beside him. The landlord nodded, and the other gave me a "Good evening," as I entered, whereupon I determined to try the gamekeeper as the more likely source of information, and:

"Is the shooting good hereabouts?" I asked, by way of opening a conversation.

My inquiry seemed hugely to amuse the man.

"None better," was the reply; "it's thick with game, sir, it is for sure—and nobody to profit, only"—he winked at the landlord—"young Jim Corder!"

The landlord emitted a deep grunt, which was evidently recognized by the other as a laugh; for he himself laughed in a wild and not wholly pleasant manner, whereby I concluded that "young Jim Corder" was a standing joke in the neighbourhood.

"You look as though you knew a hare from a partridge," said I, "so I'll take your word for it."

This remark provoked a second and deeper growl from

the landlord, and a further burst of outlandish laughter from my acquaintance the gamekeeper. Presently:

"Why, sir, if I tell you," declared the latter, "them birds all know me like I was their father, they do. I says, 'Good morning' regular, and them birds all bows to me, they does."

When the laughter had subsided, scenting possible information:

"I gather," said I, "that you get few shooting-parties nowadays?"

Gloom descended upon both my gossips.

"You're right, you are, sir," replied the gamekeeper. "He's right, ain't he, Martin?"

Martin, the landlord, growled. It occurred to me that he regarded the other with a certain disfavour.

"This 'ere country," continued the gamekeeper, vaguely waving his arm around, "is a blighted spot. A blighted spot, ain't it, Martin?"

Martin growled, whilst the gamekeeper studied him covertly.

"Since Sir Burnham went to his long rest, these 'ere parts ain't knowed themselves. I'm telling you, sir. Ain't knowed 'emselves. It's all that quiet, winter and summer alike. The Park all shut up; and the Park *was* the Park in them days—warn't it, Martin?"

Martin achieved speech; he removed his pipe, and:

"It were, Hawkins," he concurred.

Silence fell for a minute or two. My new acquaintance, Hawkins, and Martin both seemed to be pondering upon the degeneracy of Upper Crossleys, and I could not help thinking that Hawkins took a secret delight in it. Then:

"Surely the Park is still occupied by Lady Coverly?" I asked.

"Ay," Hawkins nodded. "She's kep' me on, me and the missus, she has, like the real lady she is. But things is different; things is wrong. Ain't they, Martin?" he asked, with a mischievous glance at the stolid host.

"Things is," agreed Martin.

"Best part of Park be shut up," declared Hawkins. "Horses gone, carriages gone, everybody gone; only me and my old woman."

"There must be house servants," I interjected.

"My old woman!" cried Hawkins triumphantly; "same as I'm tellin' you!"

"You mean that Lady Coverly lives alone in the place with only—er—Mrs. Hawkins to look after her?"

It was Martin, the landlord, who answered my question.

"Things ain't right," he observed, and returned to his mouth the pipe which he had removed for the purpose of addressing me.

"You don't know half of it," declared Hawkins. "What's *my* job, for instance? I ask you—what is it?"

Having thus spoken, he exchanged a significant look with the landlord and relapsed into silence. Even my offer to replenish his tankard, although it was accepted, did not result in any further confidences. Prospects of crops and fruit were briefly touched upon, but that exchange of glances between mine host and Hawkins seemed to have been mutually understood to mean that the conversation anent Friar's Park had proceeded far enough.

It was very mystifying, and naturally it served only to pique my curiosity. A certain quality of loneliness which had seemed to belong to the village, even in the brightness of the summer evening, now asserted itself potently. Seated there in the quiet little inn parlour, I recalled that many of the old-world cottages to right and left of the Abbey Inn had exhibited every indication of being deserted, and the lack of patrons, instanced by the emptiness of the bar parlour, was certainly not ascribable to the quality of the ale, which was excellent. A sort of blight, it would seem, had descended upon humanity in Upper Crossleys. It was all very curious.

Reflecting upon the matter, and sometimes interjecting a word or two into the purely technical and very desultory conversation proceeding between the landlord and Hawkins, I sat looking from one to the other, more than ever convinced that no friendship was lost between them. My position in the room was such that anyone entering would not detect my presence until he was right up to the bar, and to this sheltered seat I was undoubtedly indebted for a very strange experience.

During a lull in the patently forced conversation I heard footsteps upon the cobbles outside. Hawkins and the landlord exchanged a swift glance, and then, to my surprise, they both stared at me questioningly. Before a word could be exchanged, however, and before I had time even to surmise what this covert uneasiness might portend, a young fellow entered whose carriage and dress immediately attracted my attention.

He was attired, then, in a sort of burlesque "fashionable" lounge suit, and wore a straw hat set rakishly backward on his well-oiled dark hair. He carried gloves and a malacca cane, and his gait was one of assured superiority. He was a stoutly built, muscular young fellow, and might ordinarily have been good-looking, after a rustic fashion; but what principally rendered him noticeable was the fact that he wore surgical bandages around his neck in lieu of a collar, and that his face was literally a mosaic of sticking-plaster!

"Evening, Martin—evening, Hawkins," he said jauntily; and advancing to the bar, "The usual, Martin."

As he gave the order, and as the landlord turned to execute it, exhibiting a sort of half-amused deference, the embarrassed glance of Hawkins, who was watching me uncomfortably, drew the new-comer's attention to my presence. He turned in a flash, and I saw those parts of his face which were visible between the pieces of strapping turn fiery red. His brown eyes glared at me, and:

"Martin!" he cried, throwing out his hand in the landlord's direction, "Martin, damn you! There is a stranger here! Why the devil didn't you tell me?"

"Sorry, Mr. Edward," said the landlord, setting a glass of whisky before the excited men. "No time."

"It's a lie!" cried the other, with a wild fury which so trivial a matter did not seem to warrant. "A deliberate damned lie! You want to make me the laughing-stock of the place!"

Taking up the newly filled glass, he dashed it violently to the sanded floor, so that it was shattered to bits. Then, snatching off his hat, he held it as a shield between my inquiring gaze and his plastered face, and ran out of the room. At the door:

"Damn you all!" he shouted back at us.

I heard his quick footsteps receding. Then, as he turned the corner, the sound died away. I looked across at Hawkins. He was staring into his tankard, with which he was describing slow circles as if to stir the contents. Martin, having raised the barflap, was phlegmatically engaged in sweeping up the fragments of glass into a dustpan. It came to me all at once that these simple folk regarded the other's outburst as a personal matter. Their attitude was that of the grieved elders of a family, some member of which has misbehaved himself. But assuredly I was not prepared to concur in this shielding silence. The pressman within me demanded an explanation.

"A strange young man," I said tentatively. "Very touchy, I should think?"

"Touchy?" repeated Hawkins, glancing up quickly. "I seen him take Tom Pike by the scruff of his neck and the seat of his pants and pitch him in the horse-trough for askin' of him who his tailor was, I have."

"Indeed," said I. "A local Carpentier, no doubt?"

"Ah," said Martin, glancing at me as he returned to his seat behind the bar. "Very 'andy with 'is 'ands."

"He is evidently acutely sensitive of his present disfigurement. Might I suggest that his most recent encounter was with a barbed-wire entanglement?"

But, to my acute disappointment, Martin merely growled, shaking his head gloomily; and in this significant gesture he was closely imitated by Hawkins. Therefore:

"Is he badly disfigured?" I persisted.

"Only one is deep," replied Hawkins, glancing almost apologetically at the landlord. The unfortunate incident seemed to have drawn them more closely together. "The one on his neck. But he prides himself on his looks, don't he, Martin?"

"He do," agreed Martin.

I took the bull by the horns. I never neglect an opportunity of this nature, for however irrelevant to the matter in hand an episode may seem to be, not infrequently I have found that it is by the pursuit of such chance clues that one is led to the very piece of news that is sought.

"Drink up, gentlemen," I said, "and as the night draws on, we shall just have time for a peg of whisky before ten o'clock."

My effort proved successful, for whilst Martin prepared the ordered drinks, almost with alacrity, Hawkins became quite confidential.

"Young Mr. Edward Hines that was, sir," he confided in a church whisper. "His father is the biggest farmer round these parts, and young Mr. Edward is a terror with the gals, he is. Mind you, he's straight out about it. Comes in here, he do, and says straight out who he's after. And it's woe betide the one who takes him up on it. I'm glad my gal is up to London, with that Mr. Edward about, I am."

The drinks being placed upon the counter, he ceased, and:

"Good health!" said I. Then, "Yes—about our mutilated young friend?" I prompted.

"Well," continued Hawkins, "it's kind o' funny, ain't it, Martin?"

The landlord growled.

"Mr. Edward, he come in here three weeks back all puffed up with himself. Said he'd got an appointment with a lady down from London, what was coming all the way from West Wingham to see him. Didn't he, Martin?"

Martin corroborated.

"He see her, too," declared Hawkins, with a sort of schoolboy naïveté. "And he see her again four nights after. She give him a present—a keepsake. He showed us. Then he seen her a third time, and—"

Hawkins ceased speaking, and looked at the landlord as if mutely appealing for his aid in making clear to me what occurred at this third tryst with the mysterious "lady from London."

"Go on," prompted Martin. "Tell him. He's stoppin' here; he's all right."

I keenly appreciated the compliment conveyed by this, the landlord's longest speech of the evening, and raised my glass to him.

"Well, then," Hawkins resumed, "we didn't see him for a night or two, but on the Wednesday——"

"The Thursday," corrected Martin.

"Right you are, Martin," agreed Hawkins—"the Thursday it were. I met Farmer Hines comin' back from Wingham market as I came here mid-day. It were the Thursday. Well, then, on the Thursday young Mr. Edward he turns up after dark. Sort of slinked in, he did. There was three or four of us here, there was that night, wasn't there, Martin? 'Course it were market day. Slinked in he did, and his face was like you see it to-night, only worse. He never said a word to nobody, and nobody never said nothin' to him, not likely. Just gulped down a double Scotch and slinked out. What do you think about that for a story—eh, sir?"

He looked at me triumphantly. For my own part I must confess I was disappointed. A cat-and-dog squabble between a rustic Lothario and some local virago did not excite me so intensely as it seemed to excite my companions.

"Is that all you know of the matter?" I asked.

"No," answered Martin, "it ain't. Tell him, Hawkins."

"Ay," resumed Hawkins, "he might as well know, as he's livin' here. Well, sir, young Mr. Edward, he's very quiet about what happened to him. Maybe we shouldn't have thought so much about it like if it hadn't been that in this very bar, six months ago, he'd plagued the life out of young Harry Adams."

"For what reason?" I asked idly; the conversation was beginning to bore me. But:

"Young Harry Adams," explained Hawkins with gusto, and his former wicked look returning to his eyes, "at one time was Mr. Edward's only rival with the gals, he was. A good-lookin' young fellow; got a commission in the war, he did. He's up to London now. Well, six months ago young Harry Adams come staggerin' in here one night with blood runnin' from his face and neck. He fell down in that seat where you're sittin' now and fainted right off, didn't he, Martin? We had to send young Jim Corder (what used to come here in them days) off runnin' all the way past Leeways for the doctor. Ah, that were a night."

"It were," agreed Martin.

"Same as Mr. Edward," continued the narrator, "young Harry Adams wouldn't say a word about what happened to him. But when Mr. Edward first see him, all over sticking-plaster, he laughed till the pots nearly fell off the hooks, he did. Little did he guess his own turn was to come!"

My interest revived.

"Then in the case of, er—Mr. Adams," I said, "you never had any particulars whatever?"

"Never," replied Martin. "Time, please, gentlemen."

"Ay," said Hawkins, rising. "Time it be. Well, good night, sir. Good night, Martin."

"Good night."

Hawkins moved towards the door, and indeed was on the point of going out, when I remembered something which I had meant to ask earlier, but which, owing to lack of opportunity, I had postponed asking.

"You spoke of a gift or keepsake, which the lady from London gave to Mr. Hines," I said. "I think you mentioned that he had shown it to you. I am rather curious about this story. Might I ask the nature of the gift?"

"Ay, to be sure," answered Hawkins, standing half in shadow on the step of the bar parlour, rifle on shoulder, where I thought he made a very wild figure. "Brought it here, he did. All of us see it. That stuck up about it, he was. Not as I should have thought much of it if a party had give it to me, I do say."

"Then what was it?"

"Why—it were a little figure like—gold, *he* said it were, but brass I reckon. Ugly it were, but he says he's goin' to wear it on his watch-chain. Good night, sir."

He turned and departed, but:

"What kind of figure?" I called after him.

Out of the darkness his voice came back:

"A sort of a *cat*, sir."

And I heard his outlandish laughter dying away in the distance.

CHAPTER XII

I DREAM OF GREEN EYES

It was long enough before sleep visited me that night. For nearly half an hour I stood at my open window looking across a moon-bathed slope to where a tower projected, ghostly, above the fringe of the woods. The landlord had informed me that it was Friar's Park which could thus be seen peeping out from the trees, and as I stood watching that sentinel tower a thousand strange ideas visited me.

The curious air of loneliness of which I had become conscious at the moment of my arrival was emphasized now that the residents in the district had retired to their scattered habitations. No sound of bird or beast disturbed the silence. From the time that the footsteps of Martin the landlord had passed my door as he mounted heavily to his bed-chamber, no sound had reached me but the muffled ticking of a grandfather's clock upon the landing outside my room. And even this sound, the only one intruding upon the stillness, I weaved into my imaginings, so that presently it began to resemble the ticking of the clock on the mantelpiece in that gruesome room at the Red House.

The view which I commanded was an extensive one, and although in the clear country air I could quite easily discern the upstanding wing of Friar's Park, actually the house and the park were some two miles distant. Where the park ended and the woods began, it was impossible to determine, yet such was my curious mood that I lingered there endeavouring to puzzle out those details which were veiled from me by distance.

To-morrow, I thought, I should be seeking admittance to that house among the trees. In fact, so great was my anxiety to plumb the depths of the mystery in the hope of recovering some new fact which should exculpate Coverly, that nothing but the unseemly lateness of the hour had deterred me from presenting myself that very evening.

Yet my night of idleness had not been altogether unfruitful. I had met the scarred man, and from Hawkins I had heard something of his singular story. Now as I stood there, drinking in, as it were, the loneliness of the prospect, my thoughts turned for the hundredth time to the gamekeeper's account of what had befallen the two rustic rake-hells. I admit that the concluding part of Hawkins's story, quite evidently regarded by him as a detail of no importance, had re-awakened hope which had been at lowest ebb in the hour of my arrival.

Although it was possible that the gift of a "sort of cat" to young Edward Hines might prove on investigation to be not a clue, but a will-o'-the-wisp, I preferred to think that fate or the acute reasoning of Inspector Gatton had sent me down to this quiet country for a good purpose, and I built great hopes around the figure of the "lady down from London." Indeed, it appeared to me that there were more lines of investigation demanding attention than alone I could hope to deal with in the short time at my disposal. Except that I was determined to visit Friar's Park early on the following day, I scarcely knew in which direction next to prosecute my inquiries.

Determining that I should be well-advised to sleep on the problem, I presently turned in. And when I blew out the candle with which the chambermaid had provided me, I remember thinking that the moonlight was so bright that it would have been possible to read moderately large type without inconvenience.

I slept perhaps for two hours or more, an unrefreshing sleep disturbed by dreams of a wildly grotesque nature. Figures increasingly horrible and menacing crowded upon me; but that which proved the culminating horror and which finally awakened me, bathed in cold perspiration, was a dream of two huge green eyes regarding me with a fixed stare, fascinating and hypnotic, against which evil power I fought in my dream with all the strength of my will.

Vaguely defined as if in smoke, I could perceive the body of the creature to which these incredible eyes belonged. It was slender and sinuous, and sometimes I thought it to be that of a human being and sometimes that of an animal. For at one moment it possessed all the lines of a woman's form, and in the next, with those terrible eyes regarding me from low down upon the ground, it had assumed the shape of a crouching beast of prey. This fearsome apparition seemed to be creeping towards me—nearer and nearer, and was about to spring, I thought, when I awakened as I have said and sat suddenly upright.

One thing I immediately perceived which may have accounted for my bad dreams: I had been sleeping with the moonlight shining directly upon my face. Another thing I thought I perceived, but endeavoured to assure myself that it represented the aftermath of an unpleasant nightmare. This was a little shape streaking through my open window —a figment of the imagination, as I concluded at the time, the tail-end of a dream visibly retreating in the moment of awakening.

So self-assured of this did I become, that I did not get up to investigate the matter, nor was there any sound from the road below to suggest that the figure had been otherwise than imaginary, yet I found it difficult to woo slumber again, and for nearly an hour I lay tossing from side to side, listening to the ticking of the grandfather's clock, and constantly seeing in my mind's eye that deserted supper-room at the Red House.

And presently, as I lay thus, I became aware of two things: first, of the howling of dogs, and, second, of a sort of muttered conversation which seemed to be taking place somewhere near me. Listening intently, I thought I could distinguish the voice of a man and that of a woman. Possibly I was not the only wakeful inhabitant of the Abbey Inn was my first and most natural idea; but it presently became apparent to me that the speakers were not in the inn, but outside in the road.

Curiosity at last overcame inclination. Of the exact time I was not aware, but I think dawn could not have been far off, and I naturally wondered whom these might be that conversed beneath my window at such an hour. I rose quietly and crept across the room, endeavouring to avoid showing my head in the moonlight. By the exercise of a little ingenuity I obtained a view of the road before the inn doors.

At first I was unable to make out from whence this muttered conversation arose, until fixing my attention upon a patch of shadow underlying a tall tree which stood almost immediately opposite the window, I presently made out two figures there. Somewhere a dog was howling mournfully.

For a long time I failed to distinguish any more than indefinite outlines, nor, throughout the murmured colloquy, did I once detect even so much as a phrase. The night remained perfect, and the moon possessed a tropical brilliance, casting deep and sharply defined shadows, and lending to the whole visible landscape a quality of hardness which for some obscure reason set me thinking of a painting by Wiertz.

The low-pitched voices continued in what I thought was a dispute. Something in the voice of the woman, although I could only hear her occasionally, piqued yet eluded my memory. But it was the voice of a young woman, whilst that of the man suggested a foreigner of some sort and one past youth. Subconsciously pursuing the Wiertz idea, I know not why, I invested the dimly visible speakers with distinct personalities. The man became Asmodeus, master of the revels at the Black Sabbath, and the woman I cast for that "young witch" depicted in one of the canvases of the weird Belgian genius.

Everything in the black and silver scene seemed to fit the picture. Here was the unholy tryst, and I pictured the distant woods "peopled with grey things, the branches burdened with winged creatures arisen from the pit; the darkness a curtain 'broidered with luminous eyes. . . ."

And it was my recollection of that phrase, from a work on sorcery, which now set every nerve tingling. Closely I peered into the masking shadow, telling myself that I was the victim of a subjective hallucination. If this was, indeed, the case or if what I saw was actual, I must leave each who reads to determine for himself; and the episodes which follow and which I must presently relate will doubtless aid the decision.

But it seemed to me that for one fleeting moment "luminous eyes" indeed " 'broidered the darkness!" From out of the shade below the big tree they regarded me greenly—and I saw them no more.

A while longer I watched, but could not detect any evidence of movement in the shadow patch. The voices, too, had ceased, so that presently it occurred to me that the speakers must have withdrawn along a narrow lane which I had observed during the evening and which communicated with a footpath across the meadows.

I realized that my heart was beating with extraordinary rapidity. So powerful and so unpleasant was the impression made upon my mind by this possibly trivial incident and by the extraordinary dream which had preceded it, that on returning to bed (and despite the warmth of the night) I closed both lattices and drew the curtains!

Whether as a result of thus excluding the moonlight or because of some other reason, I know not, but I soon fell into a sound sleep, from which I did not awaken until the chambermaid knocked at the door at eight o'clock. Neither did I experience any return of those terrifying nightmares which had disturbed my slumbers earlier in the night.

My breakfast dispatched, I smoked a pipe on the bench in the porch, and Mr. Martin, who evidently had few visitors, became almost communicative. Undesirable patrons, he gave me to understand, had done his business much harm. By dint of growls and several winks, he sought to enlighten me respecting the identity of these trade-killers. But I was no wiser on the point at the end of his exposition than I had been at the beginning.

"Things ain't right in these parts," he concluded, and thereupon retired within doors.

Certainly, whatever the reason might be, the village even in broad daylight retained that indefinable aspect of neglect, of loneliness. Many of the cottages were of very early date—and many were empty. A deserted mill stood at one end of the village street, having something very mournful and depressing about it, with its black, motionless wings outspread against the blue sky like those of a great bat transfixed.

There were rich-looking meadows no great way from the village, but these, I learned, formed part of the property of Farmer Hines, and Farmer Hines was counted an inhabitant of the next parish. It was, then, this particular country about Upper Crossleys over which the cloud hung; and I wondered if the district had been one of those —growing rare nowadays—which had flourished under the protection of the "big house" and had decayed with the decay of the latter? It had been a common enough happening in the old days, and I felt disposed to adopt this explanation.

My brief survey completed, then, I returned to the Abbey Inn for my stick and camera, and set out forthwith for Friar's Park.

From certain atmospherical indications which I had observed, I had anticipated a return of the electrical storm which a few days before had interrupted the extraordinary heat-wave. And now, as I left the village behind and came out on the dusty high road, a faint breeze greeted me—and afar off I discerned a black cloud low down upon the distant hills.

CHAPTER XIII

DR. DAMAR GREEFE

As the crow flies Friar's Park was less than two miles from the Abbey Inn, but the road, which according to a signboard led "To Hainingham," followed a tortuous course through the valley, and when at last I came to what I assumed to be the gate-lodge, a thunderous ebony cloud crested the hill-top above, and its edge, catching the burning rays of the sun, glowed fiercely like the pall of Avalon in the torch-light. Through the dense ranks of firs cloaking the slopes a breeze presaging the coming storm whispered evilly, and here in the hollow the birds were still.

I stared rather blankly at the ivy-covered lodge, which, if appearances were to be trusted, was unoccupied. But I pushed open the iron gate and tugged at a ring which was suspended from the wall. A discordant clangor rewarded my efforts, the cracked note of a bell which spoke from somewhere high up in the building, that seemed to be buffeted to and fro from fir to fir, until it died away, mournfully, in some place of shadows far up the slope.

In the voice of the bell there was something lonesome, something akin to the atmosphere of desertion which seemed to lie upon the whole neighbourhood—something fearful, too, as though the bell would whisper: "Return! Beware of disturbing the dwellers in this place."

The house, one wing of which, I have said, was visible from the inn window, could not be seen at all from the gate. Indeed, I had lost sight of it at the moment that I had set out and had never obtained a glimpse of it since.

Ten minutes before, I had inquired the way from a farm-labourer whom I had met on the road, and he had answered me with a curiosity but thinly veiled. His directions had been characterized by that rustic vagueness which assumes in the inquirer an intimate knowledge of local landmarks. But, nevertheless, I believed I had come aright. I gathered from its name that Friar's Park was in part at least a former monastic building, and certainly the cracked bell spoke with the voice of ancient monasteries, had in it the hush of cloisters and the sigh of renunciation.

Although I had mentioned nothing of the purpose of my journey to mine host of the Abbey Inn or to any of his cronies—and these were few in number—I had hoped to find Hawkins at the lodge; and a second time I awoke the ghostly bell-voice. But nothing responded to its call; man, bird and beast had seemingly deserted Friar's Park.

Faintly I detected the lowing of cattle in some distant pasture; the ranks of firs whispered secretly one to another; and the pall above the hills grew blacker and began to stretch out over the valley.

Amid this ominous stillness of nature I began to ascend the cone-strewn path. Evidently enough, the extensive grounds had been neglected for years, and that few pedestrians and fewer vehicles ever sought Friar's Park was demonstrated by the presence of luxurious weeds in the carriageway. Having proceeded for some distance, until the sheer hill-side seemed to loom over me like the wall of a tower, I paused, peering about in the ever-growing darkness. I was aware of a physical chill; certainly no ray of sunlight ever penetrated to this tunnel through the firs. Could I have mistaken the path and be proceeding, not towards the house, but away from it, and into the gloom of the woods? Or perhaps the deserted lodge was that of some other, empty establishment.

There was something uncomfortable in this reflection; momentarily I knew a childish fear of the dim groves. I thought of the "darkness 'broidered with luminous eyes," and I walked forward rapidly, self-assertively. Ten paces brought me to one of the many bends in the winding road —and there, far ahead, as though out of some cavern in the very hill-side, a yellow light shone.

I pressed on with greater assurance, until the house became visible. Now I perceived that I had indeed strayed from the carriage sweep in some way, for the path that I was following terminated at the foot of a short flight of moss-covered steps. I mounted the steps and found myself at the bottom of a terrace. The main entrance was far to my left and separated from the terrace by a neglected lawn. That portion of the place was Hanoverian and ugly, whilst the wing nearest to me was Tudor and picturesque. Excepting the yellow light shining out from a window on the right of the porch, no illuminations were visible about the house, although the brewing storm had already plunged the hollow into premature night.

My conception of Friar's Park had been wide of the reality—and there was no sign of occupancy about this strange-looking mansion, which might have hidden forgotten for centuries in the horse-shoe of the hills. The stillness of the place was of that sort which almost seems to be palpable, that can be seen and felt. A humid chill arose apparently from the terrace, with its stone pavings outlined in moss, crept up from the wilderness below and down from the fir woods above.

I had crossed the terrace and the lawn, and now stood looking through the open French window from which light had proceeded into a room that evidently adjoined the hall. A great still darkness had come, and on a littered table in this room a reading-lamp was burning.

The room was furnished as a library. Every available foot of wall space was occupied by laden bookcases. The volumes were nearly all old, and many of them were in strange, evidently foreign, bindings. Items of chemical apparatus and cases of specimens were visible also, as well as an amazing collection of Egyptian relics strewn about the place in the utmost disorder.

At the table a man was seated, deep in study of a huge leather-bound volume. He was strangely gaunt, and apparently very tall. His clean-shaven face resembled that of Anubis, the hawk-headed god of Ancient Egypt, and his hair, which was snowy white, he wore long and brushed back from his bony brow. His skin was of a dull, even yellow colour, and his long thin brown hands betrayed to me the fact that the man was a Eurasian. The crunching of a piece of gravel under foot revealed my presence. The man looked up swiftly.

I started. Those widely opened black eyes were truly hawk-like in their dark intensity of gaze, and the uncanny resemblance to Anubis was heightened by them. More than ever convinced that I had made a mistake:

"Forgive me for so rudely disturbing you," I said, "but I was under the impression that this was Friar's Park, whereas I fear I have trespassed."

The intense gaze never left my face for a moment, but:

"There is no trespass," answered the man at the table, speaking in a high, harsh voice and with a marked but evasive accent. "All visitors are welcome—chance ones or otherwise. But you have certainly lost your way; this is the Bell House."

"And am I far from Friar's Park?"

"No great distance. May I ask if Lady Coverly knew of your proposed visit?"

"She did not," I said with surprise.

"Then I fear your journey has been fruitless. She is an invalid and can receive no one."

There was something peremptory and imperious in his manner which I resented, and evidently perceiving this resentment:

"I am Lady Coverly's medical adviser," added the Eurasian. "Possibly I can afford you some assistance. In any event, I fear you will have to accept my poor hospitality for the nonce. The alternative is a drenching."

Even as he spoke the hollow was illuminated by a blinding flash of lightning, and indeed his last words were drowned in the thunder that boomed and crashed in deepening peals over the hills.

In a sudden tropical torrent the rain descended, and I stepped forward into the room. Its occupant rose to his great height to greet me.

"I am Dr. Damar Greefe," he said, and bowed formally.

I made myself known to him in turn, and with a sort of stately courtesy he set a high-backed chair for me and himself resumed his former seat.

"You are a stranger to this neighbourhood, I gather?" he continued.

Now, in spite of his polished courtesy, there was that about Dr. Damar Greefe which I did not and could not like. The voice was the voice of a gentleman, but the face was a mask—a mask of Anubis; and seated there in that strange, untidy apartment, amid varied relics of the past and obscure experiments possibly designed to pry into the future, whilst thunder boomed high over the Bell House, I determined to withhold from Dr. Damar Greefe the true nature of my mission. In fact, already I regretted having told him my name—although to have given a fictitious one would have been a gross violation of hospitality unhesitatingly offered.

Even now I find it hard to explain the mingled sentiments which claimed me on the occasion of this my first meeting with a very singular man.

"I am taking a brief rest cure," I replied, "and as I am given to understand that Friar's Park is of much historical interest, I had purposed seeking permission to look over the place and if possible to take a few photographs."

Dr. Damar Greefe inclined his head gravely.

"A former monastic house, Mr. Addison," he replied, "and as you say, of great archæological interest. But the regrettably poor health of Lady Coverly makes it impossible for her to entertain visitors."

Something in the tone of his voice, which now he had lowered so that some of its natural harshness was disguised, set me wondering where I had heard it before. It needed no further scrutiny of the hawk face to convince me that I had never hitherto met Dr. Damar Greefe, but I certainly believed that I had previously heard his voice, although I quite failed to recall where and under what circumstances.

"Sir Burnham has been dead for several years, I believe?" I asked tentatively.

"For several years, yes."

Without returning to the peremptory tone which had distinguished his earlier manner, Dr. Damar Greefe coldly but courteously blocked my path to discussion of the Coverly family; and after several abortive attempts to draw him out upon the point, I recognized this deliberate design and abandoned the matter.

The storm was moving westward, and although brilliant flashes of lightning several times lighted up the queer room, gleaming upon the gaily painted lid of an Egyptian sarcophagus or throwing into horrid relief some anatomical specimen in one of the cases, the thunder crashed no more over the house. But its booming reached my ears from away upon a remote spur of the hills. I became aware of a growing uneasiness in the company of my chance host, who sat by the oddly littered table, watching me with those birdlike eyes.

"Surely," I said, "the rain has ceased?"

"Temporarily," he replied, glancing toward the terrace.

"But I should advise you to delay a few minutes longer. There is every threat of a concluding downpour to come ere long."

"Many thanks," I returned; "I'll risk it. I have already trespassed unwarrantably upon your time, Dr. Greefe. It was good of you to give me shelter."

He rose, a tall, thin figure, vaguely repellent, upon real- izing that I was set on departure, and conducted me out by way of the front door. Standing in the porch:

"At any time that you chance to be again in my neigh- bourhood, Mr. Addison," he said, "I beg of you to call. I have few visitors."

By what process, whether of reasoning or intuition, I came to the conclusion, I know not, but as I turned the bend of the tree-roofed drive and saw the deserted lodge ahead, I knew beyond any possibility of doubt that Dr. Damar Greefe had not returned to his studies, but had swiftly passed along some path through the trees so as to head me off! His purpose in so doing I knew not, but that he had cherished this purpose and proposed to act upon it I had divined in some way at the moment that I had left him in the porch.

Now, hastening my steps, I began to wonder if his de- sign was to intercept me or merely to watch which way I should turn on gaining the main road. That it was the lat- ter I presently learned, for although my unpleasant imagi- nation pictured the gaunt hawklike figure lurking amid the shadows which hemmed me in, I played the part of inno- cence and never once looked back.

Coming out into the high road, I turned sharply left, re- tracing the route by which I had come to the Eurasian doctor's abode. If he had suspected that I had intended to call at Friar's Park despite his assurance that such a visit would prove futile, then he was disappointed. A new and a strange theory to account for "the *Oritoga* mystery" had presented itself to me—a horrible theory, yet, so far as my present data went, a feasible one. Above all, I realized that I had committed a strategical error in openly seeking an interview with Lady Coverly. But I had not, when I had formed that plan, known of the existence of Dr. Damar Greefe.

I uttered a sigh of relief upon emerging upon the high road. The certainty that the white-haired Eurasian was dogging me through the trees was an unpleasant one. And now I perceived that several courses presented themselves; but first I must obtain more information. I perceived a mystery within a mystery, for I was not likely to forget that in Dr. Damar Greefe's collection I had noted a number of *Bubastite cats*.

CHAPTER XIV

THE BLACK DOCTOR

My mail, neatly readdressed by Coates, was awaiting me when I returned to the Abbey Inn. The postal deliveries in Upper Crossleys were eccentric and unreliable, but having glanced through the cuttings enclosed I partook of a hasty lunch and sat down to the task of preparing a column for the *Planet* which should not deflect public interest from the known central figures in the tragedy, but which at the same time should hint at new developments.

Many times in the intervals of writing I glanced through my open window across the valley to where the upstanding wing of Friar's Park jutted above the trees. Strange and terrible ideas flocked to my mind—ideas which must be carefully excluded from the *Planet* article. But at last the MS. was completed, and I determined to walk into the neighbouring town, some miles distant, to post it and at the same time to dispatch a code telegram to Inspector Gatton. The long walk did me good, helping me to clear my mind of morbid vapours; therefore, my business finished, and immune from suspicion in my character of a London pedestrian, I set out to obtain that vital information which I lacked.

A natural taciturnity rendered mine host of the Abbey Inn a difficult subject for interrogation. Moreover, that patriarchal outlook which had been evidenced in his attitude towards the uncouth Edward Hines clearly enough deterred him from imparting to me any facts detrimental to the good name of Upper Crossleys. But on the high road and just before entering the outskirts of the little country town, I had observed an inn which had seemed to be well patronized by the local folks, and since your typical country tap-room is a clearing-house for the gossip of the neighbourhood, to The Threshers I made my way.

The doors had only just been opened; nevertheless, as I set my foot upon the step I met the very gossip that I sought.

"Hope you wasn't caught in the shower this morning, sir?" said an old man seated solitary in an armchair in the corner of the bar-parlour. "But the country'll be all the better for the rain." He eyed me, and: "There's many a fine walk hereabouts," he averred. "There's lots come down from London, especially on a Sunday."

"No doubt," said I encouragingly, stepping up to the counter.

"There's Manton-on-the-Hill," continued the ancient. "You can see the sea from there in clear weather; and many's the time in the war I've heard the guns in France from Upper Crowbury of a still night. Then, four miles away, there's the old Friar's Park, though nobody's allowed past the gate. Not as nobody wants to be," he added reflectively.

"How is that? I understood that Friar's Park was of great interest."

"Oh, ah!" murmured my acquaintance. "Oh, ah! Maybe you was thinkin' of lookin' over it like?"

"I was—yes."

"Or, ah! Well—there's some likes a bit o' danger."

"Danger?" I echoed. "To what danger do you refer?"

He surveyed me with cunning, old rheumy eyes, and:

"What about man-traps?" he inquired. "Ain't man-traps dangerous? And what about shot-guns? Shot-guns can make a party feel sick, can't they? Oh, ah!"

"But," I exclaimed, "you surely don't mean that there are traps laid in the grounds of the Park? It isn't legal. And why should anyone shoot at visitors?"

"Maybe 'cause they're told to," he shouted. "Ay, that's the reason as like as not—'cause they're told to."

"Who are 'they'?"

"Old Gipsy Hawkins as used to be Sir Burnham's under-keeper. What's he doin' of up there at Park all day? Layin' traps and such—that's what he's doin' of. My son Jim knows it, he do. My son Jim found one of 'em—and left best part of a pair of trousers in it, too!"

These statements if true would seem to cast an unpleasant sidelight upon the character of my acquaintance of the Abbey Inn. I wondered if the "Jim" referred to was that "young Jim Corder," whose name seemed to be a standing joke with the man Hawkins (I learned later that it was so). And I wondered if Martin's mysterious references to certain patrons, whose patronage had damaged his business, might not have referred to the gamekeeper. Moreover, I now put a new construction upon Hawkins's sly amusement when I had inquired about the "shooting" in the neighbourhood.

I began to grow keenly interested, and:

"Surely you took some steps in the matter?" I asked.

"Oh, ah. My son Jim did. He lay for days for that there Gipsy Hawkins—but Hawkins was too wise for him."

"But," said I, "you could legally have claimed damages."

"Maybe," was the reply; "but I reckon they'd have asked what my son Jim was doing in the Park. Oh, ah, I reckon they would."

This point of view had not hitherto presented itself to me, but that it was a just one I did not doubt.

"What is the object of all this?" I asked. "Does Lady Coverly object to anyone entering the grounds?"

" 'Tain't Lady Coverly," confided the old man; "it's that there black doctor."

"What black doctor?" I exclaimed.

"Him they call Doctor Greefe."

"Oh," said I, "you call him the black doctor. Is he a negro?"

"He's black," was the reply, "black he is, although his hair is white. Oh, ah, there's black blood in him all right."

"And what has he to do with the man-traps in the Park?"

"Has 'em put there—has 'em put there, he does."

"But what for? Surely the property belongs not to Dr. Greefe, but to Lady Coverly."

"Belongs to her! Her own soul don't belong to her!"

I was conscious of a growing excitement. I thought that I was about to learn the very fact which I was seeking, and accordingly:

"What is the age of Lady Burnham Coverly?" I asked.

"Lady Burnham? Well, let me see; she were not more'n about twenty-five, I reckon, when Sir Burnham first brought her to the Park. Them was the days, them was. These parts 'as changed cruel since I was a young man. Then it was soon after as Sir Burnham went off to Egypt for Government, and eleven years afore he came back again."

"Did Lady Burnham accompany him to Egypt?" I asked, interestedly.

"Oh, ah, for sure she did. Poor Mr. Roger was born in Egypt. It was eight years come October they returned home to Park, and six years come September poor young Mr. Roger died."

"Then Lady Coverly must be something over forty years of age," said I musingly.

One of my theories, a wild one I must confess, was shattered by this piece of information. In short, I had conceived the idea (and the news that Lady Coverly had resided for some years in Egypt had strengthened it) that the woman in the case was none other than the mistress of Friar's Park! Her antipathy towards the late baronet had seemed to suggest a motive for the crime. But it was impossible to reconcile the figure of this lonely and bereaved woman with that of the supernormally agile visitant to my cottage in London, in short, with the possessor of those dreadful green eyes. I determined to try a new tack, and remembering that the real object of my journey to Upper Crossleys was to learn particulars respecting the early death of Roger Coverly:

"Did Mr. Roger Coverly die in England?" I inquired.

"Oh, no, sir; he died in foreign parts, but they brought him home to bury him, they did."

"Do you know of what he died?"

"Oh, ah! I have heard tell it was some foreign fever like —took him off sudden, and him only a lad. It killed poor Sir Burnham, it did."

"Then Sir Burnham died shortly afterwards?"

"Two years afterwards, and these parts has never been the same since."

"But what has Dr. Greefe to do with all this?"

"Ah, now you're asking. Seven years ago, he settled here in the big house up by the Park; part of the Park estate it

is; and there he's been ever since, him and his black servant."

"Black servant!" I exclaimed.

"Oh, ah, real black he is—not half-and-half like his
master, but as black as a lump o' coal, an' ugly—oh, ah,
he's ugly right enough. Goes up to the Abbey Inn of a
night he do, him and that there Gipsy Hawkins, the pret-
tiest pair o' rascals in Upper Crossleys. Drove all the de-
cent folk away from the place, and Martin keeps the best
beer about here, too. If I was Martin," continued the ancient truculently, "I'd know what to say to them two, I
would; ay, and what to do to 'em," he added with great ferocity.

"Oh," said I; for this unexpected clearing up of so many
minor mysteries had rather taken me aback. "Then Dr.
Greefe is not popular?"

"Popular!" echoed the old man.

He drained his tankard and set it down on the table
with a bang.

"He's been the ruin o' these parts, he has. He's worse
than the turnip-fly."

"But in what way is he responsible for these evils of
which you complain?"

The old man peered into his empty mug with a glance
of such eloquence that I could not mistake its import. Accordingly, I caused it to be refilled, thus preventing any
check in the flow of his eloquence, and:

"In what way?" he asked, his voice raised in a high quavering note. He laughed, and his laughter was pitched in
the same time-worn key. "That doctor is a blot on the
country. When Sir Burnham was alive—and afore he went
to Egypt—it was different; although, mind you, it's my belief—oh, ah, it is indeed—that him coming here had as
much to do with Sir Burnham's death as the loss of his son
what I told you about. That's my belief."

I took a sip from my replenished mug, and:

"I cannot understand," I said, "why the presence of Dr.
Greefe should have brought about the death of Sir Burnham, or the death of anybody else."

"No," said the old man cunningly; "you can't, eh? Well,
there be things none of us can understand, and things
some of us can. If you ever clap eyes on that there black

doctor, like enough this'll be one of the things you'll be able to understand."

With the idea of drawing yet more intimate confidences:

"You suggest that Dr. Greefe had some hold upon the late Sir Burnham?"

"I don't suggest nothing."

"Some hold upon Lady Burnham, then?"

"Oh, ah, like enough."

"Don't think," I added solicitously, "that I doubt the truth of your statements in any way, but what could this black doctor, as you call him, have to gain by persecuting these people?"

"There be things," replied my aged friend, "what none of us can understand, but there be things that all of us do. Oh, ah, there be; and all of us in these parts knows as Upper Crossleys ain't been the same since that black doctor settled here. Besides, first Mr. Roger went, then Sir Burnham went. Now I do read in this 'ere paper as another of 'em is gone."

He held up two gnarled and twitching fingers crossed before him.

"Did you ever hear tell of the evil eye?" he asked, and peered at me cunningly. He took a long drink from his mug. "But maybe you'll laugh at *that*," he added.

"I am in no way disposed to laugh at anything you have told me," I assured him; "and as to the evil eye, I have certainly heard of such a thing, although I must admit, and I am glad to admit, that I have never met with it."

"I do trust, sir," responded the ancient, "that such a kind-hearted gent may never meet with it. Ah, I do trust that you never may, which is to say, so to speak, as I do trust as you'll never meet that black doctor. If ever a man had the evil eye, that black doctor's got it, and old Mother Shale what lives in the cottage on the heath down against the windmill, she warned me, she did, three days after he come here. 'Mr. Corder,' she says, 'that black doctor has the evil eye!' And never was a truer word spoke. He's been the bane and blight of this 'ere place, he has."

He paused from sheer lack of breath, and having allowed him some little interval of repose:

"But what has the evil eye to do with the laying of man-traps and the shooting of visitors who may chance to cross the estate?" I inquired.

"Ah, that's it! But the evil eye, I'm told, goes with the evil heart, and that man's heart's as black as his face. Blacker," he added, on second thoughts.

"Yet you have no positive evidence that Dr. Greefe is responsible for the setting of these man-traps and the attitude of Hawkins?"

"Nobody has," declared my acquaintance earnestly. "If anybody had, we'd have had the law on him long ago."

"And is Lady Burnham often seen about?" I inquired.

"Never!" was the reply. "She ain't passed the gates of the Park this twelve months and more."

He looked about him covertly, and:

"It's my belief," he affirmed, lowering his quavering voice almost to a whisper, "that she'll never pass them gates again alive."

"Oh!" said I. "This seems to be a very cheerful neighbourhood. Yet in spite of your wishes on my behalf, I must confess I should like a glimpse of this black doctor. Does he practise about here?"

"Practise? Is it likely?"

"Then he has private means?"

"His house belongs to the estate," was the reply, "and you can't tell me he ever pays any rent. As to his means, I don't know nothing about that."

I gathered little more of interest from my acquaintance of The Threshers, but indeed I had gathered enough, and as I wended my way back to the Abbey Inn, I was turning over in my mind the extraordinary story that he had related to me concerning Dr. Damar Greefe.

Clearly the man lived the life of a pariah, and I knew not whether to pity him or otherwise. In an ignorant community it is a dreadful thing to earn such a reputation as that which evidently attached to the Eurasian doctor; and this talk of the evil eye took me back automatically to the early days of this quaint spot, where, cut off from the larger things of life, the simple folk continued to hold the same beliefs which had stirred their forefathers. In those remote times when the white brethren from the neighbouring abbey had held absolute sway in that countryside, the life history of one accused, as Dr. Damar Greefe was now accused, of possessing the evil eye, would very probably have terminated upon a pile of faggots, by order of Mother Church. It was all very strange, and apart from its importance in the eyes of the ignorant country folk, seemed to contain a nucleus of something more germane to the object of my mission than the imaginings of ancient sorcery which still lingered in the minds of the people of Upper Crossleys.

I thought how I had looked out of my window and had found in the moon-bathed landscape something which had translated my ideas to that strange picture of Wiertz. Then I had known nothing of this nebula of witchcraft which, according to popular tradition, rested upon the vicinity; yet I had pictured the night as "a curtain 'broidered with luminous eyes," and I could only suppose that my mind had become impressed by a picture conjured up by this focusing of local thought. In short, the people of the neighbourhood had created this atmosphere of desolation and of something more sinister, which I had observed in the very hour of my arrival at the little village.

So my thoughts ran as I proceeded back to the Abbey Inn, and as I had collected much new and valuable information, I determined to embody it in a long report to Gatton. Furthermore, I was doubtful as to my next step, the bold move which I made later not having yet presented itself to my mind.

Twice during the evening, however, I looked into the bar parlour, but neither "Gipsy" Hawkins nor the black servant appeared. But when at last I turned in, I closed my windows and drew the curtains. I desired no repetition of the dreams which had made hideous my first night at the Abbey Inn.

CHAPTER XV

I RECEIVE VISITORS

Over my breakfast, on the following morning, I began to formulate that plan which was to lead to an extraordinary discovery. I breakfasted in my own room, and just as I had finished and was about to light my pipe, Mr. Martin, the landlord, knocked at the door.

"Come in," I cried.

He entered, and:

"A lady has called to see you, sir," he announced.

The manner in which he made the statement evidenced a curious mixture of disapproval and respect. For my own part, it is perhaps unnecessary for me to say that my first thought, as always, was Isobel! In the very moment, however, that this idea visited me (the wish being father of the thought) I recognized its folly.

"A lady?" I repeated. "But I know no one here. Are you certain that it was for me she asked?"

"Quite, sir," replied the landlord, who was evidently flurried out of his usual calm by what I gathered to be an episode unprecedented in his memories of the Abbey Inn. "Mr. Addison, she asked for. She is waiting in the coffee-room, sir."

Wholly at a loss to understand who my visitor could be, I made my way to the little apartment at the side of the bar-parlour which Mr. Martin had dignified with the title of coffee-room. I observed, upon the bench before the door, a shabby-looking fellow whom I might have taken to be some local tradesman except that he appeared to be a chance visitor and was evidently unacquainted with Martin. He was reading a newspaper, and I saw a cup of coffee set upon the bench beside him.

This was a hazy morning, which I thought betokened another hot day, and as I entered the "coffee-room," I found it to be pervaded by a curious half-light, not unlike

102

that of summer twilight. The glow of the sun peering redly through the mist added warmth to this soft illumination, but since the room boasted only one small window it was badly lighted, even at noon.

From a little horsehair-covered sofa set before this window my visitor rose to greet me, and with my hand upon the knob of the door, I paused, for certainly this was a stranger who stood before me!

She was tall and very slender, attired with great elegance, and in her whole appearance there was something markedly foreign—or perhaps I should say, exotic. She wore a small hat which I judged to be Parisian and expensive, and from its brim depended a figured veil which effectually disguised her features, without being able, or perhaps without being intended, to disguise her brilliant, almond-shaped eyes. For one moment a dreadful idea presented itself to me; but the most appalling memory which I retained of those other witch-eyes around which so much mystery clustered, was their brilliant greenness. The eyes of my visitor, although unusually large and brilliant, were totally different in shape, being long and narrow, and apparently of a wonderful amber colour.

When she spoke, her voice was very cultured and soft, yet I started, and I know I must have been staring very hard and very rudely. There was a faint huskiness in its tone, a caress in its accents, which irresistibly reminded me of the scene in my study which had resulted in the loss of the image of Bâst.

I think I have already indicated that I am one of those who arrive at a decision somewhat laboriously; and now, convinced that my memory of the luminous eyes was threatening to become an obsession, so that I looked to find them blazing out at me from the face of every stranger whom I encountered, I forced myself to believe that a chance resemblance in my visitor's voice to the voice of that other visitor had tricked me.

"Mr. Addison," she said, "I'm afraid you will think this call somewhat unconventional, but"—she paused almost imperceptibly—"I am staying at Friar's Park, and Lady Coverly has heard from Dr. Greefe that you wish to see the house."

"Really," I murmured, "it was good of you to take so much trouble, but——"

"It was no trouble at all," she declared. "I had occasion to come this way, and Lady Coverly asked me to call and tell you that whilst she is not well enough to receive visitors, you are quite welcome to inspect the older parts of the house."

"I am much indebted," I said.

Having so spoken, I ceased, and was aware of a kind of embarrassment. For whilst I was naturally anxious to avoid unpleasant suspicions regarding a lady who apparently had gone out of her way to perform an act of courtesy, yet I could not place this elegant figure in the household of Friar's Park as depicted by my old gossip of The Threshers.

I mentally determined there and then to question Martin, and, if possible, Hawkins upon the point, directly an opportunity arose, and the former immediately my visitor had departed. But she seemed to be in no hurry to depart.

"You have never visited this neighbourhood before?" she continued, in the soft, caressing voice which persistently awakened memories of that evening in my cottage.

She re-seated herself upon the sofa, leaving me no alternative but to sit down in the only chair which the coffee-room boasted. I could not fail to notice, however, that although she addressed me as Mr. Addison, she did not volunteer her own name. Furthermore, she remained throughout with her back to the window.

"Never," I replied; "it is very interesting in many ways, I believe."

"You will find Friar's Park most fascinating," she assured me. "It stands upon the site of one of the oldest and largest monasteries in the south of England. Indeed, some parts of the house, notably the chapel and the west tower, which is visible from here I think, are remains of the original building."

She was palpably trying to interest me; and, conscious that my somewhat frigid attitude was churlish, if she was really what she professed to be—namely, a friend of Lady Coverly's—I endeavoured in turn to display an intelligent interest in the history of the old monastic house.

I do not regret that I did so. I think that I have never heard the dry bones of history clothed so fascinatingly. The knowledge displayed by my unknown visitor of the history of that old monkish corner of England was truly amazing. The Coverlys, it appeared, had played their part in that history right back to the misty times of Saxon England. The scenes conjured up by my first sight of the curiously wild country which lay between the village and the distant park land were presented now with all the colour and truth of real life. This woman seemingly was acquainted with almost every act of importance of every Coverly since the days of Canute, and with the doings of all the abbots who had ever ruled over Croix-de-Lis.

Finally, while I listened in ever growing wonder, fascinated by the extent of this strange woman's knowledge and in part, too, by the husky music of her voice, she seemed to become conscious of the passage of time, and, rising suddenly, she laughed, and her laughter again awakened a memory.

"How perfectly absurd of me, Mr. Addison," she said. "You will certainly think I am more than eccentric to sit here fulfilling the part of a local guide."

Even as she spoke the words, a sound intruded from the road outside. A heavy footstep came first—the footstep of one who approached the door of the inn; then:

"Martin!" I heard. "A moment, please."

It was Dr. Damar Greefe.

If the sound of his voice had startled me, its effect upon my visitor was truly singular. Taking a swift step towards me, she grasped my arm with her strangely slender gloved hand. Now that she stood so close to me, I realized that she was even taller than I had supposed, nearly as tall as myself, in fact. Her swift, lithe movements possessed an indescribable grace which, as I thought, and experienced a sudden revulsion, were oddly uncanny—cat-like.

"Oh, Mr. Addison," she said, and drew even nearer, so that I could feel her breath upon my cheek, "I fear that man as one fears a snake. I am going to ask a favour of you. I see that there is another door to this room, and I have a particular reason for wishing to avoid him. I don't know where that doorway leads to, but I can doubtless find my way out."

Her grasp upon my arm tightened.

"Dare I ask you," she added pleadingly, "to conceal from him, if necessary, the fact that I have been here?"

"But Martin knows that you have been here," I protested, my mind in a whirl at this sudden turn of affairs, "and the man sitting on the bench outside must have seen you come in also."

"He did not," she replied rapidly, "and Martin does not know who I am."

It was on the tip of my tongue to say, "Neither do I," but:

"Please," she pleaded; "it is not much to ask, but it means so much to me."

Thereupon, without waiting for my answer, she turned and ran out through the little doorway, which opened as a matter of fact into the larder of the inn, from which there was an exit into a kitchen garden.

I could hear Martin the landlord talking to the Eurasian doctor in the passage outside the coffee-room, and, before I had time to open the door, there came a peremptory rap, the door was opened from the outside, and Dr. Damar Greefe entered.

In spite of the already great heat of the morning, he wore a heavy black overcoat, and his white hair showed in startling relief beneath a wide-brimmed black felt hat. If I had been surprised at the tallness of the woman who had so suddenly departed, the stature of the Eurasian was curiously illustrated by the fact that he had to lower his head in order to enter the little doorway.

"Ah!" he exclaimed, peering towards me where I stood in the badly lighted room. "Mr. Addison, I believe?"

"At your service, Dr. Greefe," I replied.

"I understood that my niece was here?"

"Your niece?" I exclaimed, and my astonishment was quite unfeigned.

"Precisely."

That peremptory manner which I had previously resented in him evinced itself now; and even had I lacked reasons other than personal for foiling him, I should certainly have returned a reply far from pacific.

"I was not aware," he continued, his voice high-pitched and harsh, "that you were acquainted. Inform me."

All the time he was peering about the room suspiciously, and:

"I inform you that we are not!" I said. "But if we were, I cannot conceive that our acquaintance would concern you in any way."

"You are rude, sir!" he cried, and bent towards me so that I could see the fierce hawk face set in a vicious scowl.

"I should be sorry to think so," I said indifferently, for the Eurasian's behaviour transcended the merely annoying and was that of a lunatic. "I would not willingly provoke a sick man, and the tone and manner of your address forcibly suggest to me that your temperature is not normal."

A moment he stood bending towards me, his pose that of one about to spring, then:

"Ah!" he exclaimed. "Yes, you are right, Mr. Addison. I live much alone, and I fear my manner grows brusque. Overlook it. She has gone, then?"

"If you refer to a lady who called upon me half an hour ago—yes, she is gone."

He drew himself upright again and stood there, gigantic in the little room—a great, gaunt figure.

"Ah! And she was not my niece?"

"I lack the pleasure of your niece's acquaintance, Dr. Greefe."

"Yes. You said so. Good day, Mr. Addison."

He turned, lowered his head, and walked out of the room. When I, in turn, emerged into the passage, I saw him striding out of the inn. Martin was standing by the door of the bar-parlour looking very confused; and as I joined him, intent upon a chat, I observed that the shabby-looking stranger had departed.

"Hullo, Martin!" I exclaimed, "I thought I saw a customer here."

"When you came in there was. He went off with Cassim and Hawkins. They was goin' to show him the road to Manton."

"Cassim?"

"Ay."

Martin growled and walked behind the bar-counter.

"You have some curious residents in this neighbourhood."

"Too curious by half."

"Cassim, for instance, is not an English name."

Martin indulged in that rumbling sound which was his only form of laughter.

"English!" he said. "He's as black as your hat!"

My hat chanced to be grey, but I followed the idea nevertheless, and:

"What!" I exclaimed. "A negro?"

"A blackamoor. That's all I know or care; and dumb!"

"Dumb! And a friend of Hawkins?"

"God knows. Things ain't right."

"Do you know if—a lady—resides with Dr. Greefe?"

"Maybe—maybe not. There *is* tales told."

Substantially this was all I learned from mine host; but having lighted my pipe I sat down on the bench before the door and set my mind to work in an endeavour to marshal all the facts into some sort of order.

The reputation locally enjoyed by Dr. Damar Greefe I could afford to ignore, I thought, but from my personal observation of the man I had come to the conclusion that there was much about him which I did not and could not understand. In the first place, for any man to choose to live, solitary, in such an abode as the Bell House was remarkable. Why had the masterful Eurasian retired to that retreat in company with his black servitor? I thought of my own case, but it did not seem to afford a strict analogy.

Then, who was the "niece" so closely guarded by Dr. Greefe? And if she was none other than my late elegant visitor, why had she sought the interview? Not even my natural modesty, which in such matters I have sometimes thought to be excessive, could conceal from me the fact that she had found my society pleasing. But, since I had never seen her before, did this theory account for her visit? Recalling again that huskily caressing voice, I asked myself the question: *Had* I seen her before?

Perhaps the apparition of green eyes looking up to my window from the lane below, which on the night of my arrival I had relegated to the limbo of dreamland, had been verity and not phantasm. If that were so, then the uncanny visitant to my cottage had pursued me to Upper Crossleys!

Or could it be the fact that she had preceded me? Perhaps Gatton had not confided the whole of his ideas to me —perhaps, as I had already suspected, the heart of "the *Oritoga* mystery" lay here and not in London.

The result of my meditations was that I determined, in pursuit of my original plan, first to call upon Mr. Edward Hines; and having inquired of Martin the way to Leeways Farm, I took my stick and set out.

CHAPTER XVI

THE GOLDEN CAT

It was a perfect morning, and although the sun had not yet attained to its full power, it had dispersed the early mist, and I knew that in another hour or less the heat would once more have become tropical. During the first part of my walk, and whilst I remained in the neighbourhood of Upper Crossleys, I met never a wayfarer, and memories of the green eyes followed me step by step so that I was often tempted to look back over my shoulder by the idea that I should detect, as I had detected once before, the presence of some follower. I resented this impulse, however. I felt that my imagination was adding horrors to those which already actually existed, so that I should presently find myself unable to distinguish the real from the imaginary.

At the end of half an hour's steady tramping I saw before me a place where a wood dipped down to the wayside so that its trees cast a broad shadow across the path. I knew that the entrance to the farm lay just beyond; and pressing on past the trees I saw many outbuildings having none of that deserted appearance which characterized the neighbouring homesteads of Upper Crossleys. Twenty yards beyond the farm itself appeared in view.

There was some sign of activity about the yard, and walking briskly forward I presently found myself looking into a stone-paved place containing numbers of milk-cans. Here a woman was engaged in sweeping the floor, and:

"I have called to see Mr. Edward Hines," I said. "Can you tell me where I shall find him?"

The woman stared at me in a strange and almost stupefied manner.

"Is he a friend of yours?" she inquired.

"He is not exactly a friend of mine," I continued; "but I have very particular business with him."

She continued to stare in that curious way, and remained silent for so long that I began to think she was not going to reply, when:

"If Mr. Edward is not expecting you," she said, "I don't know that I should advise you to go in. He is not very well just now—and he is sometimes rather strange."

"I know," I said. "I quite understand; but he will be willing to see me when he knows what I have come about. Shall I find him yonder?"

I pointed towards an open door, leading to which was a neat gravelled path lined by well-kept flower-beds, and which I took to be the main entrance to the farm.

"Well, sir," said the woman doubtfully, "they'll tell you there if Mr. Edward is to be seen; but I don't advise it."

"That's all right!" I cried, and proceeded in the direction of the doorway.

I presently obtained a view of a cosily furnished room, where a white-haired old lady was bustling about engaged in some domestic duties. I paused at the threshold.

"My name is Addison," I said. "Would it be possible for me to have a few minutes' conversation with Mr. Edward Hines?"

The old lady (whom I suspected to be the mother of the youth whom I was seeking) paused in the midst of her task, and looked at me in a troubled way. It was evident enough that the reputation of Mr. Edward was the same in his home as elsewhere, and it occurred to me that his upbringing must have been a very bad one.

"Well," she replied, after this eloquent pause, "he's up in his room certainly, but he doesn't like to see visitors, I know."

"He will be perfectly willing to see *me*," I said confidently. "I have news of importance for him." And as she continued to look at me in that troubled way: "I know of his present disfigurement," I explained. "You need not be afraid of any unpleasant scenes."

"If I were sure of that," she said hesitatingly, and looked me over with a critical eye. "Does he know you, sir?"

"Oh, yes," I answered; "we have met before. I assure you it will be quite all right if you will just let me walk up and announce myself to him, Mrs. Hines."

If I had had any doubt upon the point I was soon to

learn that she was indeed the mother of the notorious Mr. Edward; for, ere she had time to reply, a high-pitched, querulous voice which I had heard before cried out from somewhere above:

"If that's anyone for me, Mother, tell him to go away! You know perfectly well I won't see anyone."

"There you are, sir," said Mrs. Hines, unable to hide her embarrassment; "I told you he wouldn't see you."

"Please give me permission to go up," I said. "He will change his mind when he hears what I have to say."

"You hear, Mother!" came the irritable voice; "I'll break his neck if he comes up here!"

Judging from the sound of the voice, I concluded that the excited young man was located in a room immediately above that at the door of which I stood.

"Don't be alarmed, madam," I said, and stepping into the room I placed my hand reassuringly upon the old lady's shoulder.

Without waiting for any further protest, I advanced to an open staircase which I had already marked as leading to the apartment above and confidently mounted. The copy-hunting pressman is not readily excluded, and a few moments later I found myself in an extremely untidy bedroom, the walls of which were decorated with sporting prints, Kirchner drawings and photographs of many damsels.

The scarred young man, his face still a mass of sticking-plaster, stood with clenched fists facing me, and:

"Get out!" was his greeting, "before I throw you out!"

"My dear sir," I said, "unless you particularly want to figure in a very undignified light as a witness in a trial for murder, sit down and listen to me."

Edward Hines hesitated, opening and closing his hands and glaring at me in a preposterous fury.

"What's the game?" he demanded. "What are you talking about?"

"I am talking of 'the *Oritoga* mystery,' " I replied.

" 'The *Oritoga* mystery'?"

His expression changed, and he dropped down into an arm-chair from which he had evidently arisen upon hearing my voice below. I observed a copy of a daily paper lying upon the carpet, and the conspicuous head-line was sufficient to show me that he had actually been reading the latest reports concerning the case at the time of my arrival. I had judged my man pretty accurately by this time, and, drawing up another chair which stood near me, I sat down facing him, holding out my open cigar-case.

"I quite understand your sensitiveness in the circumstances," I said soothingly; "but there is no occasion to suppose that I have come to remind you of your misfortune. Have a cigar. I want a chat with you."

He continued to watch me in a lowering way, but I was gradually getting him in hand. With very poor grace he accepted a cigar, lighted it, and threw the match away without offering to light mine. I did not appear to notice his churlishness, but immediately approached the matter about which I had come.

"Although I am not a member of the Criminal Investigation Department," I continued, "I am nevertheless in a sense an agent of Scotland Yard, and I must ask you to listen very seriously to what I have to say. You have in your possession a certain gold amulet——"

He was on his feet in a moment, the patches of skin visible between the strapping assuming a purple colour. A more choleric young man I had never met.

"Damn you!" he cried. "What is it to do with you?"

"Sit down!" I said sternly. "I have given you one warning; I shall not give you another. You will either answer my questions civilly here and now, or answer them in court; whichever you please. I shall not give you another opportunity of choosing. I will repeat my remark; you have in your possession a certain gold amulet in the form, I believe, of a cat."

He was choking and muttering and glaring at me as I spoke, but I stared at him coolly, and finally he resumed his seat and reached out one hand towards a chest of drawers which stood beside his chair. Pulling one of the drawers open, he took out a little gold figure of Bâst, and holding it towards me:

"Is this the thing you mean?" he jerked uncivilly.

"It is," I replied; "allow me to examine it."

He seemed rather reluctant to do so, but nevertheless I took it from his hand and looked at it closely. Beyond doubt it was of Ancient Egyptian workmanship and probably a genuine Bubastite votive offering. Raising my eyes to him again:

"Without in any way desiring to pry into your affairs," I said, "would you be good enough to tell me how this came into your possession?"

The studied coolness of my manner was having its proper effect, and Edward Hines, although sulkily, replied at once:

"A woman gave it to me."

"What was her name?"

"I don't know."

"You don't know the name of a woman who gave you a costly trinket of this kind?"

A ridiculous look of vanity appeared in his eyes.

"Is it very valuable?" he inquired.

"It may be worth as much as fifty pounds," I answered quietly.

"Really!" said he, with something approaching geniality in his tones. "Well, it's an extraordinary thing, but I assure you I don't know her name."

"Of course," I said, with Machiavellian cunning, "I don't expect you to remember the name of every girl who has loved you, but this is an unusual present to receive even from an infatuated woman."

"It's an extraordinary thing, isn't it?" repeated Edward Hines, full of self-esteem. "I can't make out the women at all; they're always giving me presents. Look at that picture-frame. I got that from a girl I had only seen three times—and it's solid silver," he added.

I glanced at the memento indicated, and observed that it contained a photograph of Mr. Hines (without the sticking plaster).

"An excellent likeness of yourself, too," I remarked.

"It's not bad," said he disparagingly. "It was done by one of the big people up in London. The girl paid for it."

"But even that," I pursued, "even that is not so remarkable a gift as this valuable piece of jewellery which I hold in my hand."

"No," said the youth, now restored to the utmost good humour by my undisguised admiration of his Don Juan-like qualities. "But the fact remains that I don't know her name to this day. What did you mean," he continued, "when you said that I was concerned in some way in 'the *Oritoga* mystery'?"

"I meant," I explained, "that the police are looking for a woman who answers to the description of your friend."

"Really!" he cried. "A tall woman, very fine figure, beautifully dressed?"

"I think it is probably the same," I said. "Had she any peculiarities of appearance or manner by which you would recognize her again?"

"She had several peculiarities by which I should recognize her," he declared, a note of resentment now proclaiming itself in his voice.

"And they were?"

Mr. Hines leaned forward, tapping me on the knee confidentially.

"I met her by accident, you understand," he confided, "on the London Road one evening about sunset. She asked me the way to Friar's Park, and I could see that I had made an impression at once. It was just an excuse to speak to me, of course. I offered to walk that far with her; she agreed, and, to cut a long story short, the usual thing, of course: she wanted to meet me again.

"Well," he resumed complacently, "I met her on the following Thursday, and we became very good friends, you understand, except that she always seemed particularly anxious to return home before dusk. All this time I never knew who she was, or even where she lived, but of course I could see how the land lay. She was some lady from London staying at one of the big houses about here, and had to show up for dinner. That night when we parted she gave me this little gold thing, and arranged to see me again."

He paused, knocking ash from his cigar and seemingly reflecting as to how he should word his next communication; but finally:

"The third time I saw her," he said, "I managed to arrange that she could not get in quite so early, you understand; and then—I don't know exactly how to tell you. I am not a chap that gets in a panic very easily; but—I may mention that the scene took place in a wood—she gave me the biggest scare I have ever had in my life."

He bent forward and again tapped me on the knee.

"My dear—Mr. Addison, I think you said your name was?—her eyes lighted up in the dark like a cat's!"

He stared at me with some return of his old truculence,

as if anticipating ridicule and prepared to resent it; but I nodded sternly, watching him as if enthralled by his narrative, whereupon:

"Yes—like a cat's!" he repeated. "And I'll admit I got in a panic. I don't know if she thought from the way I yelled that I was going to attack her or what, but the next thing I knew she was at my throat."

He uttered a sort of choking sound, tenderly touched the bandages about his neck, and fingered the plaster which ornamented his face.

"At your throat?" said I. "You mean she tried to throttle you?"

"Throttle me!" he exclaimed scornfully. "She seized me with her *teeth!*"

"But," I said, and hesitated, for I feared I might wound his curious susceptibility, "the damage to your face?"

"Damn her!" he cried. "Damn her! I had never seen her without her gloves, you understand, but she must have taken them off that night, for *this*"—he indicated his plastered countenance—"is what she did with her nails!"

He paused, staring at me dully, and then with a hint of the old ridiculous vanity entering his voice:

"But I scored after all," he said, tossing the little amulet into the drawer from which he had taken it. "If that's worth fifty pounds it will more than pay the doctor's bill, I think!"

Following a brief interval:

"Of course," I said, "you would recognize the woman again?"

"I am not so certain," declared the scarred man. "She always wore some sort of veil; but you may be sure," he added in a tone of supreme condescension, "that she was a very pretty woman, or I shouldn't have been bothering with her."

"You are quite sure of that?" I ventured to remark.

"No doubt about it at all. Most extraordinary eyes—too damned extraordinary by half!"

"Well," I said, "I am much indebted to you for your statement, and you may be confident that it will materially assist the investigation now in progress."

"Don't mention it," said Hines airily. "If I can ever do anything else for you, just let me know; but—I mean to

say I rely upon you not to bring me into it. You understand what I mean?"

"You may be absolutely certain," I replied, "that no hint
of this occurrence will ever be made public so far as I am
concerned."

I took my departure from Leeways Farm fully satisfied
with the result of the first move in the plan of campaign
upon which I had decided. Returning to my quarters at the
Abbey Inn, I spent the greater part of the afternoon in
writing a detailed account of my interview with Edward
Hines. Having completed this, I set out for the town, as by
posting my report there and not in the wayside box at
Upper Crossleys I knew that I could count upon its deliv-
ery at New Scotland Yard by the first mail in the morning.

In leisurely fashion I performed the journey, for my
next move could not be made until after dusk.

CHAPTER XVII

THE NUBIAN MUTE

I returned from the little market town beneath a sky of
tropical brilliance. The landscape was bathed in a radiance
of perfect moonlight, and under the trees which thickly
lined the way the shadows had a velvet quality rarely met
with in England, their edges showing more sharply defined
than I ever remembered to have noticed them before. But
ere long I grew oblivious even of the beauty of the night,
becoming absorbed in reflections respecting this most extraordinary case.

Every new datum acquired, instead of serving to eluci-
date, seemed only more completely to obscure the issue.
Mystery revealed itself within mystery, and this was indeed
a labyrinth, to the heart of which I sometimes despaired of
penetrating. Who was this woman whose elusive figure appeared at every turn in the case? Was she one and the
same with the visitor to my cottage who had purloined the

green enamelled statuette—and could it be that I had actually sat in conversation with her in the coffee-room of the Abbey Inn and had failed to recognize her for what she was?

Beyond doubt she had extraordinary cleverness and was a weaver of spells, so that in a sense she could temporarily disguise her personality. Whilst at one moment she was a repellent, half-animal creature, at another she was a fascinating woman of the world versed in strange lores and a most entertaining companion. What object underlay her diverse activities? Assuming that she was concerned in the murder of Sir Marcus Coverly, the purpose of her visit to my cottage was not far to seek; she had come to recover incriminating evidence and had been aided it seemed by the hand of fate.

But why had she come to visit me at the Abbey Inn, and what had she gained by this interview? Perhaps—I reflected, as I plodded along the deserted country road—she had been interrupted on that occasion by the inopportune appearance of Dr. Damar Greefe. Again, why had he appeared there at that moment if not because he had suspected her presence at the inn; and what was the relationship existing between these two singular people?

That the strange story related to me by the idiotic Edward Hines simply resolved itself into an idle adventure on the part of the mysterious woman, which she had been forced to terminate (somewhat ferociously, I admit) by the uncouth ardour of this rustic swain I seemed to perceive. But unless her visit to the Abbey Inn portended that she had selected me as Mr. Edward Hines's successor, I failed to fit it into the scheme.

I began to long for the presence of Inspector Gatton, for the assistance of his trained mind in plumbing these depths which defied my single efforts. Who this woman could be I failed to imagine; and assuming that she had been concerned in the death of the late baronet, in what way she stood to profit by it was utterly beyond my comprehension, as was the position of Dr. Damar Greefe in the matter.

On I walked and on, unconsciously increasing my pace as is my way when I am lost in abstraction; and, perhaps stimulated to greater mental clarity by the exercise, some of my doubts were dispersed and I became convinced at

last that the shadowy figure which had dogged my footsteps on the night of the crime—the owner of those blazing eyes which had watched me from my garden—the
woman who had stolen the amulet from my writing-table,
and the woman who had mutilated Edward Hines—were
one and the same as my visitor at the Abbey Inn—and the
unseen speaker who had conversed beneath my window on
the night of my arrival at Upper Crossleys!

 Here, then, was a definite chain linking the Red House
with Friar's Park, or at least with its vicinity, and now so
clearly did my ideas fit themselves each into its correct
place, that I determined upon the identity of that other
speaker who had stood in the shadows opposite the inn
when I had awakened in the night. Mentally I recaptured
the high, rather coarse tones of his voice, and remembering how, touched by the spell which had seemed to lie
upon the whole country-side, I had thought of him as Asmodeus, the master of the witches' revels, I determined
that my judgment had been not inexact. For now I identi-
fied the speaker as Dr. Damar Greefe!

So far my meditations had proceeded, and I suppose I
was about half-way on my journey towards the Abbey Inn,
when all at once I became aware again of that uncomfortable feeling of surveillance. As on that night when returning from the Red House to my cottage I had experienced a
conviction that I was followed, so now a like conviction
impressed itself upon my mind. But whereas on the former
occasion I had been less fearful than curious, now I was
aware of a positive dread of this follower whose presence I
had detected, by what sense I know not, and of a certainty
of a very grave menace.

Accordingly, I determined upon a certain plan which I
proceeded to put into execution without delay. I was traversing a stretch of moon-bathed road at the moment that
I first fell a victim to this unpleasant suspicion—which, indeed, was more than a suspicion—when ahead of me I observed a patch, some twenty yards in extent, which was entirely overshadowed by trees—for at this point the woods,
clothing a slope which ran right down to the road, closely
impinged upon the highway; and I had noticed something
at this spot, on my outward journey, which I now proposed to employ to my advantage.

Into this patch of darkness I walked then, my steps

sounding crisply along the road. On I went for some twenty yards, until I found the particular spot for which I was seeking. This was a sort of little bay or inlet, where until quite recently a heap of stones used by roadmenders had lain, and into this I marched, never once altering my pace. But having gained it, I performed an about-turn and continued to mark time there, whilst surveying the moonbathed road behind me.

The object of this trick will be evident enough; for whilst the sound of my footsteps would lead one in pursuit to suppose that I was proceeding upon my way through the shadows, actually I was staring intently back in quest of the pursuer of whose presence I had become assured.

Perhaps in spite of the cautious manner in which he had advanced he had made some slight sound which, subconsciously detected, had nevertheless intruded upon my reverie, and in this way had acquainted me with his presence. For now, continuing that steady beat, but watching intently, I saw him.

Taking every advantage of the shade cast by the hedge on the right of the road, a softly-moving figure was coming towards me!

That the tracker was desirous of avoiding observation the manner of his approach sufficiently proved; and if I had had any doubts respecting his purpose they would have been resolved in a manner painful to myself had I not had the good fortune to detect him in time.

A piece of road there was which, because of a gap in the hedge, afforded no shadow, and as the gliding shape reached this point and passed it, I obtained a momentary but clear view of my pursuer.

I was being tracked by a Nubian mute!

That one glance was sufficient to convince me of the horrible truth. The man was stripped to the waist, in order no doubt that his movements might not be impeded, and I beheld a torso like that of some Milo wrought in ebony! The cruel, animal face, the blubber lips, the partly bared teeth—all spoke of the fate designed for me. I knew the type and knew what scant mercy I could look for at his hands. Indubitably this was a mute such as is sometimes attached to the harems of great Eastern houses to this day; and even if I had known nothing of the functions of such a servitor, the fact that he carried something in his left hand would have enlightened me.

It was a *strangling-cord!*

I smiled grimly. Respecting the identity of my would-be assassin, there was little room for doubt: he was the black servant of Dr. Damar Greefe. Now, as he passed the bright patch of roadway and began to glide silently nearer through the shadows, I marked time with a lighter step, the more deeply to confuse him. Of the strange Nubian dialect I knew nothing; but taking it for granted that the man was familiar with Arabic, I raised my voice in a mournful cry, and (in the Arab tongue):

"Cassim! Cassim!" I wailed. "Satan is calling for you!"

I think I have never witnessed such an exhibition of panic fright as I now beheld. Cassim was less than ten yards away—and I could hear his teeth chattering!

"Cassim!" I cried again. "Fly! fly! Satan is here!"

A horrible tongueless babbling answered the cry. There came a scuffling, and I saw the Nubian's gleaming body leap out into the lighted roadway as he fled.

"Faster! faster! Cassim!" I wailed. "He is behind you! Ah! he is *in front!*"

Cassim staggered, turned, and then stood still, looking this way and that in a perfect delirium of fear. Finally he whirled around to the right, shrieking wildly (I think some nocturnal insect had brushed against him), plunged babbling up the bank to the hedge, and, heedless of the fact that it contained many thorns which must have cruelly lacerated his bare body, scrambled half through it and half over it into the ploughed field beyond!

Against such an enemy there is no more potent weapon than superstition. Nevertheless I kept my hand upon the pistol in my pocket and proceeded at an increased pace during the latter half of my journey; nor am I ashamed to admit that the lights of the Abbey Inn were a welcome sight, and it was with a feeling of relief that, leaving the high road behind me, I found myself again in the village street of Upper Crossleys.

What to expect next I knew not. The other party had made a false move, for I now had definite evidence of the antagonism of Dr. Damar Greefe and of his intent to cause my murder through the agency of his Nubian servant.

My plan of nocturnal operations, already sufficiently dangerous, now promised to lead me into extreme peril. I would have given much for the company of Gatton, but, if I must act alone—alone I would set out. If I am slow in planning, at least I can state with truth that I am tenacious in execution. But here, now, was open warfare, and I must look for an enemy prepared.

CHAPTER XVIII

THE SECRET OF FRIAR'S PARK

Glancing into the bar-parlour as I entered, I observed that it was empty. Martin sat behind the counter, and he seemed to be immersed in the contents of a newspaper which was spread open before him. Going up to my room, I put on a pair of puttees—which, although useless and indeed injurious for general wear, are ideal for traversing bramble-land—took my thick stick, and further looked to the condition and readiness of my pistol. Finally, slipping an electric torch into my pocket, I set out.

The bar was closing when I came downstairs. Martin stared at me dully.

"I'm going for a moonlight ramble," I explained. "Will anyone be up to let me in, or should you prefer to give me the key of the side door?"

"Never locked," was the laconic reply; "come in when you like."

To a town-dweller such a piece of information must have sounded alarming, but knowing something of the ways of these country communities, it did not greatly surprise me; and, bidding the landlord "good night," I set out.

The false move made by Dr. Damar Greefe had advanced the inquiry further than any unaided endeavours of mine could well have done. Clearly enough, the Eurasian regarded my presence as inimical to his safety. In admitting so much, he had admitted guilt of some kind. In fact,

I felt assured that he was determined at all costs to prevent my visiting Friar's Park.

Having failed in his unmistakable endeavour to remove me entirely—for so I construed the Nubian's instructions —he would undoubtedly recognize that the game was up. He was clearly a desperate man, and I realized that the only hope I had of foiling him lay in acting with despatch.

This was a perfect night, with never a cloud to mar the blue serenity of the sky; but in spite of its beauty I was more than ever conscious of that sense of loneliness and desolation which seemed to be the most marked character-istic of the country hereabouts. I met never a soul upon the highway, nor indeed did I encounter any evidence of life whatever until, turning into a narrow lane which would bring me to that road in the valley upon which stood the deserted lodge belonging to the Bell House, an owl hooted in the trees above my head.

Keenly alert to the possibility that my movements might be watched, I paused, wondering if the sound—which had proceeded from a low bough directly above me—had real-ly been made by an owl or by a human mimic. For the hoot of an owl being easy to imitate, is much favoured for signalling purposes. Taking my electric torch from my pocket, I directed its ray upward into the close foliage of the oak tree; whereupon, with a ghostly fanning of dark wings, an owl flew away.

I proceeded confidently down the sloping road amid a silence so intense that my steps seemed to create a positive clamour. Coming to the corner, I looked along to the left, where the lane, alternate patches of silver and ebony, showed deserted as far as I could see. This was the direc-tion of the gate of the Bell House, and the road, which sloped gently downwards on that side, rose in a rather sharper acclivity on my right. It was at this point that I had mistaken the way on my first journey to Friar's Park.

Therefore I proceeded to the right, seeking the entrance which I was convinced I should find somewhere within the next two hundred yards. The lane inclined gently leftward, and presently, as I had anticipated, I came upon a lodge, overgrown with ivy and but partly visible beyond the gates which barred the end of the drive.

That this was the entrance to Friar's Park I felt assured, but I had no intention of seeking admittance in the usual way. Pursuing a high wall, evidently of great age, which divided the grounds from the road, I walked on for fully three hundred yards. Here the wall, which enclosed what had once been the kitchen garden of the monastery, gave place to a lofty hedge, in which I presently discovered a gap wide enough to allow of my making my way through.

Entering I found myself in a sort of parkland, boasting many majestic and venerable trees, elms for the most part. Where the parkland ended and the woods began, it was impossible to make out, but away to my left I could follow the high wall to where, clearly visible in the moonlight which at this point was unobstructed by trees, a gate appeared.

Towards this I made my way, keeping a sharp look out for those man-traps of which I had heard, and equally on the alert for any hidden human presence. Without meeting with any obstacle, however, I reached the gate—only to find that it was closed and fastened with a stout padlock.

There was a dry ditch bordering the wall, and I followed this back towards the high road, hoping that somewhere I might chance upon a means of scaling the wall. I made slow progress, for presently I came upon a quantity of undergrowth which I distrusted keenly as it would afford admirable cover for traps. In this way I had come nearly back to the hedge lining the road before I discovered what I was looking for.

Here a fir tree grew sufficiently close to the ditch to serve my purpose. Its lower branches were within easy reach, whilst farther up I espied one which stretched out across the top of the wall. Looping over my wrist the thong attached to my stick, I scrambled up into the tree and soon found myself astride the wall.

Beneath me was a neglected orchard and beyond to the right a wilderness which once had been an extensive kitchen-garden. Directly before me lay the lodge, but the house was invisible from where I sat, being evidently situated somewhere beyond a dense coppice into which I perceived the drive to lead, for patched here and there by the moonlight I could trace it running ribbon-like through the trees.

A vine grew upon the wall beneath me, its aged tendrils of the thickness of ropes, and it afforded a natural ladder whereby I made my descent. Arrived in the miniature jungle which at some period had been a flower-bed, I set out towards the lodge, prompted to do so by the presence of a light shining out from one of the windows through a network of leaves.

I knew not if I should look for man-traps within the place enclosed by the wall, but nevertheless I neglected no precaution, picking my way through the forest of weeds which had supplanted the vegetables and sweet herbs to which doubtless this land had once been sacred. Observing even greater precaution as I neared the building, I presently found myself looking in at the lighted window, and only concealed from the occupants of the room by the presence of a tangled bush which formed a sort of natural curtain.

The room into which I was peering presented a scene of great disorder. It was a poorly furnished apartment characteristic of the rustic workman's dwelling, and was evidently the living room of the lodge-keeper. It was in process of being dismantled; cupboards and chests stood open, and my acquaintance Hawkins was engaged in packing various belongings into a large wooden box set in the centre of the floor. Upon the bare wooden table stood the oil lamp whose light I had seen shining out of the window, and bending over a number of papers, apparently engaged in making up some sort of an account, was a gipsy-looking woman whom I took to be the wife of the gamekeeper.

She had oily black hair and a very lowering and unpleasant cast of countenance; whilst the large earrings which she wore added to her gipsy appearance. An argument of some kind was in progress between the two, for ever and anon the woman would raise her eyes from her task and dart venomous glances at the man, who knelt upon the floor packing the big box. Fragments of the conversation reached me through the partly open window, and although it was difficult to follow I gathered that the woman was reproaching her husband with some alleged indiscretion which had necessitated the departure for which they were preparing. Hawkins retorted with a savage energy which displayed the darker side of the man's character, and the one which I had suspected to lie beneath his rather sinister merriment.

Having satisfied myself that the pair were deeply occupied with their personal affairs, I crept out upon the drive and began to approach the house. I had formed a rough idea of the distance at which it lay from the road, and this was proved to have been about correct. The drive swung round in a wide semicircle, and presently, majestic in the moonlight, with some of its mediæval charm restored by the magic of night, I saw Friar's Park before me.

It was a low, rambling building, bespeaking the monastery in some of its severe outlines and showing a succession of cloisteresque arches on the left, terminated by a chapel beyond which rose the ancient tower visible from the inn window—a wonderful example of Saxon architecture, and closely resembling that at Earl's Barton. There was no light in any of the windows, and indeed as I peered more closely across the wide space intervening between the end of the drive and the main entrance of the house, it seemed to me that the place was more of a ruin than a habitable establishment.

Unaware of what eyes might be watching me from any one of the numerous windows, I stepped into the shrubbery beneath the trees bordering the drive, and set out to make a detour of the house without revealing my presence to anyone who might be watching from within.

In the prosecution of this plan, I met with not a little difficulty; several times, in fact, I had to show myself in the moonlight upon the edge of the unkempt lawns, but by this device and that I finally achieved my purpose and returned to the spot from whence I had set out, without having attracted any visible notice. Here I paused to consider what I had learned.

The most notable thing was this: only one wing of Friar's Park—that remote from the tower—exhibited any evidence of occupation, indeed of being habitable at all. In other words, the greater part of the building was no more than a majestic ruin. Eyeless windows there were and crumbling arches, whilst the chapel which had looked so picturesque from a distance, proved on closer inspection to be a mere shell. A dense shrubbery grew right up to the walls of the east wing, that which was terminated by the tower, and I had been enabled to peer right in at the window of the chapel and out at a window on the other side; for the place was roofless and its floor carpeted with weeds. I could not help wondering how much of this decay dated from the days of Sir Burnham, for certainly I could not reconcile it with the character of the man as depicted by the local people.

My inquiry then was considerably narrowed down, for of the habitable apartments of Friar's Park I had only been enabled to count seven or eight, although two of these appeared to be of great extent, one of them, I fancy, being the old refectory of the monastery. My next discovery was this: that the likeliest point of entry to the house was afforded by either one of two French windows which opened upon a small lawn some twenty yards beyond the drive. But in order to approach them I should have to expose myself in the brilliant moonlight which bathed that side of the house.

I stood there listening intently, and wondering if I dared attempt the venture. Not a sound could I detect, however, and the night was so still that scarce a leaf stirred about me. I determined upon the plunge; and walking boldly forward, I approached the more easterly of the two windows.

Three stone steps led up to it, and linen blinds were drawn down within, but strengthened by the memory of the inn door which was "never locked," and hoping that the same trustfulness prevailed in Friar's Park, I turned the handle whose brassy glitter I had previously perceived from the corner of the shrubbery.

It operated smoothly, and upon giving a gentle push the window opened and I found myself standing upon a polished oak floor. I stood stock still, listening; but there was never a sound; and partly reclosing the window I pressed the button of my electric-torch and looked about me.

I stood in a long lofty room which I supposed to have been a drawing room. It was empty, containing not a single item of furniture. From my pocket I took two pairs of thick woolen socks and drew them one over the other on to my boots to deaden my footfalls. The door of this empty and desolate room was open, and stepping softly I walked out into a wide corridor, my mind filled with terrifying recollections of the Red House.

Three other rooms I explored, and although in two of them some items of massive furniture remained, covered with dust-sheets, no sign of habitation did I come upon. The whole of the ground floor proved to be vacant, and a broad uncarpeted stair suggested that the floors above were also deserted by their occupants.

I mounted softly, but the stairs creaked in a horrible fashion, so that I became hotly apprehensive before I gained the top. I had nothing to fear, however, for again empty rooms alone rewarded my search. My most significant discovery in the upper part of the house was that of a bedroom which was still almost completely furnished, and in which even the bed-linen yet remained untidily strewn about the bed. But there were thick spiders' webs stretching from the coverlet to the canopy, and a coating of dust lay everywhere.

When I finally returned to the empty drawing-room, I had convinced myself of that which I had come to seek.

Friar's Park was uninhabited!

CHAPTER XIX

THE MAN ON THE TOWER

I quitted Friar's Park unobserved, as I had entered it. Walking quickly across to the shrubbery, I began to work my way back to the point at which I must strike westward in order to reach the weed-grown kitchen garden. At the risk of encountering man-traps, I gave the lodge a wide berth and came out in sight of the wall at a point much nearer the lawns of the house than that from which I had entered.

What it was that prompted me to turn and take a final look at the house I cannot say, but before commencing to make my way through the wilderness of the kitchen garden, I know that I stood and looked back towards the ancient Saxon tower which uprose, silvered by the moonlight, above the trees that obscured from my view all the rest of the house.

Right to the embrasured crest it was sharply outlined by the brilliant moon—and as I looked I felt my heart leap suddenly; and then, almost holding my breath, I crouched, distrusting the very shadows which afforded me shelter.

For leaning out through one of the embrasures at the top of the tower, I clearly saw the figure of a man!

At first, so whitely was his face lighted up by the moon that I had no doubt of the figure being that of a man; but because he remained so still, seeming always to look in a fixed way in the same direction, again momentarily I doubted, until a slight movement betrayed the fact that my first impression had been correct.

Who he was I could not possibly tell from that distance, but of his occupation I became assured at the moment that he moved; for the moonlight glittered brightly on the lenses of the binoculars through which he had been surveying some point visible only from that elevation.

Still I watched, and again I saw the man on the tower raise his glasses and resume his scrutiny of that distant object which so closely engaged his attention. Remembering that a patch of light touched the top of the wall, spearlike, at the point where I must cross it in order to reach the fir tree, I abandoned my former precautions and hurried through the tangled weeds towards the fir which was my sailing-mark.

Hastily I scrambled up the natural ladder formed by the vine, and without pause climbed down again to the edge of the dry ditch beyond. To have looked back over the wall would have been useless, since from that point the tower would have been invisible. Nor, indeed, had I any desire to pause in my precarious journey.

That I had avoided man-traps in that hurried retreat through the weeds I knew not whether to ascribe to good luck or to the fact that none were set there, but now in the more open ground, thickly bestrewn, however, with clumps of undergrowth, I resumed all my old vigilance, and carefully retraced the path, as well as I could remember it, by which I had first arrived at the friendly fir.

When at last I found myself once more upon the high road and free of the ground of Friar's Park, I stood awhile and wondered to find myself bathed in perspiration.

There was something very eerie in the thought that I had explored those numerous rooms of the deserted house and had moreover encircled the entire building, habitable and otherwise, whilst that mysterious watcher all the time had been lurking up there in the tower! I wondered what his survey portended. If it signified that he had detected my presence at the moment that I had left the house, why was his gaze focused upon the distance and not upon the surrounding grounds? If he had not seen or heard me, then I must compliment myself upon a very successful burglarious feat.

But assuming the latter explanation to be the correct one, how much darker became the mystery of the man's presence and purpose. Who was he, and what did he do at this hour in deserted Friar's Park?

Since I had left the gamekeeper deeply engaged in his packing operations at the lodge, I dismissed the idea that the figure on the tower might have been that of Hawkins, nor was I in any way assisted in my attempts to solve the mystery by what I had seen of the man, for the distance had been too great to allow of my perceiving his face with anything like clearness.

Presently, then, I set out upon my return journey to the Abbey Inn, turning over in my mind this added perplexity which had entered the case. As Gatton had quite recently observed, every new piece of evidence which came to light in this most bewildering affair seemed merely to plunge the issue in greater obscurity than ever. My feet once set upon the slope which led to Upper Crossleys, I allowed this mood of abstraction to have its way, and the problem with which I found myself principally engaged was that of the disappearance of Lady Burnham Coverly.

As I remembered the suave assurances of Dr. Damar Greefe that the ill-health of Lady Burnham rendered it impossible for her to receive visitors, I wondered anew at the complex villainy of this formidable Eurasian. The state of the rooms in Friar's Park clearly demonstrated the fact that neither Lady Coverly nor any other had resided there for many months, perhaps many years. What then did it all mean? What was the purpose of the watch and ward kept by the gipsy-gamekeeper over the grounds and approaches to the house?

It could only mean that this was a device of Dr. Damar Greefe's to prevent any of the neighbours from seeking admittance to the house and thus learning the strange secret which its emptiness revealed.

Here, in fact, in this old monastic establishment, would seem to reside the very genius of that spirit of desolation which had touched me unpleasantly in the hour of my arrival in Crossleys. I determined to ascertain by inquiries amongst the local tradespeople, none of whom I had hitherto met, by what means the fact that no one resided at Friar's Park was concealed from those whose ordinary business activities would demand their presenting themselves at the house for orders, etc. But even as the plan suggested itself to me, I thought I perceived an answer to my question; in all probability, I determined, Dr. Damar Greefe, or the Hawkinses, who were palpably his creatures, acted as a barrier between the tradespeople and the missing lady of the Park.

But what it could all portend was a problem beyond the power of my imagination or deductive reasoning. If Lady Coverly had changed her residence for some reason, with what object did the Eurasian continue to lead everyone in the neighbourhood to suppose that she still resided at Friar's Park?

It was all a hopeless tangle, and the more I thought about it the more discouraged did I become. I seemed to get farther, too, from that link for which I sought—the link connecting the mystery with that other which I always associated with the Red House. The luminous eyes afforded the visible link; this I could not doubt. But what relation to the death of Sir Marcus did the disappearance of Lady Burnham Coverly bear? Secondly, what was Dr. Damar Greefe's place in the scheme? And thirdly (the most appalling mystery of all), who or what was the woman with the cat's eyes?

At this point in my meditations I discovered that I had arrived before the Abbey Inn, now plunged in darkness, and believing that I detected the sound of footsteps behind me, I became eventually the victim of a sort of panic which perhaps will be forgiven me under the circumstances. For emerging from these unpleasant reflections, and hearing or believing that I heard sounds of pursuit from the lonely moon-patched road behind, I know that I hurried forward to the side door and silently prayed that I should find it unfastened, as Martin had assured me that it would be.

In this particular I was speedily reassured, for the door opened to my touch—and I became conscious of a wish that there might be some means of fastening it from within! However, I could find none, but hurrying upstairs, I determined to take a precaution which hitherto I had not adopted and that night to lock my bedroom door.

Entering the room, I fumbled for a box of matches in my pocket, and presently discovering them struck one and looked about me for the candle which usually stood upon a little cabinet beside the bed. To-night, however, it had been moved for some reason and put over by the window on the dressing-table. As I made this discovery the match smouldered out, and at the moment I was about to strike another the sound of footsteps which I had formerly detected grew louder and nearer, so that I could no longer doubt that someone was running along the road towards the Abbey Inn.

A great curiosity respecting this person seized me, and without striking a match as I had intended to do, I walked to the window and looked out into the road. Twenty yards away I saw the figure of a man who seemed to be come almost to the end of his resources, for I could hear him panting as he ran. Nor did my wonder decrease when, as he came nearer and stared up in my direction, I recognized him for the shabby-looking person whom I had observed that morning sitting on the bench before the inn door.

Wondering what his presence might portend—for clearly his business was with *me*—I leaned out of the window, and as he came up to the door of the inn I saw him stagger and clutch at the post which supported the sign-board, swaying dizzily. He was clearly almost exhausted, and his voice when he spoke was a husky whisper.

"Don't light your candle!" he said.

Now, this remark, coming at such a time and in these circumstances, struck me as so ludicrous that at first I was tempted to laugh; but the man's earnest sincerity, as evidenced by his exhausted condition and the urgency of his manner, did not fail to impress me, and:

"Why not?" I asked, still leaning out of the window and filled with a great wonderment.

"Never mind," he panted. "Don't! Can I come up?"

Something now in the breathless speech of the man below struck me as oddly familiar. But yet so dense was I that I failed to recognize the truth of the matter, and:

"Certainly," I said. "I will bring a light down to show you the way, if you have business with me."

"No light!" he cried hoarsely. "If you value your life, don't strike a match!"

By this time so bewildered had I become that I scarce knew whether to descend to meet this apparent madman or to remain where I was.

"Don't hesitate, Mr. Addison!" he cried, now beginning to recover his breath. "Do exactly as I tell you!"

"Good God!" I exclaimed.

I turned and ran to the door and on downstairs. For at last I had recognized the voice of this midnight runner. Throwing open the door, I held out my hand, and the shabby-looking man extended his in return.

"*Gatton!*" I cried excitedly. "Gatton! What on earth does this mean? Why have you been masquerading in this fashion? I saw you here this morning, and you never gave me the slightest sign of acknowledgment!"

"I never intended to!" panted the inspector, staggering rather than walking up the stairs. "But I have performed one of the hardest tasks of my life to-night, and have only succeeded by a few seconds!"

We were now at the door of my room, but:

"Don't go in!" said Gatton shortly. "Let me think what we must do."

"But I don't understand at all!"

"You will understand in a moment!" was the grim reply. "You would have understood already if you had lighted your candle."

Words failed me altogether. At that we stood in the passage for some moments in silence, then:

"We have got to risk it," said Gatton, "if my theory is to be put to the test."

"Risk it?"

"Oh! I can assure you of the risk," he declared. "It will be touch-and-go. Are you game?"

"Well," I said, laughing in a very forced fashion, "this has been a night of such intense surprises that I think I can survive one more."

"Very well," replied the inspector, and there was something strange in hearing the familiar voice and dimly discerning in the reflected moonlight, which shone in at a window farther along the passage, the unfamiliar figure before me.

"What have we to do?"

"We have to take a chance of sudden death!" he answered. "But we will minimize it as much as possible."

Seeing me about to give voice to one of the many questions which literally burned upon my tongue:

"Explanations can come later," said he. "Where can I find a candle?"

"There is one on the dressing-table just to the left of the window. I will get it——"

But he grasped my arm roughly, and:

"This is *my* business! Wait here for me," he rapped tersely.

He heard the rasp of the match upon the box as I struck a light to guide him in his search. Whereupon:

"I thought I warned you!" he cried, and struck the match from my hand. "*No light!*"

With that he pushed open the door, and I saw his square figure outlined against the moon-bright open window as he crossed the room. Since he had referred to the peril which hung over us, it was with bated breath that I awaited his return, not in the least knowing what to expect. A few moments later he returned with the candlestick.

"Now," said he, carefully reclosing the door, "light the candle."

Awed by something in his voice and manner, I did as he directed without demur, noting with amazement, in the light thus created, how simple yet how effective was the disguise which my friend had adopted.

He gave me no time for comment, however, but:

"Listen," said he. "I'm going to put this candle in your room, and then you and I are going to run."

"Run?" I cried.

"Exactly. Run for our lives! Preferably upstairs. Is there any vacant room above from which we can look out in the same direction as from your window?"

"The room above is vacant," I replied, "and probably we shall find the door unlocked."

"We'll risk that, then," said Gatton. "You might start and lead the way."

"Can I use my electric torch?" I asked.

"On the stairs," replied Gatton; "but you must extinguish it when we enter the room above."

With that he thrust open the door of my bedroom, ran

in and ran out again, banging the door behind him as though pursued by devils!

Then the pair of us were racing up the stairs madly for the room above, I vaguely wondering if my companion had taken leave of his senses. Yet of the verity of the peril which he dreaded came speedy confirmation.

At the very moment that my hand touched the knob of the door above, and ere I could turn it, the whole fabric of the Abbey Inn was convulsed—the floor rocked beneath my feet, and there ensued the sound of a deafening explosion from the room below! An echo, or what sounded like an echo, sharp and staccato, came from the distant hills!

CHAPTER XX

GATTON'S STORY

"It's no good going in now," said Gatton in a weary voice; "in fact, it might be dangerous. We have to consider the possibility of fire, however," he added.

Voices of sleepers awakened and cries of inquiry sounded now from all over the inn, for naturally the household had been aroused by the tremendous noise of the explosion. For my own part, I was altogether too dazed to conjecture what had happened. But that Gatton had saved me from some deadly peril I was well convinced. Stirrings and the noise of footsteps came from an adjoining room, and presently in his night attire Martin appeared, very bemused.

"Mr. Addison——" he began, and stared from me to my companion.

"Let no one leave his room," said Gatton decisively, "until I give permission."

"Eh," began Martin heavily.

"I am a police officer," added Gatton, "and you will all do as I direct. Does anyone sleep on the same floor as Mr. Addison?"

"No, sir," replied Martin, who was not yet more than

half awake, but who nevertheless had been impressed by the inspector's authoritative manner.

Sounds of footsteps from the floor above now became audible, whereupon:

"Order all to remain in their rooms!" repeated Gatton.

Martin, raising his voice, obeyed him.

"What are your arrangements in the case of fire?" continued the inspector.

Several tousled heads were peeping down from the landing above, but no one spoke until Martin collected his ideas sufficiently to reply:

"There's buckets in the stables—and there's the well. Wilkins sleeps over the stables——"

"Can you make him hear without going downstairs?"

"I can try," was the answer.

Martin walked to a window which lighted the landing, and threw it widely open. Leaning out:

"Wilkins!" he roared. "Wilkins!"

"Ay, ay, boss!" came faintly from somewhere below.

"Tell him to stand by with fire-buckets, but not to leave the yard without orders from me," directed Gatton.

Martin issued these instructions in a voice which must have been audible at Leeways, and then stood scratching his head stupidly.

But, indeed, of all the bewildered company who gathered that night beneath the roof of the Abbey Inn, I think I was the most nonplussed of all, and turning to Gatton:

"For God's sake tell me what it all means!" I said.

"It means," he answered, and even through his disguise I recognized the old grim smile, "that only a match stood between you and eternity! Even now we cannot afford to sit down, but I am not anxious to pass your door for a few minutes. As we both have much to say, let us find a room where we can talk."

Accordingly we went up to a large empty room at the back of the inn. Through the open doorway I could hear the excited voices of the entire staff of the establishment, who had congregated in Martin's room across the landing. Never in the history of the Abbey Inn had such doings taken place.

"Perhaps," continued Gatton, "it will save time if you tell me exactly what you have done first."

"Very well," I said. "But before I begin—when did you arrive?"

"An hour and a half after receiving your code telegram! I came by car. The car is at Manton now."

"Why this disguise?"

"I will explain in a moment. But meanwhile—your own story."

At that, although consumed with impatience, I quickly outlined my movements from the time of my arrival at Upper Crossley, the inspector following me closely. The tale concluded:

"Now, Gatton," I cried, "for heaven's sake tell me what it all means!"

"I will tell you all I know," he replied slowly. "In the first place, I had two reasons for suggesting the visit to Friar's Park. I had formed an opinion that the 'cat-woman' was interested in *you*. Whether because she regarded you as dangerous or from some other cause I could not determine. And I thought of a plan for finding out if she was by any chance associated with Friar's Park. It was to send you down here (a) to make straightforward inquiries, and (b) to 'draw the cat'!"

"Very good of you!" I murmured.

"I warned you it was dangerous!" said Gatton grimly. "But I am pleased to say the plan worked to perfection. Your own inquiries have been highly satisfactory, and you have also 'drawn the cat!' Now just to show you how dramatic your discoveries really were, I will explain my second and more important reason and the one which primarily had prompted me to turn my attention to Friar's Park. A few hours before you came to the Yard the other morning—to see the bag dropped in the water by Eric Coverly—I had been in touch with solicitors who had acted for the late Sir Burnham."

"Ah!" I exclaimed. "What had they to say?"

"I was seeking information, of course, respecting the entail; in short, trying to fathom the mystery of what Eric Coverly would have had to gain by getting his cousin out of the way. I learned that financially he gained nothing but a bundle of debts. Friar's Park was mortgaged to the hilt. Furthermore, Lady Burnham Coverly had a life interest in the property under the will of her husband.

"Next, from the senior partner, a solicitor of the old

school who still retained pleasant memories of Sir Burnham's port, I learned a number of very significant details."

He paused, staring at me oddly, and the familiar expression beneath the unfamiliar disguise was very curious. Then:

"About seven or eight years ago," he resumed, "shortly after his return from *Egypt,* according to Mr. Hardacre, the solicitor, something occurred which made a changed man of his client, Sir Burnham. You will note, Mr. Addison, shortly after his return from *Egypt.* He realized upon quantities of securities, and raised a big sum of ready money, which he disposed of in some way which has always remained a mystery to Mr. Hardacre. In short, within a period of three years or less, from being a wealthy man, he became a poor one.

"Next, he sent Mr. Roger Coverly, his only child, then a mere lad, abroad in care of a tutor; Mr. Hardacre never knew for what reason, as there was apparently nothing wrong with the boy's health! He began to dismiss his servants. The greater part of Friar's Park was shut up and allowed to fall into decay. Finally, to Mr. Hardacre's surprise and grief, Sir Burnham mortgaged the property. But it was the terms of the mortgage—which I was privileged to inspect—which aroused my curiosity.

"In brief, the mortgagee agreed, in the event of Sir Burnham's death, to allow the widow to retain possession of the property for life, whether payments fell in arrears or otherwise!"

"But this——" I exclaimed.

"Is, as a friend of yours once remarked, as mad as 'Alice in Wonderland!' I agree. But to continue. At the time that this extraordinary agreement was drawn up, Mr. Hardacre went down to Friar's Park, of course; and he was a witness of several most singular and significant occurrences. For instance, on the evening of his arrival, whilst he was dressing for dinner, Sir Burnham came running to his room and begged of him to lock his door and to remain in his room until his host gave him permission to come out! He was particularly warned against admitting anyone *who might knock* in the interval!"

"Good heavens!" I cried. "And did anyone knock?"

"No one; but about half an hour later Sir Burnham came and released him. Mr. Hardacre was unspeakably distressed to observe that Sir Burnham looked white and ill; in fact, in Mr. Hardacre's own words, five years older! Again, quite by accident, on the same night, he came upon his host kneeling in the chapel—in those days it still boasted a roof—deep in prayer. An atmosphere of indescribable horror, he declared, had settled upon Friar's Park, and although, as he confessed, he had no evidence to prove the correctness of his theory, he nevertheless traced this to the person of the mortgagee. For it seemed to correspond roughly with the appearance in the neighborhood of this man—whom he now met for the first time."

Again Gatton paused, taking out his pipe and pouch, and:

"Who was this person?" I asked.

"A certain Dr. Damar Greefe!"

"Good God!" I cried. "Where is all this leading us, Gatton?"

"It is leading us slowly to the truth, Mr. Addison, and that truth, when we come to it, is going to be more horrible than we even suspect. Passing over much of Mr. Hardacre's evidence, I come to the death, in Switzerland, of Mr. Roger Coverly, under circumstances so obscure that I fear we shall never know the particulars. Of one thing, however, I am assured: there was foul play."

"You mean that Roger Coverly was—murdered?"

"I really don't doubt it," replied Gatton, who, having filled his pipe, now lighted it. "I believe he was the first victim."

"The *first* victim?"

"Mr. Addison, I agree with the late Sir Burnham's solicitor, that the spider at the heart of this web is Dr. Damar Greefe. The shock of his son's premature death led to a collapse from which Sir Burnham never recovered, and Friar's Park entered upon the final phase during which it was occupied by Lady Burnham, who seems to have been wholly under the influence of this Eurasian doctor."

"But, my dear Gatton!" I cried, "where *is* Lady Burnham?"

"In my opinion, dead!" he answered solemnly. "Oh, it sounds preposterous, but in the case of this lonely woman, who had apparently no living relatives and who was estranged from Sir Marcus and the other members of her husband's family, it was no very difficult matter to hush up the fact of her death."

"But, Gatton, you don't mean that she, too, met with foul play?"

"Most certainly I don't! It is as clear as day that the whole object of this elaborate secrecy was to *hide* the fact of her death! She was infinitely more useful alive than dead, Mr. Addison, and they hoped to keep up the solemn farce until——"

"Yes?"

"Until Sir Eric was hanged for the murder of his cousin!"

"Gatton! What do you mean?"

"He is the last of the Coverlys!" answered Gatton simply. "There would be no further danger of anyone paying off the mortgage."

"Danger?"

"Exactly. There is some secret at Friar's Park—or at the Bell House—which necessitates the property remaining in the possession of Dr. Damar Greefe—as it had virtually remained since Sir Burnham's death! So much is clear, and although Eric Coverly has persisted in his obstinate silence, one of my assistants who has been at work on the late Sir Marcus's papers made a discovery yesterday, which together with what I had learned from Mr. Hardacre and your code message, brought me down to Crossleys post haste."

"What was this discovery?"

"An invitation from Dr. Damar Greefe, dated only a short time after the death of Sir Burnham, to Sir Marcus, asking him to visit Friar's Park! The doctor explained that the state of Lady Coverly's health made it impossible for her to entertain, but he assured Sir Marcus that she was anxious to see him and to heal any breach which might exist between them. Most significant of all, the Eurasian proposed that Sir Marcus should put up *here!*"

"At the Abbey Inn?"

"Exactly. Now the 'best room' of the inn is that which you have been occupying—and it is that which Sir Marcus would have occupied had he accepted the doctor's invitation. Listen, then: all these clues seemed to point to Friar's Park, but the receipt of your message mentioning one Damar Greefe as being a suspicious party, and asking me to look up his record, quite tipped the scales. I saw, frankly, that you had made a false move, but nevertheless it served my purpose, and I determined to look into the Crossleys end of the inquiry personally, without giving Dr. Damar Greefe reason to suspect that I was in any way associated with the matter.

"I picked up one or two hints from the county police as to the geography as well as the 'notables' of the neighbourhood, and the plan which you put into execution to-night I had adopted last night."

"What! You visited Friar's Park?"

"I did. But I did not enter through the French window. It never occurred to me that it would be unfastened! I had come provided with a neat set of burglars' tools (*and* a warrant for use if necessary), and I broke into the kitchens! *I* found, as you afterwards found, that the place had obviously been deserted for a long time. I was badly puzzled. But my search was more detailed than yours. I climbed up to the top of the tower!"

"To the top of the tower!"

"Yes. I'll tell you what I found there in a minute. But, briefly, beyond learning that the story of the invalid Lady Coverly was a myth, I discovered nothing likely to help the inquiry. I seriously debated the idea of putting Dr. Damar Greefe under arrest; but finally I determined to watch him for a time without showing my hand. I had the good fortune to meet him this morning here at the Abbey Inn! Also, I saw your mysterious lady visitor! Lastly, I got into conversation with the man Hawkins, who was accompanied by your friend the mute!

"Leaving this dangerous pair, I made a rush for the Bell House, thinking I saw my opportunity to examine it unmolested. I was too late, though. One of my assistants warned me of the Eurasian's return just as I was about to enter.

"I watched the house all day. But it was not until some time after dusk that the Eurasian came out. He went to Friar's Park—and I followed him!"

"What! You were there to-night?"

"I was! I dogged Dr. Damar Greefe, determined to learn the nature of the business which brought him to Friar's Park at such an hour. I may add that it was only by the merest accident or good luck that I fathomed it after all. I had no idea into what part of the building he had gone, but, knowing that he was somewhere inside, I watched from the shrubbery. In fact, I was still in the grounds when *you* arrived!"

"Then it was you I saw on the tower?"

"Oh, no, it was not! I had thoroughly examined the tower on my previous visit, and what I found there had puzzled me badly. In fact, it was not until your admirable withdrawal from Friar's Park to-night that the horrible explanation dawned upon me—and I realized that the object of inviting Sir Marcus to Upper Crossleys was to 'remove' him! The first plan failed, of course; he never came. He went back again on duty to Russia, I believe—for a time. But when he returned—a second was adopted at the Red House. However, the murder-machine erected in accordance with the earlier plan was still there——"

"Where?" I cried in bewilderment.

"On the tower of Friar's Park! It was the appearance of *Damar Greefe* on the platform of the tower, armed with binoculars, which awakened me to the ghastly truth. The device, never used in the case of Sir Marcus, was not to be wasted, but was to be employed to remove a dangerous obstacle from the conspirator's path! I had left the car near Crossleys, you see, and never in my life have I run as I ran after you to-night!"

"But, Gatton, *what* did you find on the tower—and what connexion exists between the tower and the explosion which occurred here to-night?"

"This: a sort of miniature howitzer—I think of Krupp's manufacture, but you would be better able to judge than I—is mounted on the platform of the tower! I examined it, Mr. Addison, last night, and like a fool concluded that it had been used at some time for a local celebration and never dismounted! It was trained—as I remembered nearly too late—and laid at a certain elevation in such a way that it was evidently never meant to be moved. Yet at the time the significance of this did not strike me. How the range was found so exactly we shall probably never know; but the truth suddenly burst upon me as you made off through the bushes and as Dr. Damar Greefe came out and began to peer through his glasses—that it was mechanically set in such a manner that it could drop a small projectile into the window above the porch of the Abbey Inn!"

"Good God! It's hardly credible!"

"It isn't, I admit. But weather conditions favoured him; there wasn't a breath of wind. And that he succeeded is proved by the fact that at the present moment your room below is probably still full of poison gas! Of course, it is very small and *may* not have been a gas-shell; he may have relied, as well he might do, on the burst! But I'm taking no chances. You can well imagine that failing a knowledge of the arrangement on the tower, no explanation of the mystery would ever have been found! A thunderbolt would be the popular theory! And if any fragments of shell were found, who would ever know where it had been fired?"

"Gatton," I said, "I owe you my life. But why did this fiend try to murder me?"

Gatton smiled.

"I have a theory, Mr. Addison," he replied, "and it is this: I believe he thought that the indiscretion of a certain mysterious lady would bring about his ruin. If I am not mistaken, she has already gone far to put his neck in a halter; and he was determined to nip this latest adventure in the bud by removing the object of her——"

I felt myself changing colour, and:

"For heaven's sake say no more!" I interrupted. "It is a gruesome and horrible thought! Yet, perhaps you are right. What must we do, Gatton? These people have rendered the neighbourhood uninhabitable for themselves now, and——"

Dimly to my ears came the sound of a gun-shot.

"And have fled!" cried Gatton, springing up. "Quick! we must chance the gas!"

"Why? What was that shot?"

"A signal! Dr. Damar Greefe and 'the cat' have escaped!"

He raced out across the landing, amid a chorus of frightened inquiries from the inn staff. I followed him into a front room, and:

"This comes of turning my attention elsewhere for half an hour!" he cried angrily. "I seem to be cursed with fools for assistants!"

Throwing up the window, he leaned out. I stood at his elbow, and as I looked I saw a great red glow rising from the distant woods. The sound of a car approaching at headlong speed reached my ears, and at the same moment I saw the headlights.

"Hallo, there!" cried Gatton. "Blythe! Petersham!"

The car stopped, and a cry came back:

"We've lost him, sir! . . . and the Bell House is in flames!"

CHAPTER XXI

IN LONDON AGAIN

"Then the sudden change in the police attitude towards Eric," said Isobel, "is not due to any discoveries which you or Inspector Gatton have made at Friar's Park?"

"That I cannot say," I replied. "We have made certain discoveries, as I have already told you, but whilst they distinctly point to some criminal whose identity is not yet fully established, unfortunately I cannot say that in a legal sense they clear Coverly."

Isobel, as I had thought at the first moment of our meeting, looked very tired, and had that pathetic expression of appeal in her eyes which had hurt me so much when first it had appeared there on the morning after the tragedy. She was palpably ill at ease, and I had small cause to wonder at this. Although a veiled paragraph (in which I thought I could detect the hand of Gatton) had appeared in the Press on the previous day, briefly stating that evidence had been volunteered by Sir Eric Coverly which had led to an entirely new line of police inquiry, the item of news—which had naturally excited wide-spread interest—had never been amplified. Amid the alarms and excursions which had terminated my visit to Upper Crossleys, Gatton, I supposed, had forgotten to refer to this matter; but I did not doubt that the paragraph was an inspired one issued from Scotland Yard.

My friend's object in circulating this statement was not by any means evident to me, but as I expected to see him later that day I hoped to be able to obtain from him some explanation of his new tactics.

Many hours had elapsed since, with the flames of the burning Bell House reddening the night behind me, and throwing into lurid relief the fir groves surrounding Dr. Damar Greefe's mysterious stronghold, I had been borne along the road towards London. That Gatton had hoped for much from a detailed search of the Eurasian's establishment I knew, for I had not forgotten his anger at the appearance of the flames above the tree-tops which had told of the foiling of his plans.

Under cover of the conflagration the cunning Eurasian had escaped. Every possible means had been taken to intercept him, and whilst Gatton, inspired by I know not what hopes, had hastened to the burning Bell House, I had set out in the police car in pursuit of Dr. Damar Greefe, accompanied by Detective-Sergeant Blythe—upon whom, apparently, the onus of the fiasco rested.

In despite of these measures, the hunted man had made good his retreat, and Blythe and I had entered the outskirts of London without once sighting the car in which Damar Greefe had fled.

No communication reached me on the following morning, and I found myself, consumed with impatient curiosity, temporarily out of touch with Gatton. Then, shortly after midday, came a telegram:

"Endeavour induce Sir Eric come to your house eight tonight. Will meet him there.   GATTON."

Welcoming any ground for action—since to remain passive at such a time was torture—I called at once at Coverly's chambers. He was out. But I left an urgent written message for him, and in the hope of finding him with Isobel, hurried to her flat. He had not been there that day, however; and now I could only hope that he would return to his rooms in time to keep the appointment. For that Gatton had some good reason for suggesting the meeting I did not doubt.

Gatton and I were now agreed that Dr. Damar Greefe, if not directly responsible for the death of Sir Marcus, at least had been an accessory to his murder. At any rate, he had shown his hand—firstly, in the attempted assault upon myself by his Nubian servant, and, secondly, by the devilish device whereby he had propelled some sort of gas projectile (for this we now knew it to have been) from the tower of Friar's Park into my room at the Abbey Inn. I had, then, become obnoxious to him; he evidently regarded my continued existence as a menace to his own.

Two explanations of his attitude presented themselves: one, that my inquiries had led me daily nearer to the heart of the mystery; or, two, that the doctor's mysterious associate, the possessor of the green eyes, had adopted an attitude towards myself which the Eurasian had counted sooner or later as certain to compromise him. In short, whilst it was sufficiently evident to me that these mysterious people residing at Upper Crossleys were the criminals for whom New Scotland Yard was searching, no definite link between their admittedly dangerous activities and the crime we sought to unravel had yet been brought to light.

On the other hand, whilst it was not feasible to suppose that any relationship existed between Sir Eric, the new baronet, and the Eurasian, or the woman associated with the Eurasian, I was quite well aware that, equally, there was no evidence to show that such an association did not exist.

I longed to be able to offer some consolation to Isobel, who at this time was passing through days and nights of dreadful apprehension; but beyond imparting to her some of my own personal convictions, I was unable to say honestly that the complicity of Coverly in the murder was definitely and legally disproved.

"If only he would break his absurd silence," she said suddenly. "This ridiculous suspicion which still seems to be entertained in some quarters would be removed, of course; but his every act since the night of the tragedy has only intensified it."

She sat facing me on the settee, her hands locked in her lap, and:

"Do you refer to any new act of his," I asked, "with which I am not at present acquainted?"

She nodded slowly.

"Yes," she said; "but I can only tell you in confidence, for it is something which Inspector Gatton does not know."

"Please tell me," I urged, "for you are aware that I have

no other object but the clearing of Coverly in the eyes of the police and the public."

"Well," she continued, with hesitation, "last night he lodged with me a copy of a *declaration* which he assured me cleared him entirely. But he imposed an extraordinary condition."

"What was that?" I asked with interest.

"It was only to be used in the event of the worst happening!" she said.

"What do you mean? In the event of his being put on trial for murder?"

Isobel nodded.

"I suppose so," she said sadly; "it seems madness, doesn't it?"

"Absolute madness!" I agreed. "If he is in a position to establish an alibi, why not do it now and be done with the whole unsavoury business?"

"That is exactly what I pointed out to him, but he was adamant on the matter and became dreadfully irritable and excited. I did not dare to press the point, so of course——" She shrugged her shoulders resignedly.

Was it a selfish joy, I wonder, which possessed me as I noted the restrained impatience with which Isobel spoke of Coverly? I suppose it was, and perhaps it was even indefensible; yet I record it, desiring to be perfectly honest with myself and with others. Nevertheless, in the near future I was to regret the sentiments which at that moment I entertained towards Coverly. But how was I to know in my poor human blindness that his innocence would soon be established in the eyes of the world by other means than the publication of the statement which he had so strangely placed with Isobel?

Since, excepting the telegram, no communication had reached me from Gatton, I could only assume that he had discovered nothing in the ruins of the Bell House of sufficient importance to justify a report. Doubtless he had reported to New Scotland Yard, but that his discoveries, if any, had not resulted in an arrest was painfully evident.

My latest contribution to the *Planet* had been in the nature of a discursive essay rather than an informative article, although I had enlivened it with some account of my experiences at Upper Crossleys. But at the moment that I had set pen to paper I had realized the difficulty of expressing, within the scope of a newspaper contribution, the peculiar conditions which ruled in that oddly deserted village. And at Gatton's request I had been most guarded in my treatment of the two abortive attempts made upon my own life by the Eurasian doctor.

The appeal in Isobel's eyes, as I have said, was very difficult to resist, but, after all, I had little substantial consolation to offer; and in the circumstances I shall be understood, I think, when I say that it was with an odd sense of relief that I finally took my departure from her flat. To long for the right to comfort a woman as only a lover may do, and to suspect that this sweet privilege might have been his for the asking, is a torture which no man can suffer unmoved.

Anticipating, almost hourly, a further message from Gatton, I went first to the *Planet* offices, but although I lunched at the club and returned later, no news reached me there; whereupon I proceeded to my cottage. As I walked down the high street of the one-time village, passing that police-box at which (so far as my part in it was concerned) the first scenes of the drama actually had been laid, I was seized with wonder on reflecting that all these episodes, strange and tragic, had been crowded into so short a space of time.

An officer was on duty there as on the night when I had first made acquaintance with the green eyes of the woman of mystery; but I did not know the man, and I walked on deep in meditation, until, arriving at the Red House, other and dreadful reflections were aroused by the sight of that deserted building.

There were no spectators to-day, for the first excitement aroused by the crime had begun to subside, and I did not even notice a constable posted there. Whereby I concluded that the investigations at the Red House had been terminated, and that no more was hoped for from an examination of those premises.

Coates was awaiting me as I entered my cottage with the news that Inspector Gatton had telephoned an hour before from Crossleys confirming his telegram and stating that he would call immediately he arrived in London. This was stimulating, and I only regretted that I had not been at home personally to speak to him. Then:

"Sir Eric Coverly also rang up, sir," continued Coates,

"at about three o'clock and said that he would be calling this evening at eight in accordance with your request."

I looked at the military figure standing bolt upright just within the doorway.

"Good. Is that all?" I asked.

"That was all the message, sir," he reported.

I walked into the study in a very thoughtful mood, and from the open window contemplated that prospect of tree-lined road, now for ever to be associated in my mind with the darkest places in the tragedy in which I had so strangely become involved.

Gatton, I knew, entertained a theory that the selection of the Red House for the dreadful purpose for which it had been employed was not the result of any mere accident, but was ascribable to the fact that the place was conveniently situated from the point of view of the assassin. In short, he had an idea that the London headquarters of the wanted man, whom he had now definitely invested with the personality of Dr. Damar Greefe, was somewhere within my immediate neighbourhood!

It was a startling conclusion, and one which rested, as I thought, upon somewhat slender premises; but nevertheless I found it disquieting. And recognizing how the more sinister manifestations of that singular green-eyed creature (whom I could never think of as a woman, nor indeed regard as anything quite human) were associated with darkness—a significantly feline trait—I confess to a certain apprehension respecting the coming night. This apprehension was strengthened, no doubt, by my memories of Gatton's last words as I had been on the point of setting out from Upper Crossleys.

"With their Friar's Park base destroyed, Mr. Addison," he had said, "they will be forced to fly to that other abode, at present unknown, from which I believe they conducted the elaborate assassination of Sir Marcus. The only alternative is flight from the country, and the mechanism of the C.I.D. having been put into motion, this we may regard as almost impossible, especially in view of the marked personality of Dr. Damar Greefe. Of course," he had added, "they may have some other residence of which we know nothing, but I incline to the idea that they will make for London."

That the published paragraph relating to Eric Coverly's

alleged evidence was in some way associated with this theory of Gatton's I knew, but of the soundness of his theory I had yet to learn.

Since (as Isobel had that day informed me) the document lodged with her was a profound secret from all, Gatton's inspired paragraph could have been no more than a shot in the dark, and the fact that it had hit the mark was one of those seeming coincidences which actually rested upon a process of careful reasoning. The inspector was certain, as I was certain, of Coverly's innocence, and he had credited him with an alibi because he knew that if he would but consent to break his inexplicable silence, he was in a position to establish one. Why he had forestalled Coverly I knew not.

I made a poor and hasty dinner, for I was too excited to eat, and, returning to the study, I crossed to the book-case and took down Maspero's "Egyptian Art." I idly glanced again through those passages which Gatton had copied into his notebook—the passages relating to the attributes of Bâst, the cat-goddess. My mind rested particularly, I remember, upon the line, "She played with her victim as with a mouse."

Stifling a somewhat weary sigh, I returned the book to its place and lingered looking out of the open window into a deepening dusk. Mentally, my mood was a restless one, but it did not reflect itself physically, for I stood there leaning against the window, whilst a procession of all the figures associated with the *Oritoga* mystery raced through my mind.

And presently, as I stood there contemplating a mental image of the Eurasian doctor, I heard the telephone bell ring. The sound aroused me in a moment, and walking out into the little ante-room in which the instrument was placed, I took it up, anticipating Coates, who had immediately come in from the garden, where he was engaged at the time.

"Hallo!" I said.

A voice with which I was unfamiliar, a man's voice speaking rather thickly, replied:

"Is that Mr. Addison?"

"Yes."

"I have just arrived from Crossleys with Inspector Gatton. He requests me to ask you to meet him by the police-box at the corner of the high street immediately."

"Very good," I said. "I will come."

"And," continued the voice, "could you spare Coates with the car for an hour?"

"Certainly," I replied. "For what do you want him?"

"If he will take the car to Denmark Hill Station and be there by a quarter past eight," continued the voice, "Detective-Sergeant Blythe will meet him. There is a large box," he added, "which Inspector Gatton wishes to have taken to your house."

"Very well," I said; "Coates will start in ten minutes' time, and I will come along immediately to meet Inspector Gatton."

I replaced the telephone upon the little table and went out into the garden, whither my man had returned.

"Coates," I said, "get out the Rover."

Coates immediately ceased his gardening operations and stood upright in an attitude of attention.

"Very good, sir."

"You will just have time to get ready at the garage and return here to admit Sir Eric Coverly at eight o'clock. I am going out now to meet Inspector Gatton. But inform Sir Eric that I shall be back in a few minutes. Show him into the study and make him comfortable. You will then proceed in the Rover to Denmark Hill Station. You will meet there a man with a box—a detective from Scotland Yard who will make himself known to you. His name is Blythe. You have to bring the box back here."

"Very good, sir," repeated Coates.

And as he entered the house he was already stripping off the old shooting-jacket which he wore in the garden. For my part I slipped a light top-coat over my somewhat untidy house attire, and taking my hat and a stick, stepped quickly out along the road in the direction of the village street. A brisk walk brought me to the little sentry-box under the trees. But Gatton was not to be seen. Indeed, with the exception of several ordinary pedestrians who were obviously returning from the City to their homes (all of whom I scrutinized, thinking that Coverly might come this way), and the constable on duty at the point, there was no one about who looked in the least like either of my expected visitors.

Having waited for some ten minutes unavailingly, I spoke to the man in the box.

"Good evening, constable," I said; "I expected to meet a friend here—Inspector Gatton, of Scotland Yard—you may know him?"

"I know of him quite well, sir," answered the constable, "and should recognize him if I saw him. But he has not been here this evening."

"You have seen no one hanging about who might have been sent by him?"

"No one, sir,"

"Strange," I muttered; then: "My name is Addison, constable," I said, "and if anyone should ask for me, will you direct him to proceed to my house?" And I gave the man instructions respecting its whereabouts.

"I will," answered the constable; and wishing him "Good night," I retraced my steps, curious respecting the matter, but not apprehensive as I well might have been— and with no glimmering of the ghastly truth penetrating to my mind.

CHAPTER XXII

THE GREY MIST

I was about half-way on my return journey when I heard a car racing along the road behind me, and as it came nearer I detected the fact that it was slowing down. Ere I could turn:

"Hi! Mr. Addison!" hailed a voice.

I stopped, turned round, and there was Gatton leaning out of the car and staring towards me through the deepening dusk.

"Why, Gatton!" I said, walking up to him, "I waited more than ten minutes for you, and then gave it up."

"Waited for me?"

"Yes, by the police-box."

He stared in evident wonder at me and then at the police chauffeur who drove the car.

"Whatever prompted you to do that?" he said. "Coates must have given you the wrong message. I said I would come to the house for you, not meet you in the street."

Still I remained dense to the truth, and:

"I know you did," I replied. "I refer to the second message."

"I sent no second message."

"What!"

"Get in," cried Gatton shortly; "this wants explaining."

I stepped into the car, and as it moved onward again I explained to the inspector what had taken place. As I talked I saw his expression grow darker and darker, until finally:

"There's something wrong!" he muttered.

"Then you did not inspire the message?"

"I know nothing whatever about it. At the time you received it I was on my way from Crossleys. I have been travelling for the last hour and a half."

I stared at him very blankly. The object of such a communication was difficult to imagine, and I knew of nothing incriminating in my possession, which might have tempted the assassin to lure me from the house whilst he obtained possession of it.

In ever-growing excitement I watched the houses slipping behind us as we swept along. Then we came to the tree-lined expanse of road immediately leading to the cottage. As the car stopped, I leapt out quickly, Gatton close upon my heels, and ran up the path to the door.

From certain indications with which I was familiar, I observed that Coates was out, whereby I concluded that he had set off to meet the mythical "man with a box." But with apprehension I inserted the key in the lock and opened the door.

As I did so I beheld a most singular spectacle.

The careful Coates had closed all the windows as usual before quitting the house, so that there was comparatively little draught along the corridor. But as the door swung open I perceived a sort of grey fog-like vapour floating over the carpet about a foot in depth and moving in slightly sinuous spirals upward towards the opened door!

At this phenomenon I stared in speechless astonishment;

for whilst it resembled steam or the early morning mist which one sometimes sees upon the grass in hot weather, I was wholly at a loss to account for its presence inside my cottage!

"Good heavens!" cried Gatton, and grasped me by the arm with so strong a grip that I almost cried out. *"Look! look!"*

"What the devil is it?" I muttered; and turning I stared into his face. "What *can* it be?"

"Stand back," he said strangely, and pulled me out into the porch. "Do you notice a peculiar smell?"

"I do—a most foul and abominable smell."

Gatton nodded grimly.

"God knows what has happened here since you left," he said; "but of one thing I am sure—you must certainly bear a charmed life, Mr. Addison. There has been a third attempt at your removal."

This choking smell which now rose to my nostrils had in it something vaguely familiar, yet something which at that place and that time I found myself unable to identify; but:

"We shall have to open the windows!" rapped Gatton.

Suiting the action to the word, he took out his handkerchief, and holding it to his nostrils went running along the corridor, his feet oddly enveloped in that mysterious mist. A moment later I heard the bang of a swiftly raised window, then another, and:

"Stand clear of the door!" called a muffled voice.

A moment later Gatton came racing back again, coughing and choking because of the fumes which arose from that supernatural fog carpeting the passages.

The chauffeur now appeared upon the path leading from the gate to the porch, but:

"Stay by the car!" ordered Gatton. "Don't move without instructions."

I scarcely noted his words. For I was watching the grey fog. In the dusk I could see it streaming out, that deathly mist, and creeping away across grass and flower-beds, right and left of the door.

"Give it a chance to clear," said Gatton; "I fancy one good whiff would finish any man!"

Even as he spoke the words the nature of this vapour suddenly occurred to me, and:

"The Abbey Inn!" I whispered. "The Abbey Inn!"

"Ah!" said he. "You've solved the mystery, have you! But can you explain how this stuff comes to be floating about the floor of your house?"

"I cannot," I confessed. "But at all costs we must go in. We must learn the worst!"

"Yes, we'll risk it now," said the inspector.

Close together we entered and made our way towards the study. As we passed the doorway of the ante-room in which the telephone was placed, I glanced aside, and thereupon:

"My God, Gatton!" I groaned. "Look!"

He pulled up and the two of us stood, horror-stricken, rooted to the spot, looking into the little room.

I have said that Coates invariably closed the windows before leaving the house, but here the window was open. Prone upon the floor was stretched the figure of a man!

He wore a light overcoat, and his hat lay under the telephone table—where it had evidently rolled at the moment of his fall. The poisonous smell was more apparent here than elsewhere; and looking down at the prone figure, the face of which was indiscernible because of the man's position:

"Why, Gatton!" I said in an awed whisper—"look!—he was speaking to someone!"

"I'm looking!" replied Gatton grimly.

Grasped rigidly in his left hand the fallen man held the telephone!

"We want gas-masks for this job!" said the inspector.

His words were true enough. I had already recognized the odour of the foul stuff. It was identical with that which, as we had come down from the upper floor of the Abbey Inn, had proceeded from the room wherein the mysterious shell had exploded. In a word my cottage was filled with some kind of poison-gas!

"We must risk it, anyway," said Gatton, "and find out who it is."

I nodded, sick with foreboding. Stooping swiftly, he succeeded in turning over the prone figure, whereupon I quite failed to restrain a hoarse cry of horror.

It was Eric Coverly!

The fume-laden room seemed to swim around me as I looked down at the dreadfully contorted features over which was creeping that greenish tint which had characterized the face of Sir Marcus as I had seen it on the morning of the body's recovery from the hold of the *Oritoga*.

"Drag him out," said Gatton huskily. "He may be alive."

But even as we bent to the attempt, both my companion and I were seized with violent nausea; for the wisps of grey mist which still floated in the air were nevertheless sufficiently deadly. However, we succeeded at last in dragging Eric Coverly into the passage.

Here it became necessary to detach the telephone from the death-grip in which he held it.

I turned my head aside whilst Gatton accomplished this task; then together we bore Coverly out into the porch.

At this point we were both overcome again by the fumes. Gatton was the first to recover sufficiently to stoop and examine the victim of this fiendish outrage. I clutched dizzily at an upright of the porch, and:

"Don't tell me he's dead," I whispered.

But Gatton stood up and nodded sternly.

"He was the last!" he said strangely. "They have triumphed, after all."

The man who had driven the car and who now stood in a state of evident stupefaction looking over the gate, where he had been warned to remain by the inspector, came forward on seeing Gatton beckoning to him.

"Notify the local officer in charge and bring a doctor," said Gatton. He turned to me. "Which is the nearest?"

Rapidly I gave the man the necessary instructions, and he went running out to the car and soon was speeding away towards the house of a local physician.

I find it difficult to recapture the peculiar horror of the next few minutes, during which, half-fearful of entering the cottage, Gatton and I stood in the little sheltered garden adjoining the porch, looking down at the body of this man who had met his end under my roof, in circumstances at once dreadful and incomprehensible.

Tragically, Eric Coverly was vindicated; by his death he was proved innocent. And by the manner of his death we realized that he had fallen a victim to the same malign agency as his cousin.

I have explained that my cottage stood in a strangely secluded spot, although so near to the sleepless life of London; and I remember that throughout the period between the departure of the man with the car and his return with the doctor and two police officers whom he had brought from the local depôt, only one pedestrian passed my door, and he on the opposite side of the road.

How little that chance traveller suspected what a scene was concealed from his eyes by the tall hedges which divided the garden from the high road! It was as the footsteps of this wayfarer became faint in the distance, that suddenly:

"Come along!" said Gatton. "We might chance it now. I want to get to the bottom of this telephone trick."

He returned to the door of the ante-room, and side by side we stood looking down at the telephone which had only been extracted from the grip of the dead man with so much difficulty. The inspector stooped and took it up from the floor. The deadly grey mist was all but dissipated now, and together we stood staring stupidly at the telephone which Gatton held in his hand.

To all outward seeming it was an ordinary instrument, and my number was written upon it in the space provided for the purpose. Then, all at once, as we stepped into the room, I observed something out of the ordinary.

I could see a length of green cable proceeding from the wall-plug *out* through the open window. The cable attached to the instrument which Gatton held did not come from the proper connexion at all, but came *in* through the window, and was evidently connected with something outside in the garden!

"What does this mean, Gatton?" I cried.

Evidently as deeply mystified as I, Gatton placed the telephone on the little table, and fully opening the window, leaned out.

"Hallo!" he cried; "the cable leads up to the roof of the tool-shed!"

"To the roof of the tool-shed!" I echoed incredulously.

But Gatton did not heed my words, for:

"What the devil have we here?" he continued.

He was hauling something up from the flower-bed below the window, and now, turning to me, he held out a second telephone!

"Why, Gatton!" I cried, and took it from his hand, "*this*

is the authentic instrument! See! It is connected in the proper way!"

"I see quite clearly," he replied. "It was simply placed outside, whilst a duplicate one was substituted for it. I observe a ladder against the shed. Let us trace the cable attached to the duplicate."

The ladder was one used by Coates about the garden; and now, climbing out of the window, Gatton mounted it and surveyed the roof of the lean-to which I used as a tool-shed.

"Ha!" he exclaimed. "A gas cylinder!"

"What?"

He fingered the green cable.

"This is not a cable at all," he cried; "it's *covered tubing!* Do you see?"

He descended and rejoined me.

"You see?" he continued. "A call from the exchange would ring the bell in the ante-room here. This devilish contrivance"—he pointed to the false telephone—"is really hollow. The weight of the receiver hermetically closes the end of the tube, no doubt. But anyone answering the call and taking up the duplicate instrument would receive the full benefit of the contents of the cylinder which lies up there on the roof!"

"My God, Gatton!" I muttered. "The fiends! But why was the contrivance not removed?"

"They hadn't time," he said grimly. "They had not counted on the death-grip of the victim!"

I heard a car come racing up to the gate, followed by the sound of many excited voices.

"At last we know where the grey mist came from," I said, as Gatton and I walked through the cottage to meet the new arrivals.

"We know more than that," he retorted. "We know how *Sir Marcus* died!"

"Gatton!" I cried excitedly, as we approached a group waiting in the porch, "do you mean——"

He looked at me grimly.

"I mean," he said slowly, "that I have not forgotten the *gas-plug* in the wall of that recess in the supper-room at the Red House! The only thing I was doubtful about—the means by which the victim was induced to admit the gas into the room—is now as clear as daylight."

"You are right, Gatton," I agreed. "The same trick has succeeded twice."

"The same trick, as you say, Mr. Addison, with one trifling variation: a device which would only suggest itself to such a brain as that of——"

"Dr. Damar Greefe!" I cried.

"I believe you are right."

And now fell an awesome silence; for whilst Gatton and I stood bare-headed, the unfortunate Eric Coverly was being carried out to the waiting car, and even as I turned my eyes away in horror from that spectacle, I was endeavouring to frame the words in which I should acquaint Isobel with this second ghastly tragedy.

Here, indeed, was a new development of "the *Oritoga* mystery"; and so strangely does the mind depart from the actualities at such a moment that I found myself thinking, even whilst Gatton was talking to me, of the bold headlines which would greet readers of the Press in the morning—and of the renewed excitement which would sweep throughout the length and breadth of the land when this dreadful alibi was proven.

Over the details of that gruesome tragedy I feel myself compelled to pass lightly, for even now the horror of it remains with me. The fumes of the poisonous grey mist lingered for hours in the house, and there were official visitations, testimonies and attestations, and the hundred and one formalities which invariably accompany such a tragedy, but which I need not deal with in detail here.

Coates returned with the Rover, just as the body of the victim was being removed, and his account of what had occurred was simple enough, and followed the lines which we had anticipated. He had locked up and then gone to the garage for the car as I had directed him to do, returning to the cottage in time to admit Eric Coverly, whom he showed into the study, having informed him that I should be back in less than ten minutes. He had then proceeded to Denmark Hill railway station, only to find, as I had found, that the appointment was a hoax and "the man with a box" a myth.

"You see," said Gatton, "the scheme of the plotter was simply this: to get Coates out of the way for a long enough time to allow the substitution of the telephone to be accomplished. The fact that Coates had closed the windows before leaving the house didn't interfere very much with the scheme. It's an old-fashioned catch on the anteroom window, and I have seen the marks upon the brasswork where it was forced from the outside with the blade of a knife. For the person who opened the window to take out the real telephone and put the other in its place was easy; and all that remained was to lift the gas-cylinder on to the shed and partly re-close the window as we found it. Coates, even if he had troubled to look, would not have noticed any difference in the dusk. It is the next move, however, which I find most interesting."

Gatton spoke with repressed excitement, and:

"What do you mean by 'the next move'?" I asked.

"Well," he replied, "we have good evidence to show that the assassin possesses an almost Napoleonic capacity for working by the time-table. Witness the employment of Constable Bolton in the Red House affair—which showed that our man was perfectly acquainted with the movements of the officer on that beat and timed his scheme accordingly. Very well. . . . Having laid the telephone trap in your ante-room, did our man hurry away and make the call *in person,* which brought Coverly to the 'phone—or did he remain watching the house and give the signal to *someone else* to do it?"

"I cannot imagine, Gatton. Nor does the point strike me as important."

"No?" said Gatton, smiling triumphantly. "Then I must explain. Whereas, in the Red House, the scheme worked *automatically*—for the time of Sir Marcus's arrival was *fixed*—in the present instance someone had to watch for *your* return from the mythical appointment!"

"For *my* return?"

"Unquestionably! This scheme was arranged for your benefit, Mr. Addison. Unknowingly, poor Coverly saved you from a dreadful fate at the price of his own life! You see, they did not know that Coverly was coming here! Now, it will not have escaped your attention that he wore a soft felt hat, a light overcoat, and carried a black cane. So did *you* when you went out to keep the appointment made by the assassin!"

He paused, staring at me hard, and:

"Whoever was watching for your return," he said solemnly, "mistook Coverly for you! The moment that

Coates drove away the signal was given. It *must* have been. We were back here a few minutes later. *Now* do you see?"

"I do not, Gatton! What are you driving at?"

"At this: the telephone call *must* have been made from somewhere in the immediate neighbourhood! There wasn't time to do it otherwise. And there is no public call office within a mile *which is open after seven o'clock!*"

"Good heavens!" I cired. "At last I understand!"

Gatton looked at me, smiling in grim triumph, and:

"Dr. Damar Greefe has a residence somewhere within a quarter-mile radius of this house!" he declared. "He has betrayed himself! Then—look here."

Unscrewing the front of the mouthpiece of the false telephone, he took out the strip of cardboard upon which my number was written, turned it over . . . and there upon the back was another number!

"Just look up Dr. Brown-Edwards," he said, "He was the last occupant of the Red House, and may still be in the book."

Grasping the purpose of his inquiry, excitedly I did as he directed, and there, sure enough, the number appeared!

"The identical instrument that was used at the Red House!" cried Gatton. "Note the artistic finish with which even the *correct* exchange numbers are looked up!"

I sank back in my chair, silent, appalled at the perverted genius of this fiend whom we were pitted against in a life-or-death struggle. But presently:

"What was the object of the opening and closing of the garage doors at the Red House?" I asked, almost mechanically.

"Simple enough," Gatton replied. "Whereas here the telephone was installed, so that the bell could be rung by someone merely calling up your number—and the ringing stopped by the caller telling the exchange he had made a mistake—in the Red House, as I have discovered, the 'phone had been disconnected shortly after Dr. Brown-Edwards left the place."

"Then the opening and closing of the doors was merely a device for ringing the bell?"

"Yes. The opening of the first door set it ringing, and the opening of the second probably stopped it. Mr. Addison"—he stood up, resting his hands upon the table and regarding me fixedly—"we enter upon the final battle of wits: New Scotland Yard *versus* Dr. Damar Greefe and the green-eyed lady of Bâst. Regarding the latter, there is a very significant point."

"What is that?"

"The 'voice' on this last occasion was that, not of a woman, but of a man."

CHAPTER XXIII

THE INEVITABLE

"I very much regret having to trouble you, Miss Merlin, at such a time," said Inspector Gatton, "but as the paper lodged with you by the late Sir Eric Coverly may throw some light upon a very dark matter, perhaps you will read it to us."

I watched the play of expression upon Isobel's face with a depth of sympathy which I cannot attempt to describe. The successive trials which had been imposed upon her in so short a time had robbed her cheeks of their sweet colour, and there were dark shadows under her eyes. The tumult of my own feelings was such that I was scarcely capable of consistent thought, nor had I the moral courage to examine those emotions which stirred so wildly within me.

Late on the previous night I had performed the unhappy duty of breaking to her the news of Coverly's dreadful death. I shall never forget that black hour. Her courage, however, under all these trials had been admirable, and although I well knew what it must have cost her, she replied now with perfect composure:

"Look—I took it out of my bureau when I heard that you were here, Inspector."

She took up from the table a foolscap envelope, sealed and having her name written upon it in large and somewhat unsteady characters.

"I would suggest," said Gatton with a delicacy which

earned my gratitude, "that you read it yourself first, Miss Merlin. If there is anything helpful in it, you can then communicate it to me."

I saw Isobel biting her lip hard, but she resolutely tore open the envelope, and leaving her to read the contents, I joined Gatton at the window. We both stood staring out for what seemed a very long time, then:

"It is rather long," said Isobel in a low voice.

Gatton and I turned together, and saw her looking even more pale than before, seated by the table holding a sheet of notepaper in her hand. Without glancing at either of us, she began to read as follows, in an even and monotonous voice which I knew she had adopted to hide her emotion:

"This account of my movements on the night of August 6th will only be read in the event of my being falsely adjudged guilty of the murder of my cousin, Marcus Coverly, or in the event of my death.

"On the afternoon of that date I was informed over the telephone that my fiancée, Isobel Merlin, was meeting Sir Marcus the same night at a place called the Red House. The address was given me, and I was asked, in case I doubted the word of the speaker, to watch Miss Merlin's movements that evening.

"I had already quarrelled with my cousin respecting his unwelcome attentions, and although the result did not confirm the promise of the informant, in part at least the information was accurate. I have no idea of the speaker's identity except that the voice was the voice of a woman.

"Not desiring to trust anyone in such a matter, I myself obtained in a remote district the dilapidated garments which are now in possession of the police and respecting which they have subjected me to close examination. Attired in these, and having my face and hands artificially dirtied as a further disguise, I left my chambers by a back entrance about nine o'clock, and not having sufficient confidence in my make-up to enter a public vehicle, walked the whole of the way to College Road.

"I had little difficulty in finding the Red House, but on discovering that it was vacant, I immediately suspected a hoax. However, I determined to wait in the neighbourhood until the time at which the voice had warned me the meeting was to take place. There were very few people about, and a tremendous downfall of rain drenched me to the skin, for the only shelter afforded was that of the trees bordering the road unless I had been content to abandon my watch.

"Just before the downpour ceased, but after it had abated its first fury, I came out from my inadequate shelter and began to walk in the direction of the High Street. I had not gone more than twenty paces before I saw a cab approaching, and the man, seeing my bedraggled figure, slowed up, and to my astonishment asked me the way to the Red House.

"I immediately peered into the cab—to find that the passenger was none other than Marcus Coverly. I had begun to doubt, but at this I doubted no longer. I gave the cabman the necessary directions, and slowly following on foot I saw from the shelter of the trees on the opposite side of the road Sir Marcus dismiss the cab and walk up the drive of the empty house.

"He was alone, and since I knew that Miss Merlin had not preceded him, I could only conclude that she would be following later. Accordingly I walked slowly away from the Red House again in the direction of the High Street, and some five minutes later I passed a constable accompanied by a man wearing a light Burberry and a soft hat, whom I knew later (although I failed to recognize him at the time) to have been Mr. Jack Addison.

"I stood at the corner by the High Street until long after midnight. Twice I returned to the Red House, and once even penetrated as far as the porch; but although I thought I could detect a light shining out through the shutters of the room on the right of the door, I could not be sure of it, and there was no sound of movement within.

"These were my only discoveries, and very wretched and dissatisfied I tramped back to my chambers wondering what the visit of Marcus Coverly to this apparently empty house could mean and why he had remained there, but particularly wondering why the voice had told me this part-truth which had turned me into a spy unavailingly.

"The discovery made at the docks on the following day placed a new and dreadful construction upon the motives of the speaker, and I awakened to the fact that, although entirely innocent of any complicity, I had laid myself open to a charge of having been concerned in the murder of my cousin.

"My ill-advised attempt to conceal the garments which I had used as a disguise, and of which I had not known how to dispose, was dictated by panic. I knew the police were watching me, and I was fool enough to think that I could escape their vigilance.

"This is all I have to say. It explains nothing, and it does not exonerate me I am aware, but I swear that it is the truth.

"(Signed) ERIC COVERLY, BART."

Although she retained so brave a composure, I recognised the strain which this new and cruel ordeal had imposed upon Isobel, and Gatton incurred a further debt of gratitude by his tactful behaviour, for:

"Miss Merlin," he said earnestly, "you are a very brave woman. Thank you. I only wish I could have spared you this."

Shaking me warmly by the hand, he bowed and departed, leaving me alone with Isobel.

As the sound of his footsteps died away, Isobel returned again to the seat from which she had risen, and a silence fell between us. My own feelings I cannot attempt to depict, and I will confess that I was afraid of my humanity at that moment. Never had Isobel seemed more desirable; never had I longed as I longed now to take her in my arms.

The tension of that silence becoming insupportable:

"You will not stay here alone?" I asked in an unnatural voice.

Isobel, without looking up, shook her head.

"I am going to Mrs. Wentworth—my Aunt Alison," she replied.

"Good," I said. "I am glad to know that you will be in her cheery company."

Mrs. Wentworth was, indeed, a charming old lady, and, so far as I knew, Isobel's only relation in London, if not in England. She occupied a house which, like herself, was small, scrupulously neat and old-worldly. One of those tiny residences which, once counted as being "in the country," had later become enmeshed in the ever-spreading tentacles of greater London.

It was situated on the northern outskirts of the county-city, and although rows of modern "villas" had grown up around it, within the walls of that quaint little homestead one found oneself far enough removed from suburbia.

"When are you going, Isobel?" I asked.

"I think," she replied, "in the morning."

"Will you let me drive you in the Rover—or are you taking too much baggage?"

"Oh, no," she said, smiling sadly, "I am going to live the simple life for a week. Going out shopping with Aunt Alison—and perhaps sometimes to the pictures!"

"Then I can drive you over?"

"Yes—if you would like to," she answered simply.

I took my leave shortly afterwards and proceeded to the *Planet* office. I had work to do, but I must admit that I little relished the idea of returning to my cottage. Diverted, now, from the notorious Red House, public interest had centred upon my residence, and the seclusion, which I had gone so far to seek, was disturbed almost hourly by impertinent callers who seemed to think that the scene of a sensational crime was public property.

Coates had effectually disillusioned several of them on this point; but, nevertheless, the cottage had become distasteful to me. I realized that I must seek a new residence without delay. Shall I add that the primary cause of my reclusion no longer operated so powerfully? Of my dreams at this time I will speak later; but here I may say that I knew, and accepted the knowledge with a fearful joy, that if my new house of hope was doomed to be shattered, no spot in broad England could offer me rest again.

It was not, then, until late that night that I returned to my once peaceful abode. Coates was waiting up for me, but he had nothing of importance to report, apparently, until, when I had dismissed him, he turned in the doorway, and:

"Excuse me, sir," he said, and cleared his throat.

"Yes, Coates?"

"About half an hour ago, sir, the dogs all around started howling, sir. I thought I'd better mention it, as Inspector Gatton asked me this morning if I had ever heard the dogs howling."

I looked at him straightly.

"Inspector Gatton asked you this?"

"He did, sir. So I have reported the occurrence. Good night, sir."

"Good night, Coates," I replied.

But for long enough after his departure I sat there in the arm-chair in my study, thinking over this seemingly trivial occurrence. From where I sat I could see the light shining upon the gilt-lettered title of Maspero's "Egyptian Art," and my thoughts promised to be ill bedfellows.

Contrary to custom, I slept that night with closed windows! And although I awakened twice, once at two o'clock and again at four, thinking that I had heard the mournful signal of the dogs, nothing but my own uneasy imagination disturbed my slumbers.

Breakfast despatched, and my correspondence dealt with, I sent Coates to the garage for my little car, and since I should have another companion, left him behind and myself drove to Isobel's flat. Womanlike, she was not nearly ready, and there was much bustling on the part of the repentant Marie—who had been retained in spite of her share in the tragedy of Sir Marcus's death—before we finally set out for Mrs. Wentworth's.

Isobel was very silent on the way, but once I intercepted a sidelong glance and felt my heart leaping madly when she blushed.

Mrs. Wentworth made me very welcome, as had ever been her way. She was an eccentric, but embarrassingly straightforward old lady, and if I had heeded her simple motherly counsel in the past all might have been different.

She bore Isobel off to her room, leaving me to my own devices, for she had never observed any ceremony towards me in all the years that I had known her, but had taught me to make myself at home beneath her hospitable roof. I knew, too, because she had never troubled to disguise the fact, that she regarded Isobel and I as made for one another. Isobel's engagement to poor Eric Coverly, Mrs. Wentworth had all along regarded as a ghastly farce, and I can never forget her reception of me on the occasion of my first visit after returning from Mesopotamia.

Half an hour or so elapsed, then, before Isobel returned; and although she came into the room confidently enough, the old tension reasserted itself immediately. I felt that commonplaces would choke me. And although to this day I cannot condone my behaviour, for the good of my soul I must confess the truth.

I took her in my arms, held her fast, and kissed her.

An overwhelming consciousness of guilt came to me even as her lips met mine, and, releasing her, I turned aside, groaning.

"Isobel!" I said hoarsely. "Isobel, forgive me! I was a cad, a villain—to *him*. But—it was inevitable. Try to forget that I was so weak. But, Isobel——"

I felt her hand trembling on my arm.

"We must *both* try to forget, Jack," she whispered.

I grasped her hands and looked eagerly—indeed, I think wildly—into her eyes.

"Because my life is over if I lose you," I said, "I suppose I was mad for a moment. Tell me that one day—when it is fit and proper that you should do so—you will give me a hearing, and I will perform any penance you choose. I acted like a black-guard."

"Stop!" she commanded softly.

She raised her eyes, and her grave, sweet glance cooled the fever which consumed me, and brought a great and abiding peace to my heart.

"You were no more to blame than I!" she said. "And because—I understand, it is not hard to forgive. I don't try to excuse myself, but even if—he had lived, I could never have gone on with it, after his—suspicions. Oh, Jack, why did you leave me to make that awful mistake?"

"My dearest," I replied, "God knows I have suffered for it."

"Please," she said, and her voice faltered, "help me to be fair to—him. Never—never—speak to me again—like that—until——"

But the sentence was never completed, for at this moment in bustled Aunt Alison—in appearance a white-haired, rosy-faced little matron, very brisk in her movements and very shrewd-eyed. A dear old lady, dearer than ever to me in that she had tried so hard to bring Isobel and my laggard self together. She had, as usual, more to say than could be said in the time at her disposal. As we proceeded to the dining-room:

"Now, then, you boys and girls, I'm starving, if you're not! What a time I've had with cook, not knowing when you might be here. Cook's leaving to be married; I'm afraid she's neglected this seakale. Dear, dear! what love will do for people's minds, to be sure! Put your hair straight, Isobel, dear, or Mary will think Jack has been kissing you! I saw her kiss the postman yesterday. Mary, I mean! You're eating like a pigeon, Jack! Gracious me! Where's the pepper? Mary! Ring the bell, Isobel. I must speak to that postman; he's made Mary forget to put any pepper in the cruet, and anyone might have seen them. It isn't respectable!"

"Dear Aunt Alison!" I said, as the active old lady ran out, Mary not being promptly enough in attendance. "She loves to go running in and out like a waiter! What a friend she has been to me, Isobel! You could not be in better company at such a time."

"She's a darling!" agreed Isobel, and when I met her glance across the table, she blushed entrancingly.

Then, in a moment, tears were in her eyes; and knowing of whom she was thinking, I sat abashed—guilty and repentant. I had transgressed against the murdered man; and there and then I made a solemn, silent vow that no word of love again should pass my lips until the fit and proper time of mourning was over. Because I faithfully kept this vow, I dare to hope that my sin is forgiven me.

Luncheon at that homely house, with Isobel, was an unalloyed delight; and I regretted every passing minute which brought me nearer to the time when I must depart. But when at last I said good-bye it was a new world upon which I looked—a new life upon which I entered. I have said that to-day I venture to hope my poor human transgression is forgiven me. Yet it did not go unpunished. Little did I dream, in my strange new happiness, how soon I was to return to that house—how soon I was to know the deadliest terror of my life.

CHAPTER XXIV

A CONFERENCE—INTERRUPTED

"The case has narrowed down," said Gatton, "from my point of view, into the quest of one man."

"Dr. Damar Greefe!"

"Precisely. You have asked me what I found at Friar's Park and the Bell House, and I can answer you very briefly: nothing! The latter place had quite obviously been fired in a systematic and deliberate way. I suspect that the contents of the rooms had been soaked with petrol. It burned to a shell and then collapsed. At the present moment it is merely a mound of smoking ashes.

"Of course, the local fire brigade was hopelessly ill-equipped, but even with the most up-to-date appliances I doubt if the conflagration could have been extinguished. The men watching the house were thrown quite off their guard when flames began to leap out of the windows, hence the escape of Damar Greefe."

"You are sure he *did* escape?"

Gatton stared at me grimly.

"To whom do you suppose you are indebted for the telephone trick?" he asked. "Besides—Blythe, the fool, actually heard the car at the moment that it came out on to the high road! Oh, they bungled the thing villainously. My Marathon feat saved your life, Mr. Addison, but it looks like losing me the case! We have the Hawkins couple; but, although a graceless pair, they were more dupes than knaves. I am convinced, personally, that neither of them suspected that Lady Burnham Coverly was dead. Damar Greefe had represented to them that she had lost her reason."

"Good heavens! What a scheme!"

"What a scheme, indeed. Hawkins seems to have considered that his duty—which was merely to keep intruders out of the park—was dictated by necessity. He thought that if Lady Coverly's real condition became known she would be removed to a madhouse! He also thought that a *nurse* was in attendance."

"A nurse?"

"Yes. He assured me that he had heard and seen her! Mrs. Hawkins also was certain on the point. Neither of them was ever allowed in the house, by the way. But Damar Greefe paid them well—and they were satisfied. The identity of the 'nurse' is evident, I think?"

"Perfectly evident. But how was poor Lady Coverly disposed of—and why this elaborate secrecy?"

"Well," replied Gatton slowly, "out of the multitude of notes which I have compiled upon the case, I have worked out a sort of summary, and it amounts to this: The whole series of outrages turns upon something in the financial arrangements of the late Sir Burnham of benefit to the Eurasian doctor. It may be that Damar Greefe had some secret locked up in the Bell House which he could not very well remove, and that the greatest peril he feared was the taking over of the Park property by an heir. I assume he had complete authority over the late Lady Burnham, and his object in concealing her death—for our investigations at Friar's Park have definitely established the fact that no one had resided there for twelve months at least—was clearly this: he hoped to carry on the pretence of attending upon the invalid until—"

"Until there was no heir to the property remaining alive!" I interrupted excitedly. "Exactly, Gatton! That is my own theory, too!"

"We have now received," continued the inspector, "some particulars concerning the circumstances of Roger Coverly's death in Basle. Whilst there was no direct evidence of foul play (and at that time at any rate no reason to suspect it) I am convinced that the local physician who attended him at the hotel, and the specialist who was sent for post-haste from Zurich, were by no means agreed as to the cause of death.

"The symptoms were apparently not unlike those which would be caused by a snake-bite, for instance; but naturally one does not look for poisonous snakes in Switzerland. There was some sort of inflammation of the skin apparently"—he consulted a page of his note-book—"which might have been eczema or something similar, of course, but which according to medical evidence had no apparent connexion with the cause of his death. This was given in the certificate simply as syncope—although there did not appear to be any hereditary cardiac trouble or anything of the kind to account for a young boy of that age dying suddenly of heart failure. And there had been nothing in his life during his sojourn at Basle which would help to clear up the mystery.

"However, no doubt seems to have arisen at the time as you can well understand; nevertheless, I, personally, count the death of Roger Coverly as the first of the outrages to be laid to the credit of Dr. Damar Greefe!"

"The object of the whole thing is still completely dark to me," I declared.

"In a sense it is dark to *me*," replied Gatton; "but considering that the boy died at a time when the health of his father, Sir Burnham, was already giving cause for anxiety, I maintain that he was removed because his inheritance of Friar's Park was feared—by someone. The invitation from Dr. Damar Greefe to Sir Marcus is a very significant piece of evidence, of course; and when we consider that it reached Sir Marcus within a very short time of his return from Russia, the conclusion is obvious.

"He inherited the title on the death of Sir Burnham, and whilst he was on service in Archangel. Being in Russia I conclude that he was not accessible from the Eurasian doctor's point of view. Directly he *became* accessible, this invitation arrived; and it is perfectly clear that the fate intended for him was that which so nearly befell yourself! Remember, I have seen the gun mounted on the tower of Friar's Park, and I assure you it was not placed there yesterday. In short, I have no doubt that it was put there in anticipation of Sir Marcus's visit, and only employed in your case as a sort of afterthought.

"The Red House plot was the next move on the part of the Eurasian, and it succeeded almost faultlessly. The accident at the docks prevented the scheme being carried out in all its details, but it did not entirely dislocate the murderer's arrangements, for it left us with no better clue to his identity than the statuette of the cat."

"The presence of that statuette calls for some explanation, Gatton," I said.

Gatton very carefully lighted his pipe.

"That is true," he admitted, "but I will come to this side of the case later; at present I am summing up the evidence against Damar Greefe—who is certainly the acting partner in this series of outrages against the members of the house of Coverly. Observe the ingenuity of the Red House plot.

"He hoped by this not only to bring about the death of Sir Marcus, but also, by conviction for his murder, the death of the next heir, Mr. Eric Coverly! In fact, so well was his plan conducted, that even now—although we know poor Sir Eric to have been innocent—you will note that he has been unable to establish an alibi even by a full confession of his movements on the night of the crime! In other words, if he had not fallen a victim to the precipitancy of his enemies, to-day his name would be under as black a cloud as ever. It was with the idea of clearing him that I caused those paragraphs to be distributed to the Press, in which I anticipated the existence of such a confession as he had actually made—but, I may add, of one more convincing than that which we heard Miss Merlin read."

"Do you mean, Gatton," I said, looking hard at him,

"that by professing to have established the innocence of Eric Coverly, you hoped to draw down upon him the renewed activities of his enemies?"

Gatton looked rather guilty, but:

"I do admit it!" he said. "Nevertheless he did not fall a victim to this trap which I had laid for him in his own best interests. After all, you must admit that his death was an accident; for he suffered the penalty of your misdeeds."

"My misdeeds!" I cried.

Gatton smiled grimly.

"I say misdeeds," he continued, "although they were not conscious on your part. But it is fairly evident, I think, that whereas the unknown partner of Dr. Damar Greefe was an active enemy of the Coverlys (witness the evidence of 'the voice' and of the cat statuette), it is to Dr. Damar Greefe *himself* that you are indebted for the three attempts on your life; the first two at Upper Crossleys, and the third here in your own home by the simple but deadly expedient of substituting for your own 'phone the duplicate one which previously had been employed so successfully at the Red House! He hoped to remove a dangerous obstacle from his path and a menace to his safety."

"But, my dear Gatton, why should he regard *me* as a menace more deadly than you, for instance?"

"The reason is very plain," answered Gatton. "I don't think he paid you the compliment of regarding your investigations as likely to prove more successful than my own, but I do think that he apprehended danger from the indiscretions of his lady accomplice."

"Do you refer to the woman who visited me at the Abbey Inn?"

"I do," said Gatton shortly, "and to the woman who visited you here and stole the statuette of Bâst! The history of Edward Hines and his predecessor, which you have so admirably summarized, points to the presence in the Upper Crossleys neighbourhood of such a character as we have been seeking ever since your experience here—I refer to the cat-eyes which looked in through the window."

"I begin to see, Gatton," I said slowly.

"With what object this unknown woman visited you at the Abbey Inn I cannot conjecture, but doubtless this would have been revealed had not her visit been interrupted and terminated by the appearance of the Eurasian doctor upon the scene. From your own account she recognized that she had committed an indiscretion by coming there, and of the doctor's anger—which he was quite unable to conceal—you have told me. Note also that the next episode was your being followed by Cassim, the Nubian, undoubtedly with murderous intent. Then, recognizing that he had hopelessly compromised himself, the Eurasian took desperate means to silence you for ever."

"He did!" I said. "And came very near to succeeding. But to return, Gatton, to this problem of the image of Bâst. You see, the figure of a cat was painted upon the case in which Sir Marcus's body was found, and the image of a cat was discovered inside the case. Then, you will not have overlooked the significance of the fact that Edward Hines was the recipient of a present from his unknown friend which also took the form of a gold figure of a cat, and which I found, when I examined it, to be of ancient Egyptian workmanship."

"Right!" said Gatton, and emphatically bringing his open hand down upon the table. "I said at the very beginning of the case, Mr. Addison, that it turned upon the history of this Egyptian goddess, and I think my theory has been substantiated at every point."

"It has, Inspector," I agreed; "but I don't know that the fact enlightens us very much; for it merely indicates that the man whom you declare to be the central figure of the conspiracy is only a secondary figure, and that all we know about the person whom we may regard as the prime mover is that she is a woman—apparently possessing supernormal eyes which glitter in the dark. She is also associated in some way with the figure of Bâst. What is her relation to Dr. Damar Greefe, and in what way is she interested in the destruction of the Coverly family?"

Gatton smoked in silence for a while, staring at me reflectively, then:

"If we knew that, Mr. Addison," he said, "we should know all there is to know about 'the *Oritoga* mystery.' But I think we should have advanced a long step towards this information if we could apprehend the Eurasian. Of course, we have gathered up all the ragged details of the Red House incident: I refer to the carter who delivered

the crate and collected it in the morning, to the caterer
who supplied the supper, and so forth. As I had fully expected, none of the evidence helped us at all."

" 'The voice,'——" I began.

"Exactly! The same 'voice,' beyond a doubt, and the
whole thing worked through the means of district messen-
gers and others, telephonically instructed. No one appeared throughout, Mr. Addison."

"Yet," I said deliberately, "there was one point at which
someone *must* have appeared——"

"Yes," he interrupted; "someone dragged the body out
of that supper-room, down to the garage, and packed it in
the crate."

"You have definitely convinced yourself that the telephone device was practised there?"

"Beyond question. Haven't you seen the exchange
number? That plug where at some time a gas-fitting had
been fixed up in the wall—you remember?—proved on investigation to communicate with an empty room adjoining.
The gas cylinder was placed there, of course, and the telephone in the recess of the supper-room, where, fastened in
by the velvet curtain, anyone using the poison installation
would be suffocated almost immediately."

"Good God, Gatton!" I cried. "It's a horrible business,
and for my own part I have no idea what the next step
should be."

"I'm a bit doubtful myself," admitted Gatton; "but you
know the line of reasoning which has led me to the conclusion that these people possess a base of operations
somewhere in this district. I am having the neighbourhood
scoured pretty thoroughly, and I think it is merely a question of time, now, for us to hem in the wanted man——"

"And the wanted woman!" I added.

We were interrupted by a knock at the study door, and
Coates came in with the evening mail.

"Excuse me, Gatton," I said, for I had observed that
one of the letters was from Isobel.

Eagerly I tore open the envelope—and what I read
struck a sudden chill to my heart. Looking up:

"Gatton!" I cried, "Miss Merlin has received, by post, a
small statuette of Bâst!"

"What!"

"From her brief description I am almost tempted to believe that it is the one which was stolen from here! She is dreadfully frightened, naturally."

The inspector stood up.

"We must see it," he said rapidly, "at once; and we must see the wrapping it came in and the postmark. It is maddening," he burst out angrily, "to think that Dr. Damar Greefe may be somewhere within less than half a mile of us as we sit here now, that we could ring him up if we knew his number; but that even with all the resources of the Criminal Investigation Department at work we may yet be unable to find him! Even an outside suburb like this is a very big place to search, and the job is something like looking for a needle in a haystack!"

My own frame of mind was one of horrible doubt and indecision. I knew not what to do for the best; and Gatton had begun to pace up and down like a caged wild beast. Therefore:

"Fill your pipe," I said wearily. "A lot may depend upon our next move. To make a false one would perhaps be fatal."

Gatton stared at me almost savagely, then threw himself back into the arm-chair from which he had arisen, and was just reaching out for the tobacco-jar which I had pushed before him, when a bell rang. I heard Coates opening the front door, and wondering whom this late visitor could be, I stared questioningly at the inspector.

Came a tap upon the door.

"Come in," I cried.

Coates entered, and standing stiffly in the doorway:

"*Dr. Damar Greefe!*" he announced.

Unmoved, he stood aside; and whilst Gatton and I slowly rose from our chairs in a state of utter stupefaction, the Eurasian doctor entered, and stood, a tall, gaunt figure, towering over the burly form of Coates, in the doorway!

His hawk eyes blazed feverishly, and his face was drawn and haggard, whilst I observed with a sort of horrified wonder that he seemed to be almost too weak to stand. For, as Gatton and I came finally to our feet, he clutched at the edge of a bookcase, but recovered himself, bowed in that stately fashion which immediately translated me in spirit to the strange library in the Bell House, and:

"Gentlemen," he said, and his harsh voice rose scarcely above a whisper, "pray resume your seats. I shall not detain you long."

CHAPTER XXV

STATEMENT OF DAMAR GREEFE, M.D.

The speaker reeled, and seemed about to fall, whereupon Gatton sprang forward and placed an arm-chair, which he himself had occupied, for Dr. Damar Greefe. The latter inclined his head in acknowledgment, and sank down weakly, clutching at both arms of the chair.

For my own part, I had not yet recovered power of speech, but:

"Dr. Damar Greefe," said the inspector, closely watching the man who sat there collapsed in the chair, "I arrest you on a charge of murder. I have to warn you that anything you now say will be used in evidence against you."

The Eurasian exerted a supreme effort, straightening his gaunt body and fixing the gaze of those hawk eyes upon Inspector Gatton. When he spoke, his harsh voice had gained strength and his manner was imperious.

"Detective-Inspector Gatton," he replied, "you do no more than your duty. I have come here only with the utmost difficulty in my weak state. Therefore, you need apprehend no attempt at escape on my part. I have come with a purpose. This purpose I shall fulfil, after which"—he shrugged his square shoulders—"I shall be at your service."

"Very good," said Gatton shortly, but I noted that his face was flushed in a way which betokened repressed excitement.

Giving me a significant glance, he went out to the anteroom, and:

"Sydenham 1448," I heard him call.

Damar Greefe closed his eyes and lay back in the chair, and a moment later:

"Hallo!" said Gatton. "Detective-Inspector Gatton, C.I.D., speaking from Willow Cottage, College Road. Send two men in a cab here at once to remove a prisoner. . . . Right! Good-bye."

He came in again, and closing the door behind him, stood staring at Damar Greefe in a sort of wonderment. The Eurasian wearily opened his eyes and looked slowly from side to side. Then:

"Pray be seated, Inspector Gatton," he said. "I have a communication to make."

Gatton, with never a word, drew up a chair and sat down.

"I do not desire to be interrupted," continued Damar Greefe, "until my communication is finished. You understand? It will not be repeated."

"I am afraid," murmured Gatton drily, "it will have to be."

The Eurasian fully opened his glittering black eyes, and fixing them upon the speaker:

"It will not be repeated," he said harshly. "If I am misunderstood, inform me."

His peremptory manner in the circumstances was extraordinary—uncanny. As I had perceived in the first hour of our meeting, Dr. Damar Greefe was a man possessing tremendous force of character and a pride of intellect which clearly rendered him indifferent even to retribution.

"This point being settled," he continued, "be good enough, Inspector Gatton and"—he turned his eyes in my direction—"Mr. Addison, to give me your undivided attention."

His manner was that of a lecturer—of a lecturer who takes it for granted that his discourse is above the heads of his audience; but when I say that the statement now made by this strange and terrible man held Gatton and me spellbound I say no more than the truth. Wearily, and more often than not having his eyes closed, Dr. Damar Greefe commenced to unfold a story of nameless horrors, and save that his harsh voice grew ever weaker and weaker, he displayed not the slightest trace of emotion throughout his appalling revelations.

"I am informing you," he said, "of these facts concerning my inquiries in the realm of teratology and the subjoined province of animism, because I know that my life-work upon this subject can never now be completed. It having been necessary for me to destroy my papers and those specimens which, at hideous cost, I had accumulated during twenty years of travel through some of the most barbaric, as well as the most civilized, parts of the world, this present brief verbal account of the most important inquiry of all shall alone survive me. You are privileged. Therefore listen:

"'Two important facts contributed to my choice of a special study: the social ostracism which very early in my professional career I found to be my lot; and the fact that in myself I afforded a living example of the *hybrid*. It has been said, and not untruly, that the Eurasian hates his father and scorns his mother. Certainly, this unnatural passion is reciprocated by the parent stock, for the Eurasian is barely acknowledged by his dark brethren and hardly tolerated by the white.

"In spite of my qualifications—I am a Doctor of Medicine, a Master of Arts, and hold other degrees of Leipzig, the Sorbonne, and elsewhere—I recognized very early in my career that ordinary practise was impossible for me. I therefore turned my attention to the special study of embryology, as I fortunately possessed sufficient private means to enable me—by careful living—to dispense with the usual proceeds of my profession.

"In short, I hoped to triumph over my hereditary handicap and to build for myself a reputation which should rise above the petty disabilities of caste, and place my name upon a level with those of Haeckel, Weismann, Wallace, Focke, and the other great students who have helped to advance our knowledge of the science of evolution.

"I early turned my attention to the traditions associated with the *Cynocephalus hamadryas,* or Sacred Baboon of Abyssinia. I took up my quarters on the banks of the Hawash and succeeded in ingratiating myself with the Amharûn. The result of my sojourn amongst these strange people is embodied in my work, 'The Ape-Men of Shoa.'

"This work is unpublished and may never see the light; but briefly I may state that the Amharûn are a Semitic tribe allied to the Falashas, and have been settled for many generations in this southern province of Abyssinia. Claiming descent from Menelek, son of Suleyman and the Queen of Sheba, they have always been regarded as unclean pariahs. In part, this is due to their bestial custom of eating meat cut from living animals, but it is more particularly attributable to the periodical appearance among them of these *cynocephalytes,* or man apes, which form the subject of my work.

"My close inquiries into the physiological history of these monstrosities were only conducted with the utmost difficulty. In the first place, I found that it was customary among the Amharûn to slay the creatures at birth, but in those rare cases of survival the *cynocephalytes* were banished from the community and were compelled to lead a wild life, subsisting as best they might in the foot-hills of the desolate mountain region.

"Thus, in the first place these creatures were difficult of access; in the second place, they readily contracted tuberculosis, even in that warm, dry climate; and in the third place their ferocity rendered them more formidable to approach than any tiger in its lair. I may add here that this predisposition to pulmonary disease is (and this I have definitely established) a characteristic of all mammalian hybrids.

"Nevertheless, my studies were by no means unfruitful, since they resulted in a triumphant vindication of my theory, which, contrary to that universally received, and more closely allied to the 'exploded' Mendel's Law, ascribed the appearance of such monsters not to any strict physiological process, but to a hitherto unclassified law of embryology which I had hoped would one day take its place in science under my name.

"Armed with the results of my Abyssinian inquiry, I next proceeded to Syria, for among certain desert tribes I hoped to find further evidence to support my theory. In short, in the Arabic tradition of the jackal-man (which is allied to that mediæval and universal belief in the werewolf or *loup-garou*) and in the Indian myth of the woman who, possessing an ordinary human form by day, assumes that of a tigress by night, I thought I detected a profound truth.

"Since my life-work is destroyed, I am egotist enough to desire that credit for it should not accrue to another. I do not propose, therefore, more than lightly to touch upon the Damar Greefe Law, but I may say that in its essentials it is this:

"Such strange hybrids do actually occur periodically, and in rare cases survive; but their animal proclivities, which are physically demonstrable, and the possession of certain animal attributes (as the furry body of the *cynocephalyte*, the claws and teeth of the jackal-man, etc.) are *physical* reflections of a *mental* process taking place in the female parent."

He glared at me wildly, as if anticipating contradiction, but Gatton and I remaining silent:

"There is no physical association," he continued, "between the hybrid and that creature whose qualities and peculiarities he seemingly inherits. I have proved by a long series of elaborate experiments that a *true* hybrid of this description is a physiological impossibility. But that a *false* hybrid such as I have indicated may appear is a fact which does not rest solely upon my studies amongst the Amharûn, nor upon my subsequent inquiries throughout Assyria, Somaliland, and the middle valleys of the Yellow River."

He paused, and suddenly turning a glance of the hawk-like eyes upon me:

"As an explorer of the Dark Continent, Mr. Addison," he said, "and also, if I mistake not, something of an Orientalist, the significance of this itinerary may possibly be apparent to you. But I waste time:

"The discovery which triumphantly crowned my life's work by what some may deem poetic justice was destined also to destroy it. This brings me to the matter which has led to my presence here to-night. My preceding remarks were a necessary foreword. I come to the year 1902, when I was established in Cairo, whither I had conveyed the results of the labour of many years, and where I had taken up my quarters in a large native house not twenty yards from the Bâb-es-Zuwêla."

Gatton stirred restlessly in his chair, and my own curiosity knew no bounds.

"My inquiries at this time had nearly exhausted my always slender financial resources, and the proceeds of a small practice which I succeeded in establishing (exclusively amongst the extensive half-caste colony resident in this neighbourhood) proved a welcome addition to my income. It was due to the fact that at this time I was an active practitioner that I came in touch with the most perfect and notable example of a *psycho-hybrid* which I had ever encountered—indeed which, so far as I am aware, has ever appeared."

He paused again, as if overcome with faintness, and in anticipation of what was to come, I could scarcely contain myself, when:

"At this time," he resumed, in a yet lower voice, "and indeed until quite recently, there were but few reliable European medical men in Cairo, and during the summer of 1902 an outbreak of cholera temporarily depleted their already scanty ranks. It happened, then, that one night, whilst I sat in the huge, lofty room, once the principal harem apartment of the house, which I had appropriated as a study, Cassim, my Nubian servant, communicated to me (by means of a sign-language which I had taught him) some startling news. My immediate presence was desired at the residence of Sir Burnham Coverly, then newly appointed to a Government office, and who, with his wife, had only arrived in the country some few months earlier.

"I thought I knew the nature of the services required of me; but my employment by this typical English aristocrat, hide-bound with caste traditions as he could not fail to be, since he had spent five years of his official life in India, surprised me very greatly. I was later to learn that the services of no other medical man (or of no medical man so highly qualified as myself) were available; but even had I known this at the time I should have put my pride in my pocket, and for this reason:

"I had learned from a native acquaintance of a certain occurrence which had taken place on the very day of the baronet's arrival in Egypt; and it led me to look for a particular manifestation—in fact, I will boldly declare, since science is admittedly a callous mistress, that it had led me to *hope* for this manifestation, however unpleasant it might prove for those intimately concerned. Accordingly, having made suitable preparation, I accompanied Sir Burnham's servant back to the residence of the baronet—"

I heard the door-bell ring, and I heard Coates's regular tread as he proceeded along the passage. There was a brief, muttered colloquy, a rap on the study door, and Coates entered.

"A sergeant of police and a constable, sir, to see Inspector Gatton!"

Damar Greefe raised his thin, yellow hand. His voice, when next he spoke, exhibited no trace of emotion.

"Let them be told to wait," he said. "I have not finished."

It was wildly bizarre, that scene in my study, with the dignified white-haired Eurasian doctor, palpably labouring against some deathly sickness, sitting there unperturbed, his brilliant, perverted intellect holding him aloof from the ordinary things of life, whilst those who came to hale him to a felon's cell waited in the ante-room!

I glanced swiftly at Gatton, and he nodded impatiently.

"Let them stay in the dining-room, Coates," I said. "Make them comfortable."

"Very good, sir."

Unmoved, Coates withdrew, and I saw Gatton glance at his watch. Throughout the latter part of his strange narrative, neither Gatton nor I interrupted the narrator, therefore, I give his story, so far as I remember it, in his own words. He no longer addressed either of us directly; he seemed, indeed, to be thinking aloud.

CHAPTER XXVI

STATEMENT OF DAMAR GREEFE, M.D.
(Continued)

As I walked along through the deserted native streets—for the hour was late—I reviewed mentally the circumstances of that affair already several months old to which I have referred. Since it proved to have a very important bearing upon my own life, and unfortunately upon the lives of many others, I will briefly recount it here.

Sir Burnham and Lady Coverly, having arrived at Port Said, were proceeding by rail to Cairo when an accident farther up the line necessitated their breaking their journey at Zagazig.

Now, for a time in the spring of the previous year, I had devoted much labour to an inquiry in this place, which stands, of course, roughly upon the site of the ancient Egyptian city of *Bubastis*. In those myths, or so-called myths, of the ancient Egyptian religion which represented the various attributes of man in the guises of animals, I had perceived a nucleus of wisdom pointing to the possibility that the law which I had so laboriously established might have been known to the early Egyptian priesthood. Indeed, I was partly induced to inquire into the myths of Bâst, the cat-headed goddess to whom of old this town was dedicated, by the following two things: first, a chance reference in the pages of Herodotus; and, second, a persistent superstition that during a certain season of the year, *psycho-hybrids* occurred in this town.

By dint of close research I discovered that the date favoured by the inhabitants of Zagazig, as that upon which such creatures were born there, corresponded very closely with the Sothic month formerly sacred to Bâst, the titulary goddess of the place; corresponded, in short, with the ancient Feast of Bâst.

My inquiries at the time, however, proved futile, and beyond the fact that the town was remarkable for a singular number of semi-wild cats, I discovered nothing to support my theory. However, as I have already stated, a native acquaintance there, a very learned Moslem, to whom I had imparted during my residence some idea of the nature of my studies, sent me a long communication containing particulars of the event which had befallen Lady Coverly during her one-night's sojourn in Zagazig.

Briefly, she had learned from a native attached to the the one possible hotel which the town boasted, of the tradition associated with the place. Some other member of the party—for quite a large company had been detained in Zagazig by the mishap—unwisely pointed out to her that the favoured date was that upon which they had arrived in the town.

Nothing might have resulted from this; but by a strange fatality (or because of the operation of some unsuspected law understood by the ancients, but misapprehended to-day) the matter was sealed in a very extraordinary fashion.

Lady Coverly's room opened upon a balcony, and during the night one of those huge cats of the kind which I had observed myself to infest the neighbourhood, gained access to this balcony. Since the appearance of the creature produced so singular and disastrous an effect, it must certainly have been an unusually large specimen of its kind. I may add that, according to my Moslem friend—who, although a man of great culture, was soaked in the traditions of his religion—it was none other than a member of the *ginn,* an *efreet,* or evil spirit, and not a cat of flesh and blood, which appeared to Lady Coverly. I leave each to choose his own explanation; but let it suffice that Lady Coverly was awakened some time during the night by the appearance at her bedside of this gaunt and hungry-eyed creature. The result was an illness of a kind very dangerous to one in her delicate state of health.

Reflecting, then, upon these matters, I presently came to the official residence of Sir Burnham Coverly, and my expectations regarding the nature of the case were realized. . . .*

*   *   *   *   *

My house in the narrow street so near to the Bâb-es-Zuwêla and the minarets of Muayyâd was admirably adapted for my new purpose. For here in the very heart of native Cairo, with my great house (which had been built, as are all Oriental houses, to guard secrets) I was safe from unwelcome intrusion as one upon a desert island, whilst at the same time I was denied none of the conveniences and facilities of civilization.

Lady Coverly, then, never set eyes upon her firstborn, and Sir Burnham, who did, readily reconciled himself to the loss of such a daughter. The announcement which should have appeared joyfully under the press-heading, "Births," was unobtrusively inserted under "Deaths," and Sir Burnham being fortunately far from the haunts of the social paragraph writers, this unfortunate event aroused comparatively little comment in the English journals; beyond one or two formal condolences, it passed unnoticed.

The fever of research at last had led me into my first definite crime against society—if so it can be called. I had rescued alive the most perfect example of a *psycho-hybrid* with which throughout my extensive special inquiries I had ever come in contact. Lady Coverly never knew her un-

---

* Part of the statement which immediately followed being of a purely technical nature, is omitted here.

natural child, and Sir Burnham—as well as the old family
nurse who had accompanied them out from England—
never doubted that it had died in the hour of birth.

I set to work with enthusiasm upon my last and greatest
experiment.

To a half-caste woman upon whom I knew I could rely
—for she was deeply indebted to me—I entrusted the fos-
tering of the infant hybrid. I personally supervised every
detail of the secret nursery, Cassim procuring for me everything necessary for the rearing of this delicate and frag-
ile creature.

Over the early years of her life I will hasten. On three
occasions I despaired of preserving her existence, which,
from the beginning, had hung by a thread. The first crisis
came when she was only four months old, the second on
the occasion of her fourth birthday, the third (most
serious of all) when she was eleven, at which age she had
become a woman in the Oriental sense and was physically
and mentally comparable with an ordinary European girl
of nineteen or twenty.

With what scientific ardour did I study her development,
noting how the *cat* traits at certain periods (corresponding
to the Feast of Bâst) proclaimed themselves above the
human traits, whilst at other times the psychic-felinism
sank into a sort of sub-conscious quietude, leaving the subject almost a normal woman. Of the physical reflections
which were the visible evidence of her hybrid mentality I
have already spoken at length [*this refers to a portion of
the statement which has been deleted.*] She invariably
wore gloves out of doors and a veil to conceal the *cha-
toyant* eyes. She could, as I have explained, see as well in
the dark as in daylight, and her agility was phenomenal, as
was her power of climbing. Having her hands and feet bare,
I have repeatedly seen her climb to the top platform of the
ivy-clad tower of Friar's Park.

At the age of eleven, then, I recognized that the balance
of character was definitely established, and that the two
outstanding characteristics of the subject were—firstly (a
hereditary trait of the Coverlys), an intense pride of race
and a fierce jealousy of any infringement upon what she
regarded as prerogatives of birth; secondly, a susceptibility
to sudden infatuations which invariably terminated in a
mood of ferocious cruelty.

To one unacquainted with the Orient, thus to speak of this girl—in years a mere child—as one speaks of a mature woman, would seem strange, if not unnatural; but in the East, of course, at the age of ten a girl is counted marriageable; at the age of fourteen she is not infrequently the devoted mother of a family.

Significantly—from the point of view of the Damar Greefe Law—my ward had grown up, not as English girls grow, but, like the Easterns, as the hot-house flower grows. The point has intense interest for the scientist. At the age of twelve she was a tall, slender woman, beautifully formed, and with a natural elegance and taste which came from the Coverly stock, or possibly from her mother's side.

During eleven months of every year it would have been possible—although I considered it undesirable—for her to have appeared in public unveiled. She possessed features of perfect *Ancient Egyptian regularity*. I emphasize the point. Her eyes, during the day, were those of a handsome native woman—almond-shaped and of a wonderful amber colour. At night they appeared green.

Of her fingers, toes, and the peculiar formation of certain teeth I have spoken at length [*another reference to a deleted passage*]. I will deal, now, with those manifestations which proclaimed themselves during the Sothic month of each year formerly associated with the Feast of Bâst.

At such times, which I always dreaded—and with good cause—her innate love of admiration became so excessive as to approach nearly to mania. She hungered for homage, for praise—I had almost said for adoration.

What I may term, for convenience, the *psychic* side of her hybrid mentality, at these periods undoubtedly bordered closely upon true insanity; and learning from the Eurasian nurse to whom I have referred the whole history of her birth, my charge, to whom I had given the name of Nahémah (students will recognize its significance), began to display even more marked evidence of a sort of monomania. Bâst, the cat-goddess, became an obsession with her, and she finally conceived the idea that the attributes of that mystical and partly-understood deity were active within her: that she was Bâst, re-born. And, certainly, during one month of every year, her condition closely resembled

that which was termed in the Middle Ages "possession."
At such times, too (a phenomenon with which I have dealt
at length in my work on the subject), she evinced an antipathy towards the whole of the *canine* species which was
reciprocated in a singular way. Thus, when, contrary to
my express orders, she has wandered abroad during the
Sothic period, I have been enabled to trace her movements
by the progressive howling of dogs.

Since I had enjoined the nurse to be silent upon all
things bearing upon Nahémah's birth, I was enraged at this
breach of faith, and sent the woman away. But a new situation had been created which I found myself called upon
immediately to face.

Nahémah demanded news of her family. As I have
made sufficiently evident, it was often difficult, if not impossible, to thwart the desires of my protégée. To condense into a few words a matter which occasioned me long
and anxious thought, I may say that I made the necessary
arrangements for quitting the house near to the Mosque of
Muayyâd which had been my home for fifteen years.

I recognized the danger of Nahémah's traveling in the
ordinary way, and she performed the journey to England
in the character of an invalid under my professional care.
Equally, residence at any public establishment was out of
the question, and although I found myself compelled for a
time to court discovery by lodging Nahémah in a private
suite in an obscure hotel, I hastened to seek a house in
some quiet suburb which should reproduce as nearly as
possible the advantages of my abode in Cairo.

Such a house I discovered after about a week of feverish
questing (for apart from the ordinary dangers of discovery
to which my protégée was subject, her proclivity for ad-
ventures at the most unseasonable times greatly enhanced
the danger which I apprehended). Judge, then, of my sat-
isfaction when I succeeded in obtaining the lease of a
small villa—indeed, I might almost term it a bungalow—in
one of those odd survivals of less crowded days which are
yet counted suburbs or parts of Greater London.

This house stood alone in some two acres of ground,
and because of its lack of modern conveniences and the
comparative inaccessibility of its position, my application
was eagerly entertained by the agent interested in the leasing of the property. One week later I entered into posses-

sion, Cassim, Nahémah and myself comprising the entire household. Much of my valuable—indeed, I may say, unique—collection I had been compelled to store; for my new quarters lacked the necessary space for the purpose. But although I was unaware of the fact at the time, I was not destined to be long deprived of a suitable home for the records of my life's work.

Nahémah's demand for some understanding between herself and her family grew daily more insistent; but I might have continued to oppose opposition to her wishes had it not been for the fact that by this time my slender resources were almost exhausted.

It suddenly became evident to me that I held in my hand an instrument whereby I might force Sir Burnham Coverly to finance the new experiments upon which I had entered at this time with all the enthusiasm that a love for science inspires in the student! You may judge me unscrupulous, but the wheel of progress is at least as unrelenting. It was not, however, without much searching self-analysis that one day I presented myself before Sir Burnham Coverly at Friar's Park.

If I had had any scruples prior to that visit they were instantly dispelled by the manner of my reception. Forgetful of the service which (as he believed) I had done him in the past, Sir Burnham allowed all the prejudice of the Anglo-Indian to reveal itself in his first greeting.

Because I am a Eurasian, the worst traits which attach to such a parentage—and of which I am only too painfully conscious—revealed themselves in me. My heart hardened towards this man whose treatment of an intellectual superior was so icily, so offensively condescending. Knowing that I had it in my power to deal him a blow from which he might never recover, I toyed with him for a time; and, his manner growing momentarily more objectionable, I rejoiced to know that his very life and career were in my keeping.

His son, Roger Coverly, at that time a boy only about nine years old, as the prospective heir to Friar's Park, was cherished as an only child is always cherished in these circumstances. I pictured to myself the meeting of brother and sister! Yes; because of the refined and deliberate cruelty which Sir Burnham displayed towards myself, I retaliated with a poisoned blade. Having led the conversation in the direction of the heir, I threw away the scabbard of pretence—I launched my challenge.

Never shall I forget Sir Burnham's change of countenance. He tottered, a stricken man. With a sentence of ten words I had won my battle. Upon the details of the arrangement which presently was come to between us, I need not linger. For this statement is intended, not as a defence—for what I have done I pay the price—but as a resumé of this crowning inquiry of my scientific career.

*   *   *   *   *

At this point the speaker was seized with an alarming spasm of pain. His black eyes opened widely and his face became contorted with agony.

I sprang to his assistance; for, villain self-confessed though he was, humanity would not allow of any man's witnessing unmoved such paroxysms in a fellow creature.

But, ere I could reach his side, Damar Greefe, clenching his teeth and clutching at the chair-arms so that his knuckles gleamed in the lamplight like white marbles, turned his glance upon me, and:

"Be seated, sir," he whispered. "I desire you to be seated."

Something repellent, yet something powerful, there was in word and glance. Gatton, who also had sprung forward, hesitated. Damar Greefe raised one hand from the chair-arm and waved to us to return to our chairs. Exchanging wondering glances, we both obeyed.

Thereupon, the Eurasian doctor, whose high, bony forehead was dewed with a deathly perspiration, and whose hawk-face had assumed an indescribable leaden hue, drew from his pocket a heavy gold watch (his every movement intently followed by the alert inspector), and consulted it. His hand shook wildly as he returned the timepiece to its place. Then:

"I must hasten," he said hoarsely. "I have—only nineteen minutes. . . ."

Gatton looked at me questioningly, but I could only shake my head. The significance of the Eurasian's words escaped me entirely; but as Damar Greefe began, slowly and with palpable effort, to speak again, I saw a queer expression stealing over the face of the watchful Gatton.

CHAPTER XXVII

STATEMENT OF DAMAR GREEFE, M.D.
(Concluded)

A month later I found myself installed at the Bell House, a property belonging to the Friar's Park estate, and in the commodious apartments of this establishment I had ample room for the accommodation of my library and my priceless specimens. Nahémah was likewise an inmate of the Bell House; but recognizing the precarious nature of my tenure, I had taken the precaution of retaining the suburban villa to which I have already referred, its modest rental proving no tax upon my greatly increased resources.

Blackmail, I hear you exclaim! And so, if you wish, you may construe my behaviour, since I reply, "Science first, science last!" To have been deprived of the means to pursue my experiments at this time would have been, I believed, to impoverish the world. For not even science could reveal to me that my life's work was destined to perish amid the ashes of the Bell House.

My studies had temporarily led me into a bypath, and apprehending that a great international struggle was imminent, I had turned my investigations in a new direction. My great work, whose publication would have shattered so many scientific idols, was complete. The life history of Nahémah had crowned my inquiries into the embryology, physiology, and psychology of *psycho-hybrids*. In fact, the presence of my strange protégée promised to become something of an incubus. Later, I was to realize that she was an ever-present means of renewing those funds which the costly character of my new studies absorbed at rather an alarming rate. Perhaps I neglected my self-imposed task of studying the mental and physical development of Nahémah; for I must admit that, lost in my new work, I presently awakened to the fact that she had outgrown the control which I had formerly exercised over her.

There were unpleasant episodes. For example, in spite

of those precautions which I adopted, and of the ceaseless
vigilance of Cassim, the existence of a female inmate of
the Bell House was soon a popular scandal through Upper
Crossleys. For this I cared nothing; but far more perturb-
ing was Nahémah's behaviour on the occasion of a certain
visit of Sir Burnham's legal adviser to Friar's Park.

In some way she secretly gained admission to the house
(the episode occurred during that Sothic month whose annual coming I had learned to dread). Sir Burnham actually saw her in the chapel. He sent a messenger post-haste to
the Bell House, and I finally discovered Nahémah in hid-
ing and insisted upon her immediate return. This was only
one of several instances of her perverse behaviour, which
truly seemed to be inspired by some demon bent upon the
destruction of both of us.

Her mental activity was extraordinary, and, unknown to
me, she had followed my new researches with that intellectual ardour which she directly inherited from the Coverlys. Her ferocious jealousy of any infringement upon those
family rights denied her by her father had also developed,
it seemed; and one night, shortly after the scene to which I
have referred, entering my study, she placed before me a
proposal to which I listened with absolute horror.

I should explain that Sir Burnham, placing the repute of
his house and that of his heir above all other consider-
ations (with one possible exception: the necessity for concealing the appalling truth from his wife) had consented to
make arrangements for the support of Nahémah on the
understanding that her existence was to remain a profound
secret from the world. It was upon this understanding that
I leased the Bell House. And although, in certain wild indiscretions I had recognized in Nahémah the symptoms of
revolt against such a monastic existence, because of absorption in my new studies I had not realized how deep
was her resentment of this enforced anonymity. Certainly
I had never grasped the power and the depth of her hatred
of her brother, Roger Coverly.

Now, on this fateful night, in one of the semi-insane
outbursts which I had learned to dread, she poured out her
loathing and detestation of her brother. She was a Coverly
(such was the gist of her plaint) and the doors of Friar's
Park were closed to her; the world knew nothing of her
existence. In the event of the death of Sir Burnham, then

Roger would inherit the property, and complete disaster would be our lot.

To condense the purport of her demand, it was this: that I should test the efficacy of my new discovery by removing this objectionable obstacle from her path!

Of my subsequent behaviour I offer no defence. I am not prepared to admit that I was forced into action by the forceful personality of my protégée; in fact, I state emphatically that a chance interview with the heir during one of his visits to Friar's Park led me to regard the matter in a new light and from a standpoint almost identical with that of Nahémah.

How warning was conveyed to Sir Burnham I know not, unless by some indiscretion of Nahémah; but, instead of returning to the public school from which he had come to Friar's Park, Roger Coverly was sent abroad in haste, accompanied by a private tutor. The date of his departure corresponded with that which I associate with the beginning of my downfall.

Nahémah threatened to present herself to her mother, and painfully aware that such a course (which, nevertheless, I recognized her to be quite capable of adopting) would spell disaster, I fell in with her wishes. Two months later we were established—Nahémah, Cassim, and I—within two miles of the new residence of Roger Coverly and his tutor in Basle.

The circumstances attendant upon the death of Roger Coverly have hitherto been veiled in obscurity, and although Sir Burnham suspected the truth, in the first place he had no evidence, and in the second place, because of the existence of Nahémah, I knew that he dared not attempt to prove it.

Briefly, I had perfected that Chinese poison called in the northern provinces *hlangkûna.* By a series of dangerous experiments I had convinced myself that it was almost identical with *contarella,* the preparation made notorious by the Borgia family. Therefore I concluded that *contarella* came to Rome from the East, possibly via Palestine. Inoculating with *hlangkûna,* I found, produced death in two hours (*contarella,* one hour and forty-five minutes), leaving no trace by which the means employed could be discovered. Self-inoculation by the subject was the method which I adopted—and which Cæsar Borgia had adopted before me, so that no chain of evidence existed.

All that was necessary was for a scarf, a collar, or other article of apparel coming in direct contact with the skin of the subject, to be placed in my possession. (A glove was the Borgias' favourite medium.) It was painted with *hlangkûna* and replaced. When worn, an intense irritation was produced and a cutaneous eruption which, if scratched even very lightly, resulted in a puncture of the skin sufficient to allow the inimical elements of the poison to obtain access to the system of the subject.

I do not propose to enter into details, but so it was that Rover Coverly died. Following a brief sojourn abroad, we presently returned again to the Bell House.

This gratification of her bloodthirsty desires had done no more than to whet the feline appetite of Nahémah, and she forced me to impose new and almost insupportable conditions upon Sir Burnham, with the result, as is known, that from being a very wealthy man he became an impoverished one.

I even held a mortgage on Friar's Park on behalf of Nahémah; for by this time I had fully recognized the fact that, like a second Frankenstein, I had raised up a monster which sooner or later must devour me.

Her indiscretions threatened daily to result in exposure, and after the death of Sir Burnham, which occurred a short time later, these increased in number and audacity. The dying baronet had impressed upon his wife the necessity of following my guidance in all things. Undoubtedly he died hoping that Lady Coverly might live out her days in ignorance of the grim secret of the Bell House. This dying wish of his was gratified. The loss of her son, so closely followed by that of her husband, prostrated Lady Coverly in a mental illness from which she never recovered, although I exercised all my skill in an endeavour to restore her reason. She spent the remainder of her days in a semi-comatose state which so closely resembled death that to this present moment I do not know the exact hour at which dissolution took place.

In the man Hawkins, once a gamekeeper of Sir Burnham's, I found an instrument ready to my hand. I closed the Park to the public and took all those precautions for preserving my secret which prudence dictated: this at the cost of a reputation in Upper Crossleys which few men would have survived, but which troubled me not at all, since it left me undisturbed to those studies which to me were everything.

The death of Sir Burnham, however, had raised a new danger; for in the person of Sir Marcus Coverly, the heir, I perceived a formidable enemy, who, because of his wealth, might redeem Friar's Park, and, because of the fact that he belonged to a cadet line, might care nothing for the skeleton in Sir Burnham's cupboard.

I have said that science is callous, and I admit that it needed little prompting from Nahémah to urge me to take the next step. It is worthy of note, however, from a scientific point of view, that whilst I was prompted by motives of expediency, she was actuated solely by a lust to destroy everything that bore the name of Coverly.

My experiments for some time past had been directed to the discovery of new instruments of warfare. Particularly, I had addressed myself to the preparation of a *gas* which should possess the peculiar properties of *hlangkûna,* and by inhalation affect the lung tissues, thus producing instantaneous results. In this I had succeeded a short time prior to Sir Burnham's death, and one of the future belligerents had approached me.

For the purpose of carrying out experiments, a specially designed gun was brought from Essen and installed in a secluded part of the Park. Artillery specialists carried out a number of tests with shells of various patterns; but because I bluntly declined to divulge the formula for the making of "L.K. Vapour" (so I had named it) until substantial guarantees were given, negotiations were broken off. I retained, however, the model howitzer, as well as a number of special light shells. The gun was one of extraordinary accuracy, and it was possible, given suitable weather conditions, mechanically to train it upon a given target and without any preliminary "searching" to score a certain hit.

I caused the piece to be mounted on the top platform of the tower at Friar's Park, and having completed those mathematical calculations with the result of which Mr. Addison has since become familiar, I awaited the return of the new baronet from Russia. Shortly after his arrival, I invited him to visit Upper Crossleys.

He refused—in terms which provoked an outburst on

Nahémah's part more violent than I had ever witnessed; but on his final return to England she made it her business closely to study his habits and movements. She sought, feverishly, for some pregnable point of attack. *Hlangkûna* was tried three times—and three times failed. It was the distorted genius of Nahémah, however, which finally dictated a new line of action. She learned that Sir Marcus was paying attention to Isobel Merlin, the fiancée of Eric Coverly (who in the event of Sir Marcus's death would inherit the title).

Nahémah propounded to me a theory so strange and so novel, that I was lost in admiration of that brilliant intellect which, partly inherited from her forbears, was stimulated and brightened by a cat-like cunning which belonged to the other side of her hybrid personality.

In that district where my suburban villa was situated there were several other isolated establishments which their owners experienced some difficulty in leasing; and one of these—namely, the Red House—particularly suited the purpose which Nahémah had in view. The extensive resources now at my disposal enabled me to dispense with the usual formalities which beset the lessee and to obtain possession of the Red House without even appearing in person.

The deeper to complicate the issue, Nahémah carried out the whole of the negotiations over the telephone, and hers was the "voice" afterwards rendered notorious by the Press, which issued the directions culminating in the death of Marcus Coverly.

I recognize that the inquiries of the police have placed in your possession many particulars respecting this matter, so that I will not repeat them here, but will content myself with explaining the nature of the device employed. In this case, for the removal of the subject, I had obtained possession of an old telephone and had adjusted it to meet my requirements.

In a recess of the room which I caused Sir Marcus Coverly to visit at the Red House, I placed this duplicate telephone; the false cable communicating with the instrument was attached to a plug in the wall above, but communicated with a gas cylinder in the adjoining room. In short, what appeared to be cable was in reality tubing, and the act of taking the receiver from the hook released through the mouthpiece a sufficient quantity of L.K. Vapour to have asphyxiated a dozen men.

In order to ensure the subject's receiving the benefit of the whole discharge, I had caused a very heavy curtain to be draped in this recess, which thus became a rough gas-chamber. Following the first discharge, the subject would fall to the floor and the gas being a heavy one, he would there receive his *quietus*.

The only detail which occasioned much thought was that of the bell by which Sir Marcus should be summoned to this prepared telephone; for it formed no part of the plan for myself to appear anywhere in the neighbourhood at the time of the experiment. I was, of course, compelled to pay a secret visit to the Red House for the purpose of installing the telephone device, and at the same time I installed the bell. This was worked from a small storage battery, and I arranged that by the opening of the garage door the bell would be put in motion, and by the closing of the door at the end of the same building the ringing would cease.

A simple contrivance screwed to both doors made this possible, but I know not by whose hand the ringing would have been accomplished if it had not been for one of those brilliant suggestions of Nahémah's, which hovered between the domain of genius and that of fiendishness.

She proposed that she should ring up the local police depôt and ask the constable on that beat to lock the garage, thus making him the direct instrument for the removal of Sir Marcus!

I knew, since I myself had been a resident in this district, that a constable patrolled College Road at an hour roughly corresponding with that at which it was proposed to cause Sir Marcus to visit the Red House; and because all strategy is based upon the clock, a brief survey of the facts convinced me that Nahémah's plan was feasible.

Thus it was Police-Constable Bolton, whose evidence has appeared in the Press, who actually killed Sir Marcus Coverly! I come now to the dangerous attitude adopted by Nahémah immediately after that event.

We had had a case of suitable dimensions made for containing the body, and had had it delivered at the Red House garage, where it was received by a district messenger instructed for the purpose. Upon me devolved the task of carrying the body from the supper-room to the garage —a task which I performed shortly after the departure of Police-Constable Bolton. I packed the body, removed the telephone and also all traces of the bell-device.

The same carter had instructions to call for the case in the morning, and the garage door was left open to enable him to collect it. In short, except for these two essential visits, one before and one after the experiment, there was no occasion for myself or Nahémah to appear in the neighbourhood of the Red House.

But that cat-like spirit of impish mischief which possessed her at this season (and especially at night), together with an almost insane joy which she took in gloating over the destruction of her cousin, had led her, contrary to my special injunctions, to haunt the vicinity on the evening of the experiment. Thus, she not only witnessed the arrival of the doomed man, but also saw the constable perform the duty imposed upon him. This might have mattered little, had it not been for the presence of Mr. Addison, whom an unkind fate at this juncture involved in the matter.

For Mr. Addison Nahémah conceived one of those sudden and violent infatuations which characterized the feline element of her complex mentality. Unknown to me, Nahémah followed Mr. Addison to his home in the neighbourhood, and, indeed, was actually seen by him, I believe, on two occasions. Thus far all might yet have been well; but when later I entered the Red House to carry out the only dangerous part of the scheme, to my consternation Nahémah insisted upon accompanying me.

Prompted by that destructive devil which sometimes possessed her, she not only (unknown to me) painted a figure of a cat upon the crate, but also she placed an image of Bâst in the box with the dead man!

The premature discovery of Sir Marcus, owing to the accident at the docks, prevented the plan being carried out in all its details; but when, through certain rumours which began to creep into the Press, I learned of the presence of the statuette, I began to realize the dangerous position in which I was placed and the handicap of such an accomplice.

As a result of the scene which ensued, Nahémah, still under the worst influence of her hybrid disposition, openly visited Mr. Addison and recovered the image of Bâst! This she did in circumstances which hopelessly compromised both of us, since they revealed in a hitherto faultless plan the presence of an unsuspected party, and directed the police inquiries into an entirely new channel.

I thought it expedient to retire immediately to the Bell House, which during my brief absence in London had been in charge of Cassim, all approaches to Friar's Park being carefully guarded by the man Hawkins.

At this point I may touch upon a previous danger which had been met and overcome. Provision had been made in the will of Sir Burnham for the retention by his widow of Friar's Park and the revenues thereof; but since, in the event of her death, I should have been compelled to appear in the character of the mortgagee, it was contrary to our interests that Lady Coverly should die whilst any heir to the estate remained alive.

Nevertheless, despite all my care, this stricken woman had died six months prior to the first return of Sir Marcus from Russia. Since she had been a helpless invalid during the last years of her life, I experienced little difficulty in concealing the fact of her death. Cassim and I interred her by night in the family mausoleum, where she lies beside her husband.

In these circumstances, judge of my feelings when, shortly after the premature discovery termed in the Press "the *Oritoga* mystery," Mr. Addison one day presented himself at the Bell House! His avowed intention of calling upon Lady Coverly left me no alternative. Never, in all his days, not even when he miraculously escaped the L.K. Vapour at the Abbey Inn, did Mr. Addison stand so near to death as there—in my study!

Let me explain the situation more fully. The fatal Sothic month, which I have learned to regard with horror, commenced on the twenty-third ultimo, and does not terminate for another five days. Nehémah was—and still remains—"possessed." You will understand my employment of the term.

On the night preceding this visit of Mr. Addison's, I had traced her nocturnal movements by the howling of many dogs, and fearful of some indiscretion which might place my neck in a noose, I had followed her. I found her in a narrow footpath which leads to the Abbey Inn!

Despite entreaties, threats, she declined to give any ex-

planation of her behaviour. But finally I prevailed upon
her to return to the Bell House. The appearance of Mr.
Addison on the following morning opened my eyes to the
truth. With the scandal still attaching to the names of Edward Hines and another man, called, I believe, Adams, a
subject for gossip throughout the neighborhood, I could
not at so perilous a time risk the consequences of a third
intrigue. I determined that Mr. Addison could better be
spared by the community than I. Nahémah's next insanity
—an open visit to the Abbey Inn—confirmed my opinion.

Thereupon I committed my first mistake. Cassim, the
Nubian mute, who had been in my service for many years,
was formerly attached to a great household in Stambûl. I
shall probably be understood. I instructed him; and Mr.
Addison very cleverly playing upon his superstitious nature, Cassim failed.

My time grows short. I will touch upon my second
folly. Long before, the possibility of firing a small projectile from the tower of Friar's Park into the upper front of
the Abbey Inn had presented itself to me in the light of a
feasible experiment.

Unaware that Inspector Gatton was watching me—unaware that in my absence he had actually detected the presence of the gun upon the tower—I played my last card—
and lost.

Cassim it was who detected the fact that police were
watching the Bell House! Cassim had failed me once. I instructed him a second time.

I near the end of my statement. Destruction of all my
effects, of all evidence of my work, and, crowning tragedy,
of every trace of a life's research, was unavoidable. Knowing that every railway station and port would be watched,
and that my marked personality could not hope to escape
the vigilance of the authorities, I determined to make a bid
for freedom by seeking the shelter of my villa in London.

Cassim systematically fired the Bell House—and
perished in the flames! Under cover of the confusion
which the conflagration occasioned, Nahémah and I succeeded in making our retirement by the gate opening on
the Hainingham road.

But, in my attempts upon the life of Mr. Addison, I had
not counted with Nahémah. I had raised up a monster. . . .
That monster . . . has destroyed me. . . .

CHAPTER XXVIII

THE CLAWS OF THE CAT

The hoarse voice ceased. Neither Gatton nor I moved or spoke. Then:

"I have three minutes—or less," whispered Damar Greefe. "Question me. I am at your service."

"Where is your villa?" asked Gatton suddenly.

"It is called The Laurels——"

"The Laurels!" I cried incredulously.

"It is called so," whispered the Eurasian. "It is the last house but one in College Road! From there I conducted my last experiment with L.K. Vapour, which resulted, not in the death of Mr. Addison, but in that of Eric Coverly——"

Gatton sprang to his feet.

"Come along, Mr. Addison!" he cried. But:

"The Laurels is empty," came, ever more faintly. "In her Sothic fury, Nahémah fled. The blood lust is upon her. I warn you. She is more dangerous . . . than . . . any rabid dog. . . . Tuberculosis will end her life . . . before the snows . . . come. But there is time for her to—Ah, God's mercy!"

He writhed. He was contorted. Foam appeared upon his lips.

"*Hlangkûna!*" he moaned. "*Hlangkûna! She* . . . touched me with a poisoned needle . . . *two hours* . . . ago. . . ."

He rose to his full height, uttered a stifled scream, and crashed down upon the floor—dead!

In a species of consternation, Gatton and I stood looking at one another, standing rigidly like men of stone one on either side of that long, thin body stretched upon my study floor. The hawk face in profile was startlingly like that of Anubis as it lay against the red carpet.

Neither of us, I think, was capable of grasping the fact that the inquiry was all but ended, and that the mysteries which had seemed so dark and insoluble were cleared up and the inner workings of this strange conspiracy laid bare before us. One thought, I believe, was uppermost in both our minds: that the man who now lay dead upon the floor, a victim of one of his own devilish inventions, was no more than a brilliant madman.

If his great work on the ape-man of Abyssinia and that greater one dealing with what he called "the *psycho-hybrids*" had ever had existence outside his own strange imagination no one was ever likely to know. But that Dr. Damar Greefe was a genius whom much learning had made mad, neither of us doubted.

The whole thing seemed the wildest phantasy, and, for a time, in doubting the reality of the Eurasian's work, I found myself doubting the evidence of my own senses and seriously wondering if this possessed witch-cat, whose green eyes had moved like satanic lanterns throughout the whole phantasmagoria, had any more palpable existence than the other strange things spoken of by the unscrupulous scientist.

That Gatton's thoughts had been running parallel with my own was presently made manifest, for:

"Without a moment's delay, Mr. Addison," he said, speaking like a man newly awakened from slumber, "we must proceed to The Laurels and test the truth of what we have heard."

He crossed to the door, threw it open, and:

"Sergeant!" he cried. "Come in! The prisoner is dead!"

As the sergeant and the constable who were waiting came into the study and stood looking in stupefaction at the body stretched on the floor, I heard the telephone bell ring. I started nervously. That sound awakened ghastly memories, and I thought of the man who only a few hours before had met his death in the room where now the bell was ringing its summons.

I doubted if I could ever spend another night beneath that roof, for here Dr. Damar Greefe, the arch-assassin, and one of his victims both had met their ends. I heard the voice of Coates speaking in the adjoining room, and presently, as Gatton went to the door:

"Miss Merlin wishes to speak to you, sir," said Coates.

I ran eagerly to the 'phone, and:

"Hallo!" I cried. "Is that you, Isobel?"

"Yes!" came her reply, and I noted the agitation in her

voice. "I am more dreadfully frightened than I have ever been in my life. If only you were here! Is it possible for you to come at once?"

"What has alarmed you?" I asked anxiously.

"I can't explain," she replied. "It is a dreadful sense of foreboding—and all the dogs in the neighbourhood seem to have gone mad!"

"Dogs!" I cried, a numbing fear creeping over me. "You mean that they are howling?"

"Howling!" she answered. "I have never heard such a pandemonium at any time. In my present state of nerves, Jack, I did the wrong thing in coming to this funny lonely little house. I feel deserted and hopeless and, for some reason, in terrible danger."

"Are you *alone*, then?" I asked, in ever-growing anxiety.

To my utter consternation:

"Yes!" she replied. "Aunt Alison was called away half an hour ago—to identify someone at a hospital who had asked for her——"

"What! An accident?"

"I suppose so."

"But the servants?"

"Cook left this morning. You remember Aunt told you she was leaving."

"There is the girl, Mary?"

"Aunt 'phoned for her to join her at the hospital!"

"What! I don't understand! *'Phoned*, you say? Was it Mrs. Wentworth *herself* who 'phoned?"

"No; I think not. One of the nurses, Mary said. But, at any rate, she has gone, Jack, and I'm frightened to death! There's something else," she added.

"Yes?" I said eagerly.

She laughed in a way that sounded almost hysterical.

"Since Mary went I have thought once or twice that I have seen someone or something creeping around outside the house in the shadows amongst the trees! And just a while ago something happened which really prompted me to 'phone you."

"What was it?"

"I heard a sort of scratching at an upper window. It was just like——"

"Yes! Yes!"

"Like a great *cat* trying to gain admittance!"

"See that all the doors and windows are fastened!" I cried. "Whatever happens, or whoever knocks, don't open to anyone, you understand? We will be with you in less than half an hour."

Still in that frightened voice:

"For heaven's sake," she begged, "don't be long, Jack!"

I became aware of a singular rasping sound on the wires, which rendered Isobel's words almost unintelligible. Then:

"Jack!" I heard, in a faint whisper. "There is a strange noise . . . just outside the room. . . ."

Silence came; but vaguely, above that rasping sound, I had detected the words: "Cutting . . . telephone . . . wires. . . ."

I replaced the receiver. My hand was shaking wildly.

"Gatton!" I said. "Do you understand? *It* has turned its attention to Miss Merlin!" Then, raising my voice: "Coates! Run for the car! Hurry, man! Someone's life depends on your speed!"

Inspector Gatton grabbed the telephone directory.

"I will instruct the local police," he muttered. "Give me the exact address, Mr. Addison, and go and see the cab that's outside. If it's a good one, we'll take it instead of waiting."

Out I dashed, spurred by a sickly terror, crying Mrs. Wentworth's address as I ran. And of the ensuing five minutes I retain nothing but chaotic memories: the bewildered cabman, the police bending over the gaunt form on my study floor, Gatton's voice shouting orders. Then, we had jumped into the cab and, enjoining the man to drive like fury, were speeding off through the busy London streets. Leaving the quietude of one suburb for the maelstrom of central London, we presently emerged into an equally quiet backwater upon the northerly outskirts.

It was a nightmare journey, but when at last we approached the house for which we were bound, my apprehension and excitement grew even keener. It was infinitely more isolated and lonely than I had ever realized, behind its high brick walls.

Of the local police there was no sign, and without hesitation we ran in at the open gate and up the path towards the porch. Every window in the house was brightly illuminated, testifying to the greatness of the occupant's fear.

Gaining the porch, we stopped, as if prompted by some mutual thought, and listened.

There was the remote murmuring of busy London, but here surrounding us was a stillness as great as that which prevailed in my own neighbourhood; and as we stood there, keenly alert, distinctly we both heard the howling of dogs!

"You hear it?" rapped Gatton.

"I do!" I replied.

Grasping the bell-knob, I executed a vigorous peal upon the bell. There was a light in the hallway, but my ringing elicited no response, until:

"My God, look!"

Gatton pulled me backward out of the porch, looking upward to the window of a room on the first floor.

A silhouette appeared here—undoubtedly that of Isobel. She seemed to be endeavouring to pull the curtain aside, when the shadow of a long arm reached out to her, and she was plucked irresistibly back. The sound of a muffled scream reached my ears, and:

"Great heavens! *It* has got in!" whispered Gatton.

He raised his hand, and the shrill note of a police whistle split the silence.

The closed door was obviously too strong to be forced without the aid of implements for the purpose, and we began to run around the house, looking for some means of entrance. Suddenly:

"There's the way!" said Gatton, and pointed up to where the branches of an old elm tree stretched out before a window. The glass of the window was entirely shattered except for some few points which glittered like daggers around the edges of the frame.

"Can you do it?"

"In the circumstances—yes!" I said.

Without more ado I began to climb the elm, stimulated by memories of how I had entered Friar's Park. It afforded little foothold for the first six feet, and proved an even tougher job than I had anticipated, but at last I reached a projecting limb, the bulk of which had been sawn off. Gatton's agility was not so great as mine, but at the moment that I half staggered and half fell into the room, I heard him swinging himself on to the limb behind me, so that as I leapt to the open door he came tumbling in through the window, and the pair of us raced side by side along the corridor towards an apartment facing front from which horrifying cries and sounds of conflict now arose.

Gaining the closed door of this room, I literally hurled myself upon it. It crashed open . . . and I held a dreadful spectacle.

Isobel lay forced back upon a settee which occupied the window recess, and bending over her, having her back turned towards me, was a tall, lithe, black-clad woman who, so far as I could see, was clutching Isobel's throat and forcing her further backward—backward upon the cushions strewn upon the settee!

But instant upon the door's opening this horrible scene changed. With never a rearward glance (so that neither Gatton nor I had even a momentary glimpse of her face), the black-robed woman sprang to the window, opened it in a moment, and, to my dismay and astonishment, sprang out into the darkness.

My first thought was for Isobel; but Gatton leapt across the room and craned out, peering on to the path below. Indeed, even as I dropped on my knees beside the swooning girl, I found myself listening for the thud of the falling body upon the gravel path. But no sound reached me. That uncanny creature must have alighted truly in the manner of a cat. Through the stillness of the house rang the flat note of a police whistle. From some distant spot I heard a faint reply. . . .

* * * * *

For long I failed to persuade myself that Isobel had not sustained some ghastly injury from the attack of the cat-woman. Memories uprose starkly before me of that *hlangkûna* and of the other dreadful death-instruments of the mad Eurasian doctor. Not even the assurances of the local medical man who had been summoned in haste could convince me; for I recognized how petty was his knowledge in comparison with that of Dr. Damar Greefe. But although I trembled to think what her fate might have been if we had arrived a few minutes later, the fact remained—and I returned thanks to Heaven—that she had escaped serious physical injury at the hands of her assailant.

But, alas! to this very hour she sometimes awakes

shrieking in the night. And her terrified cry is always the same: "The green eyes of Bâst! . . . The green eyes of Bâst!"

CHAPTER XXIX

AN AFTERWORD

I wish it lay in my power to satisfy the curiosity in all quarters expressed respecting the identity of "Nahémah," the cat-woman or *psycho-hybrid,* who figured in Dr. Damar Greefe's statement. But it is my duty as a chronicler of the strange and awful occurrences which at this period disturbed the even tenor of my existence to state that from the moment in which she leapt from the window of Mrs. Wentworth's house to the path below, neither I nor any other witness who ever came forward *beheld her again.*

At the end of a quest which exercised the intricate machinery of New Scotland Yard throughout the length and breadth of the land, Inspector Gatton was compelled to admit himself defeated in this particular. And his explanation of the failure to apprehend the central figure of the tragedies which had exterminated the house of Coverly was a curious one.

"You know, Mr. Addison," he said to me one evening, "the more I think of this Nahémah the more I wonder if such a person ever really existed!"

"What do you mean, Gatton?" I asked.

"Well," he replied, "I mean that although you and I and others are prepared to testify to the existence of a woman in the case, what do we really know about her (leaving Dr. Damar Greefe's statement out of the question), except that she possessed very remarkable eyes?"

"And very remarkable agility," I interrupted.

"Yes, I'll grant you that," he said; "her agility was certainly phenomenal. But, still, as I was saying, except for this definite information, we have no *proof* outside the

statement of Dr. Damar Greefe that such a person as Nahémah ever existed, or, at any rate, that there ever was a
creature possessing the attributes which he ascribed to her.
The Laurels is an ordinary suburban house, which has
been leased for a number of years by a 'Mr. and Miss da
Costa'—Dr. Damar Greefe, no doubt, and a female companion. But of his 'great work' and so forth there's not a
trace. There are a lot of Egyptian antiquities, I'll admit,
but not a scrap of evidence; and the rooms evidently used
by the female inmate of the household are those of an ordinary cultured Englishwoman."

"But, good heavens, Gatton!" I cried. "Whatever explanation can you offer of a series of crimes which were palpably directed against the members of the Coverly family?"

"I don't say," continued Gatton, "that there wasn't a
sort of feud or vendetta at the bottom of the business. I
merely mention that we have no *evidence* to show that the
person responsible for it was any other than this Eurasian
doctor."

"But what could have been his object?"

"I could suggest several; but my point at the moment is
this: although I am prepared to grant that he had a
woman associate of some kind, I can't see that there is any
evidence to prove that she was otherwise than an ordinary
human being, except that I am disposed to think that she
was demented."

"You are probably right there, Gatton," I agreed; "and
Dr. Damar Greefe was by no means normal; in fact, I
think he was a dangerous and very brilliant maniac."

"At any rate," added Gatton, "no trace of this Nahémah
has been found, which, at the least, is very significant."

"Significant, if you like," I replied; "but for my own
part I have no ambition whatever to see again those dreadful green eyes."

"I never did see them," said Gatton musingly; "therefore I can't speak upon the matter. But when we got Dr.
Damar Greefe I think we had the head of the conspiracy.
How much of his 'statement' is true and how much the
product of a diseased mind is something we are never likely to know."

"Nor am I curious to know," I assured him. "I only desire to forget the tragedies associated with the green eyes of Bâst, and to leave the darkness of the past behind."

"And," said Gatton, with a smile less grim than usual, "you have my best wishes for the future."